OVER FRANK'S DEAD BODY

OVER FRANK'S DEAD BODY

A MEG SHEPPARD MYSTERY

BOOK TWO

VICKY EARLE

ISBN: 978-1-78324-224-5

www.vickyearle.com

Published by Wordzworth
www.wordzworth.com

This book is dedicated to my father,

Douglas Frederick Symes,

1917-1998,

who knew how to love, live and laugh.

1

Visitors

She doesn't know that I'm watching her through the glass panel beside the front door.

Kelly, my trusty border collie, heard the taxi grinding on the gravel driveway before it came to an abrupt stop, and alerted me to the unexpected arrival with a few yaps. She waits for a sign from me that this person is welcome, her body taut, her tail still.

Something stops me from going outside to greet the visitor. I watch as the woman's stocky legs emerge, followed by her chunky body encased in various shades of woolly brown. The driver places two suitcases on the stony ground as the woman retrieves her large, folded umbrella. They nod a farewell, and she walks towards the house. Kelly still doesn't know how to react because I hesitate. Astonishment at her appearance on my doorstep is replaced by a seething anger that reddens my cheeks and makes my palms wet with sweat. Kelly looks at me and decides that a growl is in order, which gives way to a confused silence as I open the door, my hands slipping on the handle.

"Hello, darling."

"I'm not your darling." I turn away from her out-stretched arms as she stumbles up onto the verandah, her umbrella waving in the air. I'm flabbergasted that she has the audacity to come here.

"Of course, you're my darling, you're my daughter." I don't want her in my home, but I let her go past me and slam the door shut behind her.

"How did you find me?" But perhaps the more interesting question is why. No, it isn't. I know the answer.

"I heard your husband, Frank, I think his name was, died in a car accident, over eighteen months ago, wasn't it?"

"Yes."

"I wanted to come over right then. I tracked down one of Frank's relatives in England and found out where you live. But your stepfather got ill and I couldn't leave. Stan's dead now."

"I know, you sent me a card." I was relieved when I read he'd died. But I didn't experience the sense of healing, or of release, that I'd expected. Nothing could undo his betrayal and violation of me, nor the hurt and pain he'd inflicted on me. In a way, the news of his death made me feel worse because it stirred up memories I'd been working hard to bury in a deep grave. I now believe I'll never fully recover, never totally emerge from the darkness.

We've ended up in the kitchen and I'm filling up the kettle like an automaton, even though I can't let her stay. My defences are working because I can't hear what she's saying, although I know it has something to do with that husband of hers. But as she moves nearer, her voice penetrates my consciousness, and I detect the scent of lavender tainted by the smell of damp wool and stale breath. She stands too close to me, watching as I grab the tea bags.

"I thought, well, now there's nothing to stop me from visiting my daughter. So here I am. Could you get my suitcases, darling?"

"No, I couldn't, and I already told you I'm not your darling." How dare she call me her darling. She should feel and act like a stranger because I've not seen her for over twenty years, and even before I left home it was as if we lived remotely from one another. Stan played us like defenceless shadow puppets. My mother and I were in the same play, but in different scenes.

"I've flown over the bloody Atlantic, at great expense, to see my daughter and this is the kind of welcome I get." She smiles with stiff lips and flops down onto one of the kitchen chairs, letting her umbrella clatter to the floor. Kelly slinks over to my side, the hairs on her back bristling. She doesn't like her either. I'd hoped never to see her again. I've worked so hard to banish the flashbacks and to build strength to get on with my life.

"You can't stay here. Chuck is due home tomorrow."

"Who's Chuck? That's an American name if ever I heard one."

"He's my partner, and he lives here with me."

"Not married then?"

"None of your business. I'll make a reservation at the Vannersville Inn and arrange a taxi to take you there."

"You must have plenty of room here. Why won't you let your poor old mother stay?"

"Because your behaviour has always been the antithesis to the meaning of the word 'mother'."

"I'm not well, you know."

I stop pouring the tea and pick up my phone to arrange a room and a taxi. She wiggles her chunky frame as if trying to anchor herself onto the chair. She lets me know she has no money and follows that predictable pronouncement with a story about frequent headaches and dizziness she's suffering from. I don't want to hear it. I want to block all of it out.

As she embellishes her stories of illness, I grow doubtful that she'll leave.

But she does.

I heave an audible sigh of relief as the taxi turns out of the driveway. Her invasion of my home has brought uncertainty and confusion, as well as pain. I'm not surprised that she wants money. No doubt she thinks I'm rich, as many others assume. But I am surprised that she's made the long journey from England to ask. She can't possibly care about me any more than I care about her. And she'll be back tomorrow. A shiver goes down my spine despite the beads of sweat on my forehead.

Kelly brings me back to my senses. She whines, reminding me it's time to put the horses in. It's a relief to have chores to turn my attention to. The hay and water are ready and waiting for them, but the horses must be led into their stalls from the paddock, and fed their carrots and grain. I put on my thick, familiar jacket, that smells faintly of molasses and pine wood-shavings, grab my gloves and we're outside in the sparkling dusk. An early dusting of snow glitters as the sun sinks with a pink shimmer.

My mobile beeps. At last, the long-awaited text message from Chuck. But it's not what I'd hoped for. He's not coming home tomorrow. There's nothing more. There's an ominous gap in the communication which makes my stomach flutter and my heart pound. I'll reply when I get back into the house, since the horses demand my full concentration. Whatever happens, the animals have to be cared for. But I find I want to rush the horses into their stalls, and to usher the cats into the safety of the feed room, but they won't be hustled. Everything seems to take an eternity, as slow as the molasses that's mixed with the horses' grain and smells so sweet.

Of course, I do eventually get back to the house, Kelly at my side with her bright eyes and wagging tail. In my text to Chuck I ask if anything is wrong, and he replies he needs time to think. That doesn't sound good and I don't know what to make of it.

I want to see him. I search the internet for information on the writing conference, which I recall he said was being held in Kentucky. Nothing comes up. I try numerous keywords, and other locations, but the only conference that appears to be a possibility is being held in New York and is not due to start for several days. My hands are shaking. Something is wrong with our relationship, and I've been blind to it.

I still blame myself, at least in part, for Frank's disappearance. He faked his own death over eighteen months ago and I wonder if I could have helped him, could have supported him, could have made a difference. I'd been wallowing in my own self-pity and didn't see his suffering. He'd lost the love of his life, his wife Louisa, to cancer, about two years after their marriage. I couldn't replace her in his heart. We had a marriage of convenience. He was a government minister and wanted a beautiful wife by his side. And I wanted to marry him since I thought, given that I'm damaged goods, I'd never find anyone to love me. He offered me the lifestyle I craved, the horses, the country, and the lack of financial worry. But evidently it hadn't worked out as well for him as it has for me. He staged a car accident, and they found his car scrunched up on large boulders in a fast-moving river going out to the lake. His body wasn't found, but he wanted everyone, including me, to believe he was dead. Only a few people know that he's still alive and we've decided to leave it that way. That's what he wanted.

So, am I going to lose Chuck too? Have I been blind to what he's thinking and feeling? Am I still in a narcissistic funk?

I sit and stare at my computer screen, having lost my appetite and my motivation to do anything at all. My mobile beeps again, and I snatch it off the table as my heart misses a beat. But it's not Chuck. I might have let him slip away, out of my life, and I'm not sure if I can bring him back.

The text is from my racehorse trainer, Neal Carvey. He confirms that everything is on track for Rose, one of my two racehorses, to run in the Errol Stakes Race tomorrow. This race has been a long time coming for Rose, whose official racing name is Alusio: which I belatedly worked out is an anagram of Louisa. And my racehorse Speed's official racing name is Scarfin, an anagram of Francis. When I realized Frank had named the two racehorses after he'd married me, it stung a little. If I'd realized this before he disappeared, would it have made a difference? Would I have been able to do anything to help him, to help our marriage?

aBeating myself up won't achieve anything. I'll focus on the Stakes Race. At least it will help me get through tomorrow, and then I'll think about my next steps towards finding Chuck. I must call Joanna and ask her to keep an eye on Kelly when I'm out at the track, and to put the horses in the barn if I'm not back in time.

Joanna moved into the area about four months ago. It's not easy to get to know neighbours when living in the country, but Joanna made a point of introducing herself and offering to work on a casual basis. She knows a little about horses, but not much, which is unfortunate, because there are times when I could do with some knowledgeable help. Chuck was hired by Frank to be our gardener, but had worked at the track for a while, so he could pitch in if I needed assistance with the horses. But he has been doing less and less on the farm, and going away more and more often, despite the fact that he moved in to live with me several months ago.

Joanna can be pushy and nosey, and occasionally unreliable, but she looks after Kelly sometimes, and has done a few odd jobs for me. She's grateful for the cash. She and her out-of-work husband, who I haven't yet met, live in a dilapidated clapboard house which is precariously close to a collapsing bank-barn. The barn's galvanized steel roof is peeling off in strips and curling up, as if someone is attacking it with a blunt paring knife. The stone foundation has cracks which are large enough for rats to run through, and the wooden plank walls threaten to give way. I often think about Joanna and her husband living in the shadow of the disintegrating barn as it threatens to topple on top of them.

I find out that Joanna is available tomorrow, but my stomach is still tied up in knots. Even my anxiety over Chuck's puzzling disappearance is no match for the gut-wrenching pain I feel knowing that my mother is in the same country as I am, and in the vicinity, and will be coming here again, to my home, my sanctuary.

During the years of abuse, my mother did nothing. She would not even make eye contact with me, and we barely spoke. My dog, Bertie, was my companion, and the only one who gave me unconditional love. Once he died, I left. My stepfather couldn't threaten to harm Bertie anymore. I fled to Canada, hoping I could leave the hurt behind in England, but it came with me as if it was glued inside my brain and my heart, not to be dislodged.

My mother's presence will bring back the dreaded flashbacks. And, even if Chuck was here, he wouldn't be able to help because I've not confided in him about the brutality I suffered from my stepfather's abuse. I haven't found the strength to tell Chuck since I'm afraid it would drive him away for good. But perhaps that's what has happened in any case, somehow.

I pick up the flashlight. The days are too short now: December has just arrived. Kelly stretches and wags her silky tail. She knows it means we're going for a walk. The dusting of snow is not enough to discourage her, but it's enough to reflect the moonlight. The crisp air tingles my hot cheeks as we wander into the paddock, and then into the large field at the back of the property. The coyotes howl and yip, but Kelly knows better than to join in the chorus of barking dogs which has risen in response. She's content to follow curious scents and trails, running back to check on me from time to time. I turn to make my way to the barn. I want to make certain that everything is in order. I might have missed something when I put the horses away because I was distracted by Chuck's text message.

Eagle and Bullet blink their eyes at the sudden bright light as I walk in, their heads lolling over the stall doors. I double-check that they have plenty of hay and water.

The cats are piled on top of one another in the feed room. I adopted them from the humane society where I worked, and they are gentle, loving cats. That's where Kelly and I met, too. She was a stray, just like the cats. I suppose I was a stray once.

My visit to the barn has made me feel a bit more settled, but it hasn't worked as much magic as I'd hoped. I have a defeatist attitude about sleep tonight. It's not going to happen.

* * *

After a restless night of tossing and turning, followed by pacing backwards and forwards in the kitchen with a cup of herbal tea clasped in my hands, it's a relief to see the sun rising. The temperature is already high enough to melt the snow and to soften the ground. It's good to breathe in the fresh air as Kelly and I walk on the worn path to the barn. The warm, welcoming whinnies of the horses lift my spirits as I scoop up their grain rations and drop them into their feed buckets.

Once back in the kitchen, I make an effort to think of food. I must eat something, but nothing interests me. I give Kelly a biscuit and settle on a piece of toast, but I nearly drop the bread when the landline phone rings. The sound startled me. This phone isn't often used.

"Is that Meg?"

"Yes."

"This is Annabella. Do you remember me?" Her warm Italian accent is kind to the senses. Annabella is the beautiful opera singer whom Frank left me for after his faked death. They were lovers. Frank was also a significant sponsor of her up-and-coming career. But it all came to an abrupt end when he left her without warning.

"Of course I remember you. How are you?"

"Good. I have some news. I am not sure if you want to know, but I will tell you. I feel we are like sisters because Frank left us both." Her laugh is like a soft sigh floating across the Atlantic.

"What news?"

"My agent, my hard-working faithful agent and assistant, Simeon, found out that Frank left Paris with a make-up artist who was on tour with an American opera company. I cannot remember which one. She is American, and Simeon, he is very clever you know, found out that Frank and Tammy went to Kentucky."

"I thought Frank didn't want to return to North America."

"He did not say that. He said he would not return to Canada or go to England. He was going to start a new life. Remember? Another new life!"

"With this make-up artist, Tammy."

"It is hard to accept his behaviour. I have more understanding of how you must have felt when you found out he left you to be with me. To leave for another woman, it is hard."

"I know, but he isn't well. He needs help."

"Will you find him and see him?"

"No. I've decided to let him be dead. That's what he wants. He's chasing an impossible dream, the dream that Louisa will be reincarnated somehow, and that he'll find her."

"It is sad, but my blood is still boiling. I only have small sponsorship, not a quarter of what Frank was contributing. He dropped me like a hot potato."

I thank her for letting me know Simeon has found out Frank's whereabouts. I'm not sure why her agent needs to know. Perhaps he has some naïve idea that he'll be able to convince Frank to resume his sponsorship of Annabella, but I can't imagine that there's any possibility of that happening.

Kelly must have missed someone driving up to the house because the doorbell chimes, taking us both off-guard. The button is rarely pressed, since Kelly usually hears the grinding of the gravel as tires crunch their way up the driveway, well before anyone reaches the door.

"Murray! How nice to see you." I've got to know Murray, Frank's brother, more since the spring. He has graduated, if that's the right term, from the Lighthouse Rehabilitation Centre, and is doing well as a recovered alcoholic. I hope.

"I'm good. How about you?"

"Not bad. Any special reason for your visit?"

"Yes. I've found out that Frank's in Kentucky and I wanted to tell you." There's something different about his speech, as if he's putting effort into the articulation of each word.

"I heard about it this morning. How did you know?"

"It wasn't hard to find out. I connected with Simeon. Not sure if you know about him. He's Annabella's agent."

"Yes, Annabella told me that Simeon discovered where Frank is."

"I'm going to talk to Frank."

"What about?"

"I want to reconcile with him. The last conversation we had before he disappeared was an argument about the trust fund he'd set up for me, and I don't feel good about that. I want him to see me as the person I really am, not the alcoholic he knew me as for most of his adult life."

"Have you told him you're coming?"

"No, I want it to be a surprise."

"It'll be that, for sure." This is a terrible decision on Murray's part. I hope his desire to seek reconciliation with Frank has nothing to do with the fact that he's not satisfied with the funds Frank gave him before his disappearance, or with the trust fund that Frank left him in his will. We now know that Frank has a lot more money than was distributed after his faked death.

In the past, it seemed that Murray's quest for more money was the only motive for his wanting to see Frank, and that their difficult and contentious relationship, full of hurt and blame, was exacerbated by these frequent demands for money. When Murray confronted his brother, demanding cash, it would always result in an altercation. From what I gathered, Murray resented Frank's wealth and success, and believed that their parents' support of Frank's schooling had given him an unfair advantage over his younger brother, who struggled. Murray was overshadowed by Frank's brilliance at school where his older brother was the star pupil. And eventually Murray gave up trying. His parents gave up on him too and put their total support behind Frank and his education. It's not clear to me what came first, Murray's alcoholism or Murray's surrender and despair.

But Frank wanted Murray to get better. He was willing to fund rehabilitation programs and wanted to avoid supporting him in his drinking.

Curiously, after Frank's disappearance, Murray admitted himself to the Lighthouse Rehabilitation Centre and emerged as a different person. Not only does his face and body have softer contours, his complexion is clearer and his eyes have a sparkle. He walks with a bounce in his step, and I like to think he's regained some of his dignity. It would be great for Frank to see his brother doing so well, but my intuition tells me the meeting will not result in reconciliation. One important matter is that Frank wants everyone to believe he's dead. And the more people who connect with him from his past, the more he'll be pressured into vanishing again to somewhere where he cannot be traced by anyone from his past. Despite everything, I care for Frank and he's still my husband, and I think his wishes should be respected, even if no-one agrees with them.

A twinge of concern flits into my thoughts. What if Murray has started drinking again?

"Don't you think it'll be upsetting for Frank if you show up? He wants to be presumed dead."

"I'm sure he realizes by now that we know he's not dead. Simeon has let the cat out of the bag, if no-one else has. I've made up my mind."

I look for signs of drinking, but none is apparent. His hands aren't shaking, he doesn't appear anxious as he sips on a mug of tea and his eyes still have their sparkle, although perhaps they have a little less glimmer. I'm not absolutely sure.

"Any signs of the Humane Society changing their mind?" Murray asks.

"And re-hiring me after they've fired me? I don't think that's likely." I don't want to discuss it. It's still too recent and raw. I know why I was fired from my job as Executive Director. The Board of Directors put financial security above animal welfare. At least, that's how I see it. The Board ordered me not to respond to any more complaints about puppy mills in the area because we were using up our contingency fund. We raised some extra funds through a special appeal, but there wasn't enough to meet all the need. I couldn't leave the animals to suffer, so I used some of the precious contingency fund (as well as some of my own money of course). Our supporters expected us to use their money to help the animals, not to build up a bank account.

"Will you look for another job?"

"Maybe. But it won't be easy. Management skills are often viewed as not being transferrable from one field to another. In any case, I'd much prefer to work in animal welfare, and there aren't any other humane societies in Vannersville."

"I think it's grossly unfair. I bet that lawyer friend of yours, William Porter, could at least get you a decent settlement."

I don't reply. Usually I enjoy Murray's company, but I want him to leave. I don't want to talk about Frank and I don't want to talk about my dismissal. I stare into my empty mug, discouraging further conversation. He pushes himself up from his chair and puts his black woollen jacket on. He pats Kelly and gives me a quick hug. I wonder how the meeting of the two brothers will go. I wish I could be a fly on the wall. But perhaps not.

2

The Race

Almost as soon as Murray is in his car, the landline phone rings again. It's getting a work-out today.

"Hello." A weak, breathy voice squeaks into my ear.

"Who is it?"

"Your Mum. I've had a fall in my room."

"Oh. Are you hurt?"

"Can you come?"

Of course, I have to go even though it's the last thing I want to do. And Kelly must come with me. Since she was kidnapped, I don't leave her alone and out of my sight unless there's no other option. I couldn't bear to lose my beloved dog again, my best friend.

It takes us about five minutes to get out of the house and into the pickup truck.

Once we arrive at the Vannersville Inn, I have to leave Kelly, but I park the truck under my mother's window where I'll be able to check on it, and lock the doors.

The receptionist is expecting me and gives me a key card for my mother's room. Her face is smooth, pale, and expressionless. I don't think my mother could have told her she's had a fall.

I'm not sure what to expect as I approach her room. Perhaps she's lying just inside. I'm cautious and tentative as I open the stiff door. My mother is on the floor in the middle of the room, with her head on a pillow and the cordless phone beside her. She's reading a book.

"What happened?" I ask. She startles, snatches her reading glasses off her face and looks at me. "You seem to be handling it very well. You have a pillow, the phone, your reading glasses and a book."

"Oh." She moans. "Your poor mother had to crawl over to the bedside table to get them."

"Why can't you get up?"

"I think I've broken something."

"I don't think so."

"It's so nice that my darling daughter came."

"What do you want?"

"I want my darling daughter back."

"I have never been your darling and never will be. I'll call an ambulance if you need to go to the hospital and I'll pay the hospital bills if your insurance won't cover the costs, but that's it. I have business to attend to."

"Aren't you worried about your poor mother? You came, didn't you?"

"No, I'm not worried. I believe you're fine. Shall I call the ambulance?" I have my mobile in my hand which I raise above my head as I grind my teeth and my face flushes with anger.

"I think I'll wait and see how I am by lunchtime."

"I have to go." I leave the room. I wait about thirty seconds outside the door, and then open the door a crack with as little sound as possible, and see my mother on her feet. Oblivious to my spying, she throws the pillow on the bed and chucks the book across the room, confirming my suspicions and giving me an instant tension headache. But I don't have the will to confront her at the moment.

As I walk towards the truck, I take a few deep breaths and check my mobile, which reveals no evidence of communication from Chuck. I try calling him a couple of times, but he doesn't answer. I'm disturbed by his silence.

Kelly's in the truck, her nose dabbing at the window, her bright eyes following me. She has been the only faithful and loving constant in my life during the past few years. People have come and gone, but she's always at my side like a security blanket, protecting me from the hurt, comforting me. Our relationship is uncomplicated and forgiving. She is easy to love and accepts me as I am. I need her unconditional love today and will miss her when I leave to watch Rose's race. It's somewhat consoling that Joanna has agreed to stay on the farm with Kelly, since at least she won't be alone.

We make our way back to the farm where I must get ready to go to the racetrack. This is Rose's third stakes race this year. She had a rocky start to the season, primarily due to what I believe was incompetence on the part of her previous trainer. Stakes races are high-level races for which the horse must usually be nominated and a nomination fee paid. Few racehorses make it into one stakes race, let alone three in one year. And Rose has exceeded all expectations by winning two. Despite Chuck's disappearance and my mother's appearance, I'm looking forward to her race and to being part of the event.

* * *

As I drive to the racetrack, my thoughts drift back to Chuck. I carry a sense of loss at the belated realization that Chuck and I have gradually drifted apart, which causes me to question whether what I'd thought was love had been merely wishful thinking. I grip the steering wheel, telling myself that I shouldn't dwell on these unhelpful thoughts.

My arrival at the racetrack helps me to shift my focus back to Rose's race. I'll have time to visit the backstretch, although I don't want to disturb the trainer, Neal or the groom, Linda. But most of all, I don't want to agitate Rose.

As I step into the shedrow, I catch a glimpse of Linda, and am pleasantly surprised. She's clean and tidy, wearing a new pair of jeans, a smart black windbreaker and a clean purple cap. Neal's stable colours are black and purple. The horses look elegant when they go out to train in the mornings, with black saddle pads trimmed in purple, and with purple polo bandages wrapped round their legs (which they wear for protection).

"You look great, Linda."

"I'm glad you're here." She sounds breathless and her frown is so pronounced it's making her eyes look smaller.

"Oh no, there isn't something wrong, is there? Is Rose okay?"

"Sorry. She's fine, great. It's something else." Tears roll down her cheeks.

"Is Neal okay?"

"I'm fine." He steps out of the stall to our right, and Rose puts her head over the mesh gate as Neal closes it. "But let's get out of Rose's sight. I don't want her picking up on our stress as we talk."

Neal's dressed in a suit, hoping to be photographed later in the winner's circle. He strides ahead and Linda has difficulty keeping up with us. Despite the strenuous physical exercise she endures every day, her rotund body is no less spheroid, and her short steps are no less wanting. Neal leads us to his modest office, which is at the end of the shedrow. It's about six feet square and houses a rusting fridge, a coffee maker on a small metal table, a couple of chairs, a tall, leaning cupboard, and numerous hooks on the walls with a myriad of horsey things hanging from them. There's no window, but the door is always open when Neal is around. Linda enters the office, puffing and red in the face. Neal insists we sit down on the two plastic chairs.

"So, what on earth is the matter?" I ask.

"A jockey was killed this morning," Neal says. Tears run down Linda's hot cheeks. Neal hands her a couple of tissues. "The official take on it is that he was thrown from his horse just as they were about to start a timed work."

"But that's not right." Linda almost chokes and blows her nose.

"Linda and I saw what happened. We were there watching one of our horses being breezed." Neal hands Linda another couple of tissues. "It looked like Juan blacked out and slumped forward, frightening the horse, which bolted, and Juan was thrown, landing on his head."

"It was the worst thing ever." Linda breaks into sobs.

"The reason we wanted to tell you is that there's something fishy about it."

"We want to find out the truth." Linda looks at me with red, puffy eyes and a runny nose.

"And we think you'd be able to find out what happened. I knew Juan. He was a good kid. He hadn't been at this track for very long, but he was doing well most of the time. He was a champion jockey at a track in the States."

"I don't think I'd be any help." I need this like a hole in the head. Too much is out of control in my life at the same time. "What about the police?"

Linda snorts and then blows her nose again.

"Accident," Neal says. "It seems like no-one else thinks it's suspicious, so they're not listening to us. But no-one was close to Juan when it happened, not like us. And we both agree. Hope you'll help. We can't think of anyone else who has the connections and would be able to ask questions without getting people uptight."

Neal and Linda look at me while the silence hangs unseen but felt, expecting to be broken. I can't ignore their eyes. They remind me of Kelly's eyes when she's asking me for something. I can't resist their appeal.

"I mean it when I say I don't think I'll be able to help." I let out a sigh. Linda's frown deepens as she looks at me with unwavering intensity. "But I'll do what I can."

"That's great." Neal shakes my hand. Linda gets to her feet, wipes her nose again, and hugs me. I'm not comfortable with physical contact, but her embrace, limited by her rotund body, doesn't make me feel smothered, and she releases me after a couple of seconds, letting me breathe again.

"No time to talk more," Neal says, as he grabs a lead-rein off one of the hooks. "Linda and I need to get Rose ready for the race. We'll see you track-side."

I walk out of the shedrow in a bit of a daze, and almost collide with a large grey thoroughbred. After profuse apologies to the hot-walker and the horse, I emerge from the barn and come close to stepping into the water-sodden ditch. I'm discombobulated. As I climb into my truck, I make a concerted effort to focus on one thing only, Rose's race. That's what I've come for and have been looking forward to. But what is Chuck up to? And is there really something suspicious about the jockey's death?

By the time I make it to the grandstand, the horses are being led by the grooms from the backstretch to the saddle-up area which consists of individual stalls inside the building. It's disappointing that the jockeys won't be mounting outside. I like to see the horses walking around on the grass among the trees, but the weather has turned too bleak and cold for the athletes, both horse and human, to be exposed when not in motion.

Rose looks good. Her chestnut coat gleams, she is lean and muscled, light on her feet and tossing her head with impatience. I imagine she can't figure out why it takes so long to start the race. The official checks her tattoo inside her upper lip, and the saddle is applied with the aid of another official. Neal checks and double-checks the tack and, at last, the jockey is on her back and they start the long walk to the front of the grandstand for the post parade. The announcer informs the spectators of the name of each horse, the jockey, the trainer and the owners. Rose's odds are 2:1 and she's the favourite, which I'm inclined to believe is a bad omen. My legs are trembling and my hands are shaking. There are nine other horses in the race, all talented performers, all looking magnificent, and all with hard-working teams behind them.

It seems to take a long time for the starting-gate to be driven into place, and for the horses to collect behind it. I remind myself to breathe as she's loaded into the gate, and we all wait for the horses to be released. As the gates fly open Rose stumbles, and veers a bit to the outside, losing precious time and increasing the distance she'll have to run. She's second-from-last going into the first turn. The jockey is hovering over her back, flexing his knees with her stride and letting her go at her pace. Along the backstretch piece of the track, she picks up her speed. She moves up behind the four front horses as they enter the turn before the home-stretch. But she's got a lot of catching up to do. The four horses in front are battling it out and the announcer is focussed on them, not considering Rose in the equation. But I haven't given up on Rose yet, and I can see she hasn't given up either. The jockey just has to show her his whip, and it acts as a cue for her to lengthen her stride. She finds a new gear, and her talent, courage and competitiveness radiate. The announcer picks up on her move.

"Alusio is closing in. She's challenging the leaders."

The four front runners are tiring, but Alusio appears to be gaining power and speed. It's as if she's grown wings: her strides seem effortless. She crosses the finish line with a last-minute surge, winning by a head.

I don't notice Neal beside me until he grabs me and gives me a quick hug before I have time to think about it. Linda is on her way to meet the horse. Neal and I follow quickly.

I lead the horse into the winner's circle that is reserved for stakes races. Alusio, although still catching her breath, poses for the picture (she's become quite the ham), and then gives everyone trouble because she's so proud and pleased with herself. After the saddle has been removed, and it and the jockey have been weighed, Neal throws a light-weight blanket on the sweaty horse, so she won't get chilled as Linda leads her back to the barn.

A racetrack official presents me with a glass vase, which will be engraved later, as the photographer takes a couple more pictures. What's Chuck doing right now?

After a quick celebratory drink of sparkling white wine with Neal, I drive home, hoping that Kelly is fine, and that Chuck is back so that we can talk. But his Jeep isn't in the driveway and there's no sign of my beloved, beautiful dog, Kelly. My heart sinks under the weight of growing concern as I pull up in front of the house.

I find a note from Joanna saying she's sorry, but she had to leave. Most of the time she's reliable, but sometimes her behaviour is odd. Now and then she looks at her phone and, without explanation, and with only a quick "sorry, have to go", she drops everything and leaves. I'm left to deal with the consequences. I haven't, so far, lost my patience with the situation, but leaving Kelly alone could be the tipping point, especially if something has happened to her.

Kelly bounces out of the family room and greets me as if I've been gone for a year. She breaks all the rules: jumps up, licks my face, runs into the kitchen, chases Cooper, the kitten (who leaps onto the counter which is out of bounds), barks and jumps up at me again. I restore order by feeding both of them their supper, and sit down at the kitchen table and stare out of the window at the paddock. In the dim light of the early evening, I see the silhouettes of the horses.

They should have been put in their stalls two hours ago. Joanna has let us down.

I check my mobile as I reach for my barn jacket. No message from Chuck.

Bullet and Eagle seem content in the half-dark as Kelly and I make our way along the familiar path to the barn, but they move towards the gate as we pass by. Bullet whinnies, with little enthusiasm, but with enough conviction to get the message across that it's time to go in. I'm glad I have everything set up ready for them, so it won't take long to get them settled and fed. A wave of weariness overcomes me and my energy wanes as I fill up the scoop with feed from the bin. My eyelids feel heavy and I think I'd fall asleep if I curled up on the floor of the feed room. I must be exhausted.

The moonlight reflects off the fresh sprinkle of fluffy snow, illuminating our way back to the house. Despite the crisp, fresh air, I drag my feet and let my body stoop as I give in to my tiredness. One good thing is that I don't have to rush to get everything done in the morning so that I can get to work. No, that's a bad thing. My stomach knots as I recall my abrupt and impersonal dismissal. I received a registered letter with no explanation and no severance pay. I miss my job. I miss helping the animals and trying to make a difference every day. I'd taken about a year off after Frank disappeared: I felt I wasn't functioning well enough to work. That might have been a mistake, in retrospect. I went back to work at the end of this spring, and that's when puppy mills became a hot topic and the public became more aware of the appalling conditions which are, more often than not, the reality of these breeding factories. We got lots of calls and rescued hundreds of dogs and puppies. Some of them couldn't see because of the matted fur around their eyes, others were flea-infested, some malnourished, all were filthy and nearly all were terrified. Many required urgent veterinary care. A few had to be euthanized, and those who remained needed many hours of patient socialization.

I believe the Humane Society should respond to such cruelty. I don't want to think of animals that should be rescued continuing to suffer for the sake of maintaining a contingency fund.

I feel even more weary as these thoughts weigh me down. I try calling Chuck again, but no answer. I take a defeatist attitude with me again as Kelly and I go upstairs to bed. Despite this wretched tiredness, there's too much buzzing in my head for me to sleep a wink.

3

Mother

I wake to find sunlight bouncing off millions of dancing dust-mites. It's later than usual. Kelly and I had a good night despite my conviction that it would be a long, sleepless one. And, for once, Cooper the kitten didn't wake me up with his raspy tongue exfoliating my nose. He's leaping into the air, apparently attempting to catch the sunbeams.

But dark thoughts flow over me as I put my warm feet onto the cool floor and stand up. Where is Chuck? Is his disappearance permanent? Am I never going to have an opportunity to talk with him about us? And my mother; what am I going to do about her? I'm sure she's here to extract money from me. She must think I have pots of cash, but I don't. Frank upheld his part of the bargain, which was laid out in our marriage contract, by providing a fund which generates enough income to cover usual farm operating and personal living expenses.

As I push my mother out of my mind, the dark recollection that I've lost my job lurches back into my consciousness. I loved helping to make a difference for animals, and my job loss leaves a hole in my life. And it leaves a hole in my wallet. Although I made regular significant donations to the humane society, the remaining income helped to pay some racehorse training bills. I force myself to let go of that thought and to unravel my clenched fists. I have a lot to be thankful for. At least I'm alive, not like the poor jockey whose tragic death tumbles into my mind. Neal and Linda want me to investigate, but I wonder how I'm going to cope with that on top of everything else.

Kelly looks up at me and wags her tail. I swear she's smiling at me. It never fails that some of her radiating positivity seeps into my being. I make a conscious effort to change my perspective. Investigating the death of that poor young jockey might not only get answers for the family and for Neal and Linda, but could help me as well by providing a distraction away from the self-pity I'm inclined to wallow in.

My motto for the day is to be more positive and optimistic.

Kelly and I find that the snow has all melted in the warmth of the bright sunshine, which is more reminiscent of spring than of early winter. The horses toss their heads and paw at their rubber mats in their stalls, using all the body language they can to tell me they want out, now. Once in the paddock, they kick up their heels, chucking large divots of thawed earth high into the air behind them. The ground is fast becoming muddy and the horses' hooves will churn it up, necessitating some reseeding in the spring. But I don't care about the extra work because they're having such a great time. They're acting as if it's already spring, living in the present and making the best of the day.

* * *

Kelly and I return to the kitchen as Neal calls me on my mobile.

"Rose is doing well after that fine win," Neal says.

"That's great. I'm glad she's not showing any ill effects. She ran so well and had to make up some distance."

"Yes. And Speed is doing well too. The racing season is almost over, as you know. I think it's time to ship them to your farm."

"Okay."

"By the way, I've been approached by a couple of trainers who have clients interested in buying Rose. They're talking six figures. And one of them is also interested in Speed. You've said before that you're not interested in selling, but I thought I'd better check."

"I don't think I want to." I realize I'm not as sure as I have been. Is it because I've lost my job? The horse-racing business is one of the riskiest ventures one can take on. Everything can go up in a puff of smoke with an injury, an illness, or the loss of the will to race, resulting in a lot of "investment" going down the drain.

"They're worth quite a bit at the moment, and you never know what the future's going to hold, so I'd understand if you want to consider it. Should I get more information?"

"No, not right now, Neal. But I'll bear it in mind. Thanks." My mind feels like it's cluttered with too many things, too many issues, as if my brain's made of honeycomb with a swarm of bees buzzing around in a frenzy.

Neal suggests how and when he'd like to have the horses shipped.

As I put my phone down on the kitchen table, I see that I have a text message from Murray. He's leaving for Kentucky today and will let me know how the meeting with Frank goes. I don't have a good feeling about it.

I phone Chuck again, and still there's no answer. This time I leave a voice mail, even though I believe it's futile. I sit at the kitchen table, wondering what to do about it, when someone knocks at the outside kitchen door, stirring Kelly into a convulsion of barks until she realizes it's William.

William Porter, the lawyer I met in the spring, is the person instrumental in rescuing Kelly from her kidnapper, as well as in helping me to uncover what really happened to Frank when he disappeared. He often drops by and stops for a chat. I've grown to enjoy his company and to value his friendship.

"I really wish you'd let me contact the Board of the Vannersville Humane Society. They owe you severance pay," he says as he makes himself a mug of steaming coffee. Chuck brought his coffee maker with him when he moved to the farm, and it's proven to be useful for several of our visitors who were previously offered only tea or water.

William has lost the paunch which used to protrude over his belt threatening to burst the buttons on his well-worn shirts, and his head is less spheroid, revealing a strong bone structure. And his dark eyes have a fresh twinkle. It's great to see that he's on a healthier track in his life.

"You know I don't want you to do that. Thanks anyway."

"Is it because I'm not a labour lawyer? I know a good one, if that's what the problem is."

"No, it's nothing to do with that. The reason I don't want to go that route, however much I'm legally owed, is that any money I receive would be money not available to help the animals, and I'd feel like a hypocrite. I want them to spend their money on rescuing abused and neglected animals."

"It's the principle of the thing. You could get the severance pay you're eligible for, and then you could donate it straight back to the humane society. At least then you'd get a tax break."

"It's not worth the aggro. Honestly, I've got too many other things on my mind." I don't want to dwell on my job loss. I'd rather focus on the other things that are swirling around in my life, churning up my emotions.

"You sound frustrated. Is there something I can help with?"

Since I have no-one else to turn to whom I trust, I take him up on his offer.

"Yes. Top of my priority list is to find Chuck."

"What do you mean? You don't know where he is?"

"No, I don't. He said he was going to a writing conference in Kentucky, but there isn't one. The only one I can find will be in New York, and it hasn't started yet."

"I presume he hasn't connected with you? Have you reported him as a missing person?"

"He has connected, sort of. He texted he needs time to think." My hand is trembling. I try to hide it by putting my hands in my lap and gaze into my mug of lukewarm tea.

"I'm sorry to hear that." William leans back in his chair and sighs. "Meg, perhaps that's all he needs, time to think, and then he'll be back and the two of you can talk."

"I've no idea what's going on."

"It might not be easy to find him if he doesn't want to be found."

"I need to find out what went wrong." I get up from my chair and make a fresh mug of tea. Losing Frank, and then losing Chuck so soon afterwards, is eroding the little courage and confidence I'd painstakingly nurtured inside me. The flimsy foundation I've been trying to rebuild my life on is wobbling precariously. Despite my insecurity, I desperately want to hold on to the possibility that one day, I'll have a long-lasting, intimate, fulfilling relationship. I can't explain why I want this so much.

William puts a warm, soft hand on mine as I sit down, holding my mug.

"I'll help of course." We sit in silence for about a minute. "What else can I help with? I've time to do something more."

I'm grateful for the nudge. It's good for me to be occupied, especially in solving puzzles. And William's offer of help acts as encouragement.

"There is something else. You remember Neal, my trainer at the track?"

"Yes."

"He and the groom, Linda, have asked me to look into the death of a jockey which they think is suspicious." I give William the information that I have.

"Still sounds like it could've been an accident. But I'll do whatever I can to help, for sure."

The day ends with my motto of being more positive and optimistic lying on shaky ground. But William's friendship and support have helped to boost my resilience, and I resolve to dig deeper for more fortitude.

* * *

The next day, as I slip and slide on the path to the barn, I marvel at the ice which has encased every branch, fence rail, pine cone, and blade of grass. This new fairy-land glistens and glitters in the early morning sun. The ice-storm has resulted in a power failure for a large area which includes the farm. I expect it will be some time before electricity is restored because we're in a rural area, which is assigned a lower priority. Losing our power means we lose water, since we use an electric pump to bring the water up from the well. Another thing to cope with. But I'm not dealing with this at the moment, which leads me to admit that I've done nothing about anything during the past couple of days, despite my resolve.

And my attempts to block out Chuck's deliberate disappearance are not working. It's not easy to put him behind me and pretend he was never a part of my life.

I return to the house with a promise to take some steps towards finding Chuck. I'm a few seconds from the kitchen door when a taxi enters the driveway. Kelly goes dashing towards it, barking, and I assume it must be someone we don't know because she continues to bark. An umbrella appears, used as a cane, and then a foot emerges to land gingerly on the ice-encrusted gravel. I've tried to forget that my mother is in town, but she's here, large as life, taking baby-steps towards the verandah. I go into the house and through the kitchen, and meet her at the front door.

"Oh, darling! I've never seen anything like this ice. This is terrible. How can you bear it?" The taxi hasn't left. For a second, I vainly hope this is going to be a fleeting visit. "I told him you would pay. I don't have enough Canadian dollars."

"You can pay with a credit card." Having become temporarily deaf in both ears, my mother makes her way to the kitchen while I snatch up my purse and pay. I feel anger and resentment bubbling up inside me before she's even sat down. I fill up the kettle, and then remember the power is out, so I grab two bottles of water instead.

She pulls out a crumpled copy of the Vannersville Times from her large, brown, leather purse and throws it onto the kitchen table with a flourish.

"I thought you cared about animals," she says. She sits down and folds her chubby arms, leaning them on the table. I notice the pronounced veins and age spots which hadn't emerged by the time I left England. "You certainly wouldn't think so if the front page article is anything to go by, dearie."

"I'm not your dearie or your darling." I turn my back on her to pour the water into glasses.

"They say that you're not responding to cruelty complaints because you'd have to dip into your precious contingency fund. What kind of humane society is that?" She must know more about my life here than I would have guessed.

"Interesting."

"Is that all you have to say? The animals are suffering. The RSPCA wouldn't stand by and do nothing to help those poor puppies."

"Neither did I, and I got fired over it."

She fidgets on the chair as if it's grown prickles.

At this moment, the kitchen lights flash back on, the fridge purrs and the furnace rumbles. It's always a relief when power is restored. I plug in the kettle, and it's hissing drowns out the silence between us.

I mull over why my mother has made the long trip to see me. It's as if she's come simply to enrage me. Her behaviour confounds me.

"You know your father deserted us, don't you?" She says, smiling with straight, tight lips. She lost the first round, so she's on another tack.

"He didn't. And why would you want to mention my father?" I get up and thump two mugs onto the counter. I'm glad they didn't break. I like these mugs.

"I think it's time you heard the truth. He left us high and dry."

"You've forgotten that I have his diary which the army returned with his personal effects, after he was killed by that bomb. I know exactly where he was and what he was doing until the day before he died."

"Well, he still left us, didn't he? He shouldn't have been a soldier."

"And you married that monster soon afterwards."

"Stan wasn't a monster."

"He most certainly was. I defy anyone to dream up a viler villain than he was, other than perhaps you. You did nothing, that was your crime. While your husband abused your daughter over and over again, you did nothing."

"Stan didn't do anything, darling. It was all in your youthful imagination. You've always had a good imagination."

"Do not call me darling ever again." My fury is so hot and passionate it's as if there is a fiery glow enshrouding me. I feel as if I'm about to burst with rage. "I can't understand how you can be so delusional. For once and for all, stop the denial for God's sake. You need to face up to your neglect, your lack of love, your lack of protection for your only daughter. I'm your flesh and blood. Are you incapable of any compassion or empathy? How could you let him do the things he did to me, night after night, year after year?"

"I don't know what you're talking about." Her hands are shaking and there are beads of perspiration on her brow. She isn't looking at me. The power goes off again and we're left in sombre lighting, in deathly silence, except for the relentless ticking of the clock.

"Yes, you do. There must have been a poison in your relationship with Stan, something really foul, or otherwise you're a hard-hearted, sadistic, hateful person. I don't want to see you ever again."

"Stan said he'd leave me if I said anything to anyone. I needed him."

"You needed a lecherous abuser of your daughter?"

"I was alone. Your father ran off."

"He did not run off. He was killed in the goddam war. Stop the lies, now. I'll get Dad's diary. You need to face the truth for once. I'm permanently scarred and damaged because of Stan and because you didn't do anything about it. How do you expect me to feel about you?"

"Okay. I did know. I did." She sobs as she lowers her head onto her arms, which are crossed on the table.

My eyes catch movement in the hallway. I'm sure I saw some brown curls bounce out of view, and I run to the front door. There's no doubt that the person in the hallway was Chuck. He's driving off in his Jeep, sliding a bit on the ice as he brakes at the end of the driveway. My heart sinks down into my stomach and I feel sick. I sense there's no point in tearing after him.

"And now I've probably lost Chuck forever because of you," I yell as I slam the kitchen door. Kelly slinks under the table, with her ears pressed close to her head, as if she expects the sky to fall. It has fallen. On me. I feel the weight of the universe come down, making it difficult for me to breathe. I gasp and sit on the chair with a thud and hold my head in my hands. I expect tears of sadness, rage and fear to roll down my searing cheeks, but nothing happens. My heart thumps as I listen to my mother's soft sobs.

I pick up my phone and send a message, pleading Chuck for a chance to talk with him.

"I'll go back to the Inn," my mother says, as she lifts her head. Her eyes are bloodshot and her mascara has smudged. She looks older and frailer, but my anger is so strong that it won't allow me to have any sympathy or compassion for this woman.

As the taxi leaves, the lights in the kitchen come back on again. I hope it's more permanent this time. While I keep some fresh water at all times in a trough in one of the spare stalls in the barn, horses drink a lot, especially when they're eating dry hay rather than moist grass. We had a power-cut for three days once, when there was a much thicker layer of ice coating everything. We were able to keep warm, but we had to truck water from a neighbour's house. He had a generator. Frank didn't think it was necessary to get one since a power-cut of that length happens so infrequently. I'm wondering if I should have one installed. But I can't contemplate that at the moment, it's going to be put on the back burner.

A text from Chuck, at last. He asks why I didn't tell him the truth about my past. He must have heard most of what went on between me and my mother. I don't know how to answer. Because I thought I'd lose you if you knew since I'm damaged goods; because I want to forget (but I can't); because I don't want the flashbacks to return; because it hurts; because. What do I say?

The doorbell chimes, bringing me back to the here and now. A police officer stands at the front door as I open it. He looks so sombre and serious and colourless in his black uniform that I think he's here to tell me that Chuck has been killed in a terrible accident, probably on the same bend that he and Tom were hurt and where Frank faked his car crash. But no, he's here to tell me, once I've sat down, that Frank's body has been found. But the curious thing is that he's been dead for a matter of hours, not for eighteen months, as the police would have assumed. He was found shot in a barn in Kentucky. He tells me in a monotonous, slow voice that his death is presumed to be a suicide and is not considered suspicious. He doesn't ask me many questions. I am visibly shaken and trembling. I think I see a glimmer of compassion in his soft brown eyes, which contrasts with his stiff, official, uniformed presentation.

I have grieved Frank's death once, and have continued to consider him dead even after I knew he was alive, because that's what he wanted, and I knew I wouldn't see him again. But the shock of his second, 'real' death knocks me off-balance as if I've been thrown from my horse, hitting the ground with a painful thud. The police officer asks if I knew Frank had survived his crash in the spring, and all I can do is mumble incoherently and let the tears roll down my cheeks. He asks if anyone could come and stay with me, and I say no.

But once he leaves, and as soon as I close the front door behind him, I send a message to Chuck telling him that Frank is dead. I make a lot of spelling mistakes even in such a brief message. My thumbs won't work properly on the tiny keyboard.

I find Murray standing in my kitchen: I have no idea how he got here. Kelly senses something is wrong because she's back under the kitchen table, her head lying between her paws, her eyes wide.

"Have you heard about Frank?" His speech sounds slurred. I do hope he hasn't been drinking.

"Yes, I know. He's really dead this time."

"They found his body in his stables. I just got back from there."

"They suspect suicide. I can't believe it."

"No, I can't really, either. But he was anxious about the fact that so many people knew he was alive." Murray notices my quivering body, my moist red eyes and my stuttering speech. "It's a shock, isn't it? You sit down. I'll find some herbal tea bags and make us some tea. No guarantees what it will be like."

He must be stronger than I am. Other than some slurring of his speech, he seems to be coping.

"How did your meeting with Frank go?"

"He was agitated, sort of uptight. I thought his skin looked pale and drawn. That could support the suicide theory, perhaps."

"He must have said something."

"He said he planned to leave Louisa's Acres because he wanted to be disappeared. He didn't want anyone from his past bothering him."

"Oh, so we would bother him." This isn't what I meant to say.

"He'd guessed that we knew he has millions stashed somewhere and thought we'd be after some of it. And, most of all, Louisa's death still tormented him. I'm sure of it. He was still trying to run away from the pain."

"I wish he'd got help. I wish I'd been more aware."

"There's no point in any of us looking back with regret."

"I do it all the time." I accept the mug of tea which has bits floating in it. The tea bag must have burst. "Did you see Tammy, you know, the American make-up artist he left Paris with?"

"She showed me the way to Frank's office in the stables."

"Did you see anyone else?"

"I was hoping you wouldn't ask me that."

"Why?"

"Because I saw Chuck. I was going to see Frank again the day I was due to fly back, but Chuck was going into the stables. I assume he was going to Frank's office. I got the hell out of there."

I feel as if I've been punched in the stomach. Chuck said he was going to Kentucky to attend a writing conference, but I couldn't find any indication that there was one being held there. What reason did he have for meeting with Frank?

4

Jockeys

Murray has left and I don't remember him going. The tea is cold, and bits are congealed around the inside of the mug, which is enough to make me go off herbal tea for good. My brain has become encased in a fog of confusion and anxiety, so much so that I can't move. Cooper jumps onto the kitchen table which, along with the counter, is off-limits. He purrs and rubs against me, his tail high in the air, his whiskers twitching. Kelly nudges my leg and whines. If I didn't know better, I'd think they were telling me to get a grip and do something. And they'd be right. I'm a resilient person. I tackle problems and deal with them. I just have to get hold of Chuck and find out what he's been up to, send my mother back to England, and unearth what caused the jockey's death.

The best way for me to clear my head, so I can think straight, is to go for a walk. I find my ice grips and stretch them over my barn-boots, grab my thick work coat, gloves and hat, and we all leave the house for a tour of the fields. It was a mistake to let Cooper out of the house. I have to watch him carefully since he has no fear or common sense, making him easy bait for a coyote or even a fox.

Kelly doesn't mind sliding on the ice. Four-wheel drive is a definite asset. Cooper is so light he doesn't seem to notice, but perhaps he has his claws out. His tail's still in the air, his sleek, tabby fur is shining in the rays from the setting sun. But as we enter the big field, I pick him up and put him inside my coat with just his head out. He's purring so loudly I wonder if I'll be able to hear the chickadees or the cardinals.

As we turn for home, the horses are standing in their run-in shed, not risking much moving around on the lumpy, frozen, ice-covered ground. I should have put them in the barn about an hour ago, but they're not agitated and are patiently waiting. I'm getting too hot from the fluffy little body wriggling inside my thick jacket and, with some reluctance, I put Cooper back in the house. He's warmed up my heart as well as my body. His love of life and the pleasure he derives from the simplest of things are infectious. I'm sure he's helped me to put things in perspective and to nurture the resolve I need to move forward. And Kelly's unconditional love, which radiates from her faithful large brown eyes, rebuilds some of my lost confidence. I am more determined and feel stronger as we walk towards the barn.

Once we've put the horses safely in their stalls, and have fed and watered them, Kelly and I return to the house to find Cooper on the kitchen counter lapping milk out of the small jug which Murray must have left there (although we didn't need milk with the herbal tea). I have to teach this kitten some manners, but not today. I put him on the floor where Kelly gives him a lick, which nearly knocks him over. I tip the milk into Kelly's bowl and put the jug in the dishwasher.

My thoughts drift back to Murray's visit with Frank. He didn't tell me what they talked about, and I wonder if there was any reconciliation.

It would have been even more disturbing for Murray if he'd gone down there, found Frank, and then they'd had another one of their arguments. And how would Frank have felt about Murray turning up? I guess he would have assumed that Murray was there to ask for money. And what on earth was Chuck doing there? Was he asking for money? The Chuck I think I know wouldn't do such a thing. But the Chuck I think I know wouldn't have gone to see Frank in the first place.

I need to tell Annabella that Frank is dead. I bet no-one has thought to tell her. The easiest way to connect with her is through her efficient agent-come-assistant, Simeon. I never know which country she's in, so don't know which time-zone applies, so email is best, which Simeon manages for her. She might have a personal email address, but I don't know it. I'll let Simeon know that I'd like to talk to Annabella about something important.

I still can't conceive of a plan to track Chuck down, so, until I have more to go on, I'll keep myself busy by looking into the death of the jockey. It probably won't take very long to find out what happened. Tomorrow I'll start by talking to the other jockeys who knew Juan the best, as well as those who were around when the incident occurred.

* * *

I sit in the cafeteria, which is close to the barns in the backstretch, and wait for Pedro. He's the fifth jockey today. I've not had any luck with the first four. I made appointments to meet them in between their rides, through their agents. I figured out which jockeys were on the training track at about the same time as Juan, because they did timed works which were recorded with each horse's name. Then I found out which jockeys usually rode those horses.

I wasn't thinking clearly when I contemplated this investigation. It's going to take up a lot of time and will need dedication if I'm to find out the truth. But I've started now, and there's no going back.

Pedro saunters into the cafeteria, holding his crop, and takes his helmet off as he reaches the table where I'm sitting. He has a dark complexion, bright brown eyes and a broad grin revealing straight white teeth. As I stand to shake his hand, I feel out of proportion. It's as if I've gained two feet in height while losing all sense of grace. Pedro, despite his diminutive stature and slim build, is dignified and has a firm hand-shake. I can tell he has no idea why I want to chat with him. I don't offer him anything to eat to accompany his skim milk, because I assume he's on a regimented diet so that he can maintain the low weight that racing demands.

"Are you a journalist or something?"

"No. Neal Carvey asked me to help him find out what happened to Juan. Neal and his groom were close by when Juan was killed. I'm not an official, just a racehorse owner."

His smile has gone, but he looks unruffled.

"How do you think I can help?"

"You were on the track that morning and I thought you might have seen something."

"No, didn't, sorry."

"Can you think of any reason why someone would want to hurt Juan?"

He doesn't answer, but slowly and without fuss, glances around the room, moving his chair without noise so that he can scan the myriad of tables. There's only one other customer I can see, and he's chatting with the cook, and the server is stocking the fridge with fresh sandwiches. We're sitting at a table which is about twenty feet away from where the three of them are.

"There's only one guy I can think of who'd do something to Juan."

"And he is?"

"You're not recording this, are you?"

"No, and I don't need to remember who told me anything. I just need some leads, something to go on."

"There's this guy, Dominic Marcel, who runs a race-fixing thing. Juan was one of his jockeys."

"I've never heard of anything like that."

"It's here and at most other race-tracks, I guess."

"How does this Dominic fix races?"

"He has about six jockeys in his pocket. He pays them to pull the horses up short. They'd be the favourites."

"It's linked to gambling obviously."

"Yep. The horses with the longer odds win, and Dominic cashes in."

"The owners of the good horses lose out."

"The trainers as well. And it makes the whole racing business dirty."

"How does he get the jockeys to play along? He'd have to pay them a lot, wouldn't he? You jockeys get a percentage of the winnings."

"Yep, but there's a lot involved in Dominic's gambling. Word out is that he runs his own betting business, illegal of course. He rakes in enough money that he can make it worth their while. But, as I said, I have no proof. Can't give you anything more than what's being whispered in the corners of the jockeys' room."

"This is very helpful. It gives me a lot to go on."

"I hope you get enough evidence to convince the officials to investigate. I'd like the scum who do this stuff to go to jail and not come out again. I love the horses and racing, and this sort of shit spells a whole lot of trouble for the business."

"I agree. You've been a great help. Thanks."

"Another thing. It'd be a good idea to talk to Juan's wife. Got to go now, have a ride."

"Thanks. Thanks a lot."

* * *

Juan's agent goes out of his way to be helpful. He not only gives me the contact information for Juan's wife, but sets up a time for me to meet her this afternoon.

It's a cold, blustery day, but the moving, dry air is vaporizing the ice, making it safer to walk and drive. Kelly and I make our way to the new walking trail, that was constructed to encircle the racetrack. Even though there are only a few patches of ice, I nearly tumble twice as I watch the horses on the well-groomed training track rather than heeding where I'm putting my feet. I'm enraptured by these sleek athletes with their pulsating puffs through flaring nostrils. Their smoky rhythmic exhalations are synchronized with their strides, creating a mesmerizing fluidity of movement and sound.

As we return to the pickup truck, it feels as if some of the horses' energy and calm focus has seeped into me. I take a deep breath.

* * *

Juan's apartment is about ten minutes from the track, on a busy road close to a strip-mall. There are twenty storeys. What captures my attention are the rusty streaks running down from the rotting balconies, which are peppered with orange patches encircled by peeling paint. I leave Kelly in charge of the truck, which I've parked close to the building and locked, and find my way into the lobby, which is strewn with junk mail and flyers. I miss the farm and I've only been away from it for about four hours.

Susana opens the door but turns away to sit down on the sofa. Her raw grief is palpable and fills the room, which is in semi-darkness. We have some awkward moments when I'm not sure what to say, and she's not sure what to do. She stands up and takes a couple of steps towards the kitchen, but then changes her mind. I'm not one to beat around the bush, and I think she appreciates me getting to the point. I explain to her why I'm here, that Neal and Linda don't believe Juan's death was an accident, and that I want to find out the truth. This grabs her attention and she looks directly at me and tells me she's eager to share what she knows.

"Juan was a great jockey. He was going to be big. His problem was that he was honest. He didn't want anything to do with that race-fixing thing," Susana says.

"Tell me about it."

"When he started at the racetrack, he was told that he had to be part of this ring, or he wouldn't stand a chance of being a top jockey. We wanted to leave, but we'd given up a lot to come here. We stayed. And later we found out it was lies."

"What ring exactly?"

"A group of about six jockeys, all working for one person. He'd tell them when they should hold their horse back in a race, so it wouldn't win, or wouldn't be in the top three. I think the instructions could change though."

"Do you know who runs the ring?"

"Juan mentioned a man called Dominic. I've forgotten his last name."

"What do you think happened to Juan, and why?"

"Why? He wanted out of the ring. He hated the dishonesty, the trickery. And he knew he could be successful and earn enough money without being in it."

"What happened?"

"He was told that Dominic could make sure that he lost his jockey's licence, and there were threats from Dominic's men. They came here, two of them, and told him he was in the group for good. If he said anything or didn't play by the rules, he'd be beaten up and they couldn't say that his family, meaning me, would be safe." Susana yanked a tissue from a box she had beside her on the sofa, dabbed her eyes and blew her nose, and chucked the tissue onto the floor to join numerous others.

"What did Juan do?"

"He couldn't believe that anyone would carry out such threats in Canada, this beautiful country. So, he didn't do what Dominic wanted him to in the races that weekend. Juan believed nothing would happen. He really thought Dominic wouldn't do anything."

"So, you think Dominic had something to do with Juan's accident?"

"I think they must have done something to him. Injected him or something. I don't know. He wouldn't fall like that. I heard he blacked out before the horse started to move off." She sobs, with her head in her hands, rocking on the sofa. I touch her arm. It's at times like this that I wish I was comfortable with physical contact. She needs lots of hugs.

"Who told you that?"

"I don't remember." She raises her head and looks at me. "I've had so many calls from his jockey friends and from trainers and riders. It's been good, but it's been hard too. I don't know who said it."

"I suppose we all think being a jockey is dangerous, and perhaps we don't ask as many questions as we should when something like this happens."

"I know that being a jockey is dangerous. Juan lost a good friend who was thrown and then trampled, but that was in a race. It's not supposed to happen when he's sitting on a horse before the horse starts its work." She looks at me with piercing, watery brown eyes which look like pools of dark sorrow.

"Tell me more about Dominic, Susana. Anything you know. It could be helpful."

"I don't know much. I'll try to remember." She puts her head in her hands again, and her voice becomes muffled. "Juan told me that Dominic runs a gambling business, that's why he wants to fix races, so he can make lots of money. He has men who work for him. Juan met Dominic once. He told me he was short, about the same height as Juan, so he wondered if he'd been a jockey once and that's how Dominic knows so much about the business."

"That makes sense. Anything else?"

"Some of the jockeys had to work together in races now and then, to make the right thing happen for Dominic. And I remember Juan saying that the agents had a hard time getting the right mounts for them sometimes. They are good jockeys, but they're often being paid to lose, so it could be hard to get them back on the good mounts that Dominic wanted them on."

"You've been so helpful. I'm going to do my best to get to the bottom of this."

Susana thanks me and apologizes for not offering me anything to drink. I give her my contact information and find myself compelled to give her a quick hug. And I leave the grieving widow with a lot more determination to find out what happened to Juan.

* * *

"You don't know me, but I'm Tammy," a soft, breathy voice with a trace of an American twang says into my phone. "Frank and I came together to Kentucky from Paris. I hope you knew about that." I can hear her body trembling through her words.

"Annabella told me. Her agent or assistant, Simeon, found out. It was a shock to hear about Frank." I clear my throat. "How did you know how to contact me?"

"Through Simeon. He knows everyone, it seems." She sniffed. "I'm shaken up about Frank."

"I'm sorry." I search for some more words, but they don't surface.

"I expect you wonder why the heck I'm calling." She makes a poor attempt at a giggle, which is overtaken by a sob almost before it emerges.

"I'm listening."

"I'm sure you've been through an awful lot. I feel bad about calling you. But you knew Frank better than me, and I reckon you'll understand. I'm counting on your help."

"Okay." I'm intrigued, but still the right words evade me.

"Fred, I mean Frank, didn't commit suicide." Sniff. "I know he faked his death over eighteen months ago, and you thought he'd died in a car crash. That must have been hell for you. But you thought there was something that didn't add up and you found out what happened. This doesn't add up. He's dead, that's for sure, but he didn't shoot himself. No way."

"Why do you think it wasn't suicide?" I've tried so hard to move on. It hasn't taken long for me to realize that I'd rather bury myself in finding out what happened to the jockey, Juan, than entangle myself in Frank's death again. Once is more than enough.

"Because there was no note. I know Fred would leave a note."

That was exactly what I thought, and I was right, when he disappeared over eighteen months ago.

"Is there anything else that makes you think it wasn't suicide?"

"We haven't long been at this beautiful farm, and he'd just bought some racehorses and set up a racing business. He'd hired barn staff, including a manager. He didn't like handling the horses himself, he said. And he was looking forward to the racing season. I have to sell all the horses now, and let the staff go." I hear a couple of whimpers. "Sorry, I'm not coping well at the moment."

"He had plans to stay, then?"

"Yes and no. He was real annoyed that some people had found out that he was here. I guess he was thinking of changing his identity again and moving to somewhere more isolated, but I know he wanted to continue with his plans to race and breed. He was so enthusiastic. I sure can't believe he killed himself." She sniffles and blows her nose.

"He changed his name at least once, obviously. You mentioned the name Fred."

"He'd changed it to Fred Simpson."

"I wonder how he got identification and travel documents."

"Don't know. All I know is that I miss him and the person who murdered him should be brought to justice. But the cops aren't interested. They treat me as some kind of hysterical woman, and have written his death off as suicide."

"You told them what you think and they haven't followed up?"

"No, they haven't. They don't want to listen. There's been some school shooting. It's real bad. They're buzzing around that place like flies, and the media is stuck on it. I can't get anyone's attention for a murder of a foreigner in a horse barn. It's crazy. Do say you'll help."

"I'll think about it." I must be nuts. I'm juggling too many things in the air already. But, knowing what I do about Frank, even though I haven't seen him since the day of his faked car crash, I think Tammy is right and that he wouldn't commit suicide. My curiosity is piqued and I should want to know the truth. I am his widow, after all. (I don't like the word "widow". It sounds just as it should: black, lonely, abandoned).

I travelled through the grieving process when I thought I was a widow, but when I found out that I wasn't a widow, that Frank was alive, Frank remained lost to me. My bereavement intensified, mixed with hurt and guilt: hurt, because Frank didn't confide in me, and guilt, because I should have seen signs of his distress and been able to reach out to him and help him. Now that I've recovered from the shock of the news of his death, I have no more grief left in me for Frank. I've exhausted my capacity to mourn the loss of my husband. But Tammy has made me realize I do want to find out what happened to him; for the second time. But I don't have a clue how I'm going to get the answers.

5

Louisa's Acres

The early winter storm which was predicted and made much of in the media, has started. I've grown cynical about the hype. And William must feel the same way because he's on his way and bringing supper, which I'm grateful for. The animals have eaten better than I have today.

Ice pellets tap at the windows, tantalizing Cooper, who is springing up and down off the countertop, where he's not allowed to be, trying to catch them. Kelly is under the kitchen table, sprawled out on her side, her paws paddling as she dreams of chasing rabbits, perhaps. But the kitchen seems empty. I sit motionless, feeling a chill creeping over me, hoping that William has some useful information that will mean I'll be able to talk with Chuck soon, in person. I wish neither Murray nor Chuck had gone down to Kentucky to see Frank.

William's intense dark eyes are narrowed as he bursts through the kitchen door. He has a bulky scarf wrapped around his neck, covering half of his face, and a black toque pulled down, sitting on the bridge of his nose, leaving a narrow band for breathing and seeing. He's told me before that he feels the cold with much more intensity than he did before he lost weight. The expense of buying warm jackets and gloves of good quality was something he hadn't bargained on.

Being a man of little resourcefulness in the kitchen, he's brought salad, pasta and garlic bread from the local restaurant. Kelly and Cooper like the smell of it all, and so do I. It's the kind of comfort food that tempts my appetite, which is just what I need this evening.

"You didn't tell me about Frank," he says.

"I didn't know what to say." I should have called him right away.

"That's what friends are for. I could have been here for you."

"I know."

"I hope you consider me a friend?"

"Of course." To hear him acknowledge he wants to be thought of as a friend is strangely heart-warming and comforting. I should say more, but the right words don't percolate to the surface. "I'm sorry, William. I think my brain's a bit addled. Thanks for bringing the food. That's a lifesaver." I smile weakly. "Did you find out anything about Chuck?"

"We did some phoning around, and found out that he stayed at the Vannersville Inn for two nights, and left this morning on the airport shuttle bus. We weren't able to find out anything else, except conjecture. One Inn employee thought he might be headed for the US."

"I'm sure he wouldn't go back to Kentucky. The only thing I can think of at the moment is that he's going to the writers' conference in New York." To think that he'd been so near, and was staying in the same place as my mother. Perhaps if I'd visited her, I would have seen him. I put my fork on my plate and slump into my chair. "I should go to New York."

"Perhaps that would be a good idea." He sounds so hesitant and doubtful that I'm certain he's telling me it's not.

"Tammy called me today. She's the woman Frank was living with in Kentucky. The police aren't listening to her and don't consider his death to be suspicious. But she's convinced that Frank didn't commit suicide and has asked for my help in finding out who murdered Frank and why.

"Eventually the police will listen to this Tammy, and if she has evidence to support what she's saying, they'll review the case."

"I have to admit I'm concerned that both Chuck and Murray were down in Kentucky to see Frank around the time of his death. The police might consider them to be suspects. What would you do if you were in my shoes?"

"You might want to get a head-start on the investigation, to prevent that from happening."

"I suppose that should be the priority. I wish I could talk to Chuck in person."

"I'm sure you do. You asked me what I would do. My primary concern for you both is that Chuck could find himself accused of murder. I would look into Frank's death, and I'll help in any way I can. And that should go without saying." He raises his eyebrows, and his eyes linger on mine for a second.

"I know you'll help." I look down at my plate, feeling his mild reproach for not leaning on him, as a friend should, when I heard of Frank's death. I have let half of my pasta go cold, but it's still moist and tasty, so I eat a bit more. I'm so appreciative of William's thoughtfulness that I want to eat as much of it as I can possibly manage.

"You don't have to eat any more if you don't want to. Don't do it to please me." William rinses off his plate and puts it in the dishwasher and puts on the kettle as if he lives here, and then makes himself a mug of coffee.

"I'm enjoying it," I say. He doesn't miss a thing. "I'm going to eat a bit more. I've been thinking about what you said, and it makes sense for me to go down to Kentucky as soon as possible."

"Sounds like a plan."

"Did you find out anything that might be useful in the investigation into Juan's death?"

"Dominic Marcel was a jockey some years ago. And then he got his thoroughbred trainer's licence. His Ontario licence was suspended about one year later, for nearly two racing seasons, so he went to Florida. After about six months, his Florida licence was suspended for nearly three seasons. It appears that the infractions were similar and were related to doping horses, using restricted drugs. He hasn't reappeared as a jockey or a trainer since."

"I suppose that's when he started his gambling business." I give him an overview of my conversation with Susana.

"Poor woman. What she says sounds feasible. And, by the way, I heard Dominic lives very well, but that's not sufficient evidence on its own."

* * *

As soon as William leaves, I get busy making travel plans for Kentucky. One reason I've been reluctant to leave so quickly is that the horses will be coming home from the track the day after tomorrow. I phone Joanna, hoping that she'll be able and willing to look after Kelly, Cooper and all four horses including helping the shipper to unload the two arriving from the track. I hope to spend just one full day in Kentucky, so she'll only have to manage the farm for less than three days, including my travel time.

Joanna says she'll drop in to chat about the horses. I tell her I don't think she needs to come, especially since there's a storm warning, but she comes anyway.

"Are you okay?" I ask as Joanna comes in the kitchen door. Her blonde hair is tied back, making her face seem gaunt and more angular. I wonder if she's losing weight. Somehow, it doesn't feel right to confront her with her recent dereliction of duty, and I don't want to dwell on it. I just have to hope she doesn't drop the ball this time.

"I'm okay. Just thought I'd come and find out what I need to do when the horses come."

"You look tired."

"Yeah, I am. Tell me about the horses. I've never helped unload any off a trailer before."

I'm able to assure her that Speed and Rose will be well-sedated for the trip and that they should be relatively easy to handle. She asks a lot of questions, which increases my confidence that she'll be able to assist the shipper when the horses arrive.

"Is there anything I can do for you this evening?" She fidgets on the chair, as if it's become prickly, and ignores Kelly's request for a pat on her silky head. Something is bothering her, but I don't know what.

"No, there isn't. Is it okay, though, if I call you if something comes up before I leave? Chuck hasn't come back from the conference yet."

"Yeah, fine." She grabs her shabby coat from the back of her chair. I'd like to give her one of mine. I could spare one that would be in a lot better condition. But it's hard to do something like that without offence. I watch her amble down the driveway into the darkness. It's as if she's lost the spring in her step.

My thoughts revert to what William said: I must do what I can to ensure that neither Chuck nor Murray are wrongly accused of Frank's murder. I can't sit still and let that happen.

* * *

I'm uncomfortable in this rental car. It's low to the ground, cramped and makes me feel as if I could be crushed in a flash by a falling branch or a speeding pickup truck. I miss Kelly and I miss home, but remind myself that I'm on a mission and need to keep focused, for the sake of Chuck, Murray and Frank.

I'm on the road that leads to the farm which Frank leased. It reminds me of an English country lane with grass verges, stone walls and trees, although the latter are in regimental rows, pruned and standing to attention. The grass has a light covering of snow and the temperature is cooler than I'd expected, being about freezing. I'm surrounded by the most beautiful horse farms I've ever seen. The oak rail fencing is immaculate, straight and painted, with not a horse-chewed mark on it. I can't see a horse anywhere, but the pastures, from what I can tell through the dusting of snow, are well maintained and would be lush in the spring.

I find the farm and know that I have the right place because "Louisa's Acres", carved out of a large piece of oak, is mounted between two stone pillars. That must have cost Frank a bit. My eyes moisten at the thought of Frank's unending grief for Louisa. The tragedy of her death lived on, eating away at him, and never died, until now. Perhaps he did commit suicide. People have taken their own lives for less.

The sweeping asphalt driveway is bordered by trimmed shrubs surrounded by mulch, and the occasional specimen tree. Order and symmetry rule the day here. My farm is messy, eclectic and shabby in comparison.

I pass the enormous stone barn with its large oak doors. It looks brand new, as if no-one has ever stepped foot in it, let alone a horse. There's not one piece of wood-shaving, straw or hay anywhere. I notice a couple of cars parked at the back as I make my way to the mansion. The house is also made of stone with the doors, window-frames and trim made of oak. The finish on the wood gives it a warm honey colour, softening the stone, which is primarily grey. The driveway is circular. There is a concrete fountain, about five feet tall, which is shaped like a stallion rearing up, although no water is spouting out of its mouth into the pond surrounding it. A large perennial garden surrounds the whole shebang. I'm almost overwhelmed by the opulence and feel out of place. My car seems too small, my clothes too casual and I should have put on some make-up.

"You must be Meg." Tammy runs down the wide stone steps and gives me a hug before I have a chance to grab my purse out of the car. She's sobbing on my shoulder, and I'm wondering how I'm going to console her.

"Tammy, I'm so sorry." She steps back and blows her nose on a couple of tissues she has in her hand.

"It must be awful for you, too. Come in out of the cold. What am I thinking to keep us out here?"

I follow her into the huge foyer.

"Frank leased this furnished. It was his dream to have a horse farm in Kentucky," she says. I didn't know this. It's the first I've heard of it. I've come to the conclusion that there was a lot about Frank I didn't know. My stomach feels unsettled. "Let's go into the kitchen. There aren't any staff in the house anymore because I can't pay them. Frank wanted staff to do everything." Now, that sounds like Frank. I insisted on doing the barn chores, but he wanted staff for just about everything else, even at our modest farm. "You don't look good, Meg. Was your flight okay?"

"I'm fine. The flight was okay and the bed-and-breakfast place is great. I dropped my bag off there before coming here."

"If you come again, you must stay here. I should have asked you. I'm sorry, I'm not doing well myself, and I'm not thinking straight."

"I'll be fine. Do you like tea? I can make it. I could do with some."

"That would be nice. I usually drink coffee, but I know there's tea here somewhere."

The kitchen has so many cupboards, I think it might take me a week to find tea. I assume, though, that things are just as orderly inside as they are outside. There's a kettle, so tea must be close by, and I'm right.

"It's real nice to have you here. Someone who knew Frank and knows he wouldn't commit suicide." Tammy wriggles herself onto one of the high chairs positioned at a granite counter, which runs along a large window overlooking the paddocks. I can imagine Frank here, watching his horses grazing. We sit in silence for about a minute.

"Tell me what you know. Start from the beginning."

"Okay." Tammy turns to face me. She fell in love with Frank almost the instant she met him. As she tells me this, I see luminosity in her dewy eyes. She must have truly loved him, and she must have believed that he loved her. And perhaps he did. His death is even sadder if he had finally come to terms with his first wife's death. But I recall the name of the farm engraved on the large oak sign. Perhaps he hadn't.

Tammy relays how they travelled from Paris, and that money appeared to be no object. Everything was first class. He had previously found out about this farm and leased it sight-unseen.

"He wanted to race thoroughbreds?"

"He wanted to race and to breed. He bought mares and yearlings from sales, and he had a couple of two-year-olds as well. There were about forty horses, but there are only a few left in the barns now. I've been sending them to auctions, with the help of the barn manager."

"How did he get all the horses? Did he go to the sales himself?"

"No. I remember him mentioning someone who was doing this for him. I'm pretty sure he paid him a commission."

"Do you remember the name? It might be helpful, in case a transaction went wrong, or perhaps this person might know something."

"Dominic, I think."

"Dominic Marcel?"

"Could be. Not sure if I heard Fred, Frank, use his last name."

"It seems he's a bad actor. I wonder if Frank knew who he was dealing with?"

"My mind's a fog at the moment. But I know Frank was pleased with the horses, and I wouldn't be surprised if Dominic did well out of it all."

"I expect he did. From what I've heard, it's all about money with him. Tell me more about Frank and the reasons why you think he didn't commit suicide. I know it's difficult to talk about."

"He was planning for the future and excited about racing. He was even thinking of sending three of the two-year-olds to Florida to train. He'd selected about three trainers. I think Dominic helped him with that, too. But I guess he knew several people had figured out that he was Frank Sheppard, even though he never used that name. He let it drop that we might have to move. But he didn't sound desperate, more like frustrated."

"What about the circumstances surrounding his death?"

"I've been talking to the police. I think I've got their attention at last. They said they'll check his gun for fingerprints. It was on the floor beside him. I reckon they won't find any. The killer would have wiped them off, wouldn't he?"

"If the gun's clean, it should steer them away from suicide." It must have been traumatic for Tammy to see Frank lying dead on the barn floor. I don't want to concoct an image of his body left in the barn to grow cold and stiff. I divert my thoughts by studying Tammy's facial expressions and body language. I must keep my emotions in check, otherwise I won't be of any help.

"That's true. But they're still wrapped up in that awful school shooting. It's sent shock-waves through Kentucky. I don't expect them to move quickly."

"How many people knew where the gun was kept?"

"Lots of people. Frank kept it in an obvious place, in the drawer of his desk, and he wanted staff to be aware. I don't know if he was expecting trouble. Perhaps he was. I didn't think of that until now." Her watery blue eyes are accentuated by a thin line of dark grey, and a faint touch of blue-grey eye shadow. I assume that the subtle but effective use of make-up is reflective of her training as a make-up professional, as well as of her innate artistic ability.

"That makes it difficult to narrow down. Remind me who visited the stables that day and when."

Tammy crosses her long, slender legs and pushes her shiny blond hair behind her shoulders. Her posture is rounded, aging her. Perhaps it has something to do with stooping over to put make-up on the faces of numerous performers.

"Murray, his brother, showed up the day before. Frank had told me he was an alcoholic, but he seemed okay. Just tense, I guess. I showed him to Frank's office in the stables. I didn't know he was coming, and it was obvious Frank wasn't expecting him."

"Why do you say that?"

"Because Frank said something like 'what are you doing here?' I don't think the visit was great because it didn't last long, and when I asked why he didn't invite his brother into the house, Frank didn't want to talk about it." Tammy fidgets on the stool and gazes out of the window without seeing.

"You don't know what their meeting was about?"

"No." She turns her head to look at me, as if she's recalled something important. "Then, the day Frank died, someone called Chuck showed up. He was pleasant, but I thought he was nervous. The barn staff told me he and Frank had an argument. They were worried. They said they thought it was something to do with money. I didn't see him leave, so no clue how long he was there. I think you know him?"

"Yes, I do." I gulp a mouthful of tea and nearly choke. "I can't figure out why he was visiting Frank though, and have no clue why he'd be talking about money with him, let alone arguing." I have to turn my face away from Tammy and look out of the window. I hope she doesn't notice the tremble of my bottom lip, which I clench in my teeth. Chuck had no business going to see Frank, and certainly no reason whatsoever to discuss money with him. I'm flabbergasted, but try not to reveal it. Nevertheless, I can't believe that he killed Frank.

I sit more upright as if to rid myself of the emotions that are threatening to pierce my protective shell and beat me down, and regain my composure.

"Tell me more about this Dominic guy."

"None of the barn staff liked him or his guys. I know that much. Frank tolerated him. I guess he was so excited about setting up his stables that he didn't pay much attention to what Dominic was like. He delivered what Frank wanted, and perhaps that's the only thing that mattered."

"He didn't mention Dominic's illegal gambling business and his race-fixing?"

"Gee, I'm not sure."

"Perhaps Frank found out about Dominic's activities, and then things went bad between them. It might be a good idea to mention to the police that Frank was dealing with Dominic. I believe he's our most likely suspect at the moment."

"Gee, Meg, that's great that you already have a suspect. I'll tell them for sure."

"Was there anything on Frank's computer?"

"He had a smart phone, but not a computer. He sometimes used my laptop if he wanted to watch a race. I checked his phone, but I could only find text messages to and from that guy, Dominic, and a couple to me about nothing. He hadn't set up a list of contacts or anything like that."

"Anything in the text messages to Dominic?"

"You can read them if you like. There's nothing I could see."

Tammy's right. I find nothing in the text messages. They're all brief messages dealing with horse business.

Before I leave, I have a look around the magnificent stables, including Frank's office, the door to which is off the wide aisle. There's nothing of Frank's here. It's a large, impersonal space with no photographs, paintings or memorabilia. The huge oak-framed windows look out over the paddocks towards the woods. From Tammy's description, I find where Frank's body lay with the gun on the floor close by, in the middle of the fifteen-foot-wide aisle between the stalls. Fortunately, it's harder than I thought to visualize him lying here. And it seems an odd place to commit suicide. The more likely spot would be in the office, sitting at the desk, and with a note in front of him.

The staff has all left for the day, and the few remaining horses are munching on their hay. Their chomping sounds bounce off the oak stall walls and reverberate among the solid rafters in the vaulted ceiling. One of the horses drinks out of the water bowl attached to the automatic watering system, which hisses and sputters. They are oblivious of me and I feel solitary, alone with Frank's ghost. I shiver and retrace my steps.

* * *

There's no Joanna in sight as I enter the house. Kelly greets me with such enthusiasm I wonder if she's been alone for hours. We make our way to the barn, Kelly jumping up close by my side. I don't think she wants me to leave her alone ever again.

There should be four horses in the barn, but there are only two, Eagle and Bullet. They seem okay, but I expected to find Speed and Rose here too. Neal arranged to have them shipped today, saying this was the only time that worked for everyone, other than me, of course.

Back in the house I find a note on the kitchen table from Joanna. "Carl and I put the horses in the stalls. I've fed Kelly, and she's in the house. There's another power-cut and Ewert wants me home. Best, Joanna." Where are the horses? When did she leave? Why didn't she text me? I phone her.

"Joanna, the horses aren't here."

"What do you mean?" Her deep voice has a strange squeak.

"I mean that Speed and Rose are not in the barn."

"Carl and I put them there. You can check with him." She hangs up. I've no time to dwell on her strangely abrupt response.

I phone Carl the shipper.

"Carl, Scarfin and Alusio are not in the barn. I just want to confirm that you did ship them today from the racetrack. Neal Carvey would have made the arrangements."

"Sure did, to your farm. Your barn manager helped me unload. Doesn't know much about horses, does she?"

"She isn't my barn manager. The horses are missing."

"They were there all right, when I left." He sounds unperturbed. But I'm becoming more and more agitated. How do two horses go missing? I phone Neal.

"Neal, the horses left today, right?"

"Carl picked them up this morning about eight."

"Well, they're not here."

"Did he take them to the wrong barn?"

"No, he says they arrived and were put in their stalls with the help of my neighbour. But they're not here."

"There must be some logical explanation." Neal is being exasperatingly calm and matter-of-fact. It makes me want to scream.

"All I can think of is theft." My teeth chatter as my stress level rises exponentially.

"Difficult for people to get away with stealing racehorses, they have registration tattoos inside their top lips as you know."

"I know, but,"

"I bet whoever has taken them will find out that they can't race them, and will return them. I wanted to talk to you, by the way."

I'm stamping my feet as if I'm a two-year-old having a tantrum with my face flushed and hands sweating. I'm not in the mood to talk about anything that's not related to getting Speed and Rose back home safely.

"Neal, I'm desperate to find my horses."

"I'll do some calling around. I'm sure they'll be easy to find. They're big, you know." His attempt at a chuckle makes me more irritated and impatient with him.

"Neal, I'm very anxious about them."

"They're good horses, and I know you care about them. But I can't see what anyone would want with them. Unless,"

"Unless what?"

"Someone could be on the lookout for a ringer." A ringer is a fast horse that looks like a horse that is slower, and is substituted fraudulently into a race in order to make money, both with bets and the purse. "But the tattoos would be an issue. Not sure if there are ways of changing them. The documents wouldn't be difficult."

"Oh, no. I hadn't thought of that. Then we could be dealing with professional fraudsters. Someone like Dominic Marcel." I feel nauseated.

"Look, I'll do what I can. I know some people who'll help. But I wanted to tell you that Linda and I have been going over everything that happened that morning, before Juan died. And we think there's something important that I promised Linda I'd tell you asap. So, here goes. Linda saw Ferris, another jockey, hand Juan a coffee as he was walking towards the shedrow to pick up his ride."

"Okay." I snap my response. I feel as if I've downed ten cups of coffee. I'm so much on edge.

"We think the coffee could have been poisoned."

"Mm." My legs feel weak as I stand by the ancient wall phone, twirling the cord in my fingers and rolling my eyes.

"There should be an autopsy. I think it's called that."

"Okay. Got it. Please do what you can to find Speed and Rose. I have to go." I hang up the phone and slump into a ball on the floor. Kelly licks my ear, which, beyond all that makes sense, gives me a lift. If she has confidence in me, that gives me a bit of hope that perhaps I can get myself out of all the messes I'm in. It isn't rational, but I don't feel rational at the moment. I'll cling onto anything as I hang like a spider on a flimsy thread, waving in the breeze with no control over most of what's happening to me.

6

Dominic

The more I toss and turn in my bed, disturbing Kelly, the more certain I am that Dominic Marcel must be the villain. I've decided that he must have killed Juan, stolen my horses and murdered Frank. It seems so obvious that I have a hard time not calling the police to tell them.

With an ache in my heart, I feed Eagle and Bullet, clean out the stalls, refill the water trough, and plug the submerged heater in to keep the water free of ice. It's cold, but the patchy ice in the paddock is now covered with a fine layer of snow, which is safer for the horses.

The last person on earth I want to see is my mother, but she's sitting at the kitchen table when Kelly and I return to the house.

"You look like something the cat's dragged in." She says as her eyes drift back to Cooper, who's on the table batting a tea bag around. "I was going to make tea, but thought you'd want to make it when you came in."

"You'd look like hell too if your horses were stolen."

"I can see them in the field."

"Not those, my two racehorses."

"Oh, those. I saw a man take them."

"What?" I nearly drop Cooper as I remove him from the table to place him on the floor.

"It was Chuck, that man who should be called Charles. He took them. I saw him do it yesterday when you weren't here."

"What did he look like?" I can't believe Chuck would do something this hideous to me, or to the horses. My mother leaves the room and comes back in about a minute, holding a framed photo in her hand which belongs in Frank's office. She has a broad grin on her face, which accentuates the deep wrinkles under her eyes.

"That's Frank, not Chuck. Stop your lies. And stop hurting me. You're going to leave. Now." I'm too tired to yell, but I want to scream, slam doors, and throw things, including my mother, out of the door. Instead, I put my jacket on and Kelly and I get in the truck. I need to think, to sort things out.

I drive a short distance down the road to where a hiking trail starts. It's only a short loop, but it'll give me respite for about twenty minutes. Exercise in the fresh air, with Kelly at my side, invariably helps to clear my mind. I need to get rid of the frustration and fogginess I'm feeling.

My mobile rings as we're entering the trail. It's Tammy.

"I can't understand it, Meg. The police just called and the only fingerprints on the gun were Frank's."

"That doesn't make sense."

"You sound like you're sick."

"I'm pretty upset. My two racehorses have been stolen."

"Gee, that's bad. Meg, I'm sorry. Do you think there's a connection?"

"Between Frank's death and my horses?"

"I don't know. Perhaps that's silly."

"Perhaps it's not. Neal, the trainer, said they could have been stolen to be ringers." I have to explain what a ringer is. "You said you weren't aware of any concerns that Frank had about his business dealings with Dominic Marcel. Are you sure?"

"I told you, Dominic, if it's the same guy, was helping Frank set up his stables."

"Do you remember anything more about Frank's dealing with Dominic?"

Tammy hesitates, and I wonder if I've lost the connection. But just as I'm about to check if she's still there, she replies. "Gee. I forgot Frank invited him into the house for a drink several times. How could I forget that? Let me think. Mm, Frank talked to me afterwards about a couple of things. Yeah, there was something about race-fixing, I think he called it. I didn't understand what he meant. It's coming back to me. Yeah, Frank said Dominic boasted about having a race-fixing business at three racetracks, including Vannersville, and he told me he was going to look into it because that's where he'd raced horses before. I wish I'd remembered this earlier. Frank was sure mad about it."

"I'm glad you've remembered. This could be very helpful. But I suppose, because the fingerprints are Frank's, that the police are now absolutely certain that he committed suicide."

"Well, no. That was one of the things I wanted to tell you. I had to tell the police about the row Frank had with that man Chuck, and it got their attention."

"I can't believe Chuck's capable of murder. And I can't think of any reason for him to want to kill Frank."

"Gee. I'm sorry. I reckon they should do an autopsy, and I told the police that. You know, like on those television programs. Then we'd know." She sniffles. "I've been trying real hard to remember everything because it doesn't make sense that Frank killed himself."

"Tell me about Chuck."

"The barn staff heard the argument between Frank and Chuck, and told me, and said it was about money. But I now remember that I heard the beginning of it, as I left the barn. Not the words, but it was loud. I was scared they might fight or something. I know you don't think Chuck could have done it, but the argument sounded that bad that I can't help wondering if he came back to kill Frank. That's why I told the police. They said they can check the bullet to confirm it came from Frank's gun. That gun found lying next to Frank was fired, by the way. That's another thing I wanted to tell you."

"Oh, okay." This doesn't sound good for Chuck, but, since Frank's gun was fired, it also sounds like the suicide theory could be resurrected. But I can't believe that Frank killed himself any more than I can believe that Chuck killed Frank, argument or not.

We finish our conversation, but as I put my phone back in my pocket, I worry. I worry about the implications for Chuck of what Tammy has told the police. And the fact that Murray is the only other person she knows of who visited Frank around the time of his death. As far as she knows, Dominic wasn't there. But it's likely that a killer would be careful not to be observed, so it doesn't rule him out, or anyone else, for that matter. It would be a big help if I knew the motive.

* * *

Kelly and I complete the trail without any more interruptions, but when we return to the truck, I notice a piece of paper tucked under one of the windshield wipers flapping in the breeze. It can't be a ticket because I'm parked off the road in a small lay-by which is often used by people walking the trail. The note is written by hand on the back of a window-envelope and says that if I want my horses back, I must pay $1million in cash, one week from today, and call the number on the envelope to find out where to leave it.

My reaction isn't as explosive or emotional as I might have expected.

This can't be the work of a professional, not the way someone like Dominic would act. That's perhaps a good thing. But it might mean the horses are not being well cared for. That's a bad thing. I have someone's handwriting and an envelope, which might help to trace them. And they must have been close-by just minutes ago. I look around. Kelly is sniffing the ground surrounding the truck. She probably knows who it is. But she doesn't find a trail to follow and I don't find any evidence that gives me clues where the person came from or went to. So, we go home.

My heart feels even heavier when I find my mother still here. Why is she determined to hurt me?

"There's a message from the police for you to call them. They said it was about Francis Sheppard's death. You said he was dead a year and a half ago. Now look who's been lying. Miss goody-two-shoes."

"Frank faked his death. But he's dead now. I'm not talking about it." I banish Cooper from the cupboard out of which I'm retrieving Kelly's bag of kibble. I have to keep functioning, even though there is so much whirling around in my brain and pummeling at my heart.

"Oh, he left you, did he?" She's enjoying herself, sitting up straight with folded arms. Let me never, ever, be like her. I don't respond. I'll find some energy to get her to leave once I've finished looking after all the animals. Cooper is crunching on a piece of Kelly's kibble which I dropped on the floor, while the dog waits patiently for me to put her bowl down. I put fresh water in the other bowl, and Cooper bounces over and dips his paw in and licks it. It's an inefficient way of drinking water, and I'm surprised he tolerates getting his paw wet. His antics momentarily distract me a little.

"What did he die of?"

"He was murdered."

"Oh, how exciting! Do you know who killed him?"

"No. But I'm going to find out." I turn to face her. "You must leave now. I'm calling a taxi." She puts up some resistance, at the same time as asking me a myriad of questions about Frank, which I don't answer, but she leaves when the taxi arrives.

* * *

As I get dressed the next morning, I feel queasy and light-headed. I forgot to eat anything yesterday evening. I'll make sure that the animals are not the only ones who eat this morning. After the barn chores and my breakfast of porridge and toast, which was difficult to digest, I pick up my mobile and there's an email from Tammy waiting for me.

> *"Hi Meg, the Kentucky State Police just called and said that the bullet found in Frank didn't come from his gun! It's now a homicide investigation!"*

Not long afterwards, I get a call from an RCMP (Royal Canadian Mounted Police) officer. He tells me that Francis Sheppard has been murdered and that the RCMP is assisting in the investigation through Foreign Affairs. One suspect is Charles Alexander Murphy. Do I know him? Mr. Sheppard's partner, Tammy, advised that Charles lives at this address. The Kentucky State Police believe Charles was at the scene on the day of Mr. Sheppard's murder. This is a serious matter in that Charles Murphy is a suspect, so I could be an accessory after the fact if I fail to give information on his whereabouts. I respond that I don't know where he is, but he might be at a writers' conference in New York. Did I have to say that? Shivers go up and down my spine and my breakfast is in danger of being regurgitated. I'm asked various questions, including whether he owns a gun, which he doesn't to the best of my knowledge. Do I know of any possible reason for him to want to kill Mr. Sheppard? No, I don't. I try to stop trembling and to get my brain functioning. I tell him that Frank was involved with Dominic Marcel, who told him he ran a race-fixing business, which angered Frank. I explained why I think this is important and could lead to Dominic wanting Frank out of the way. I can hear the officer clicking on a keyboard and he tells me that Dominic Marcel is known to the police. They will be checking out all leads.

I sit down at the kitchen table, feeling as if I've been dragged through a lengthy interrogation under a hot, blinding spotlight. But it could only have been a few minutes, and I'm in my cool, comfortable kitchen. But Chuck certainly is in deep, hot water.

William texts me he's coming over, if okay with me. I'll be glad of his company and it doesn't take long for him to appear, thank goodness. I don't think I've moved an inch since the phone call from the RCMP. I must be stunned, although I should have seen it coming. I blabber out all the information I have while William listens. He's a good listener, which is perhaps indicative of his profession as a lawyer. I include everything that I know about the horses, Juan, Chuck, and even my mother (but nothing about the abuse I suffered in my past). It's cathartic to talk about it all to someone who understands. The weight of all these troubles has lightened, just by sharing it all with William.

"I can do some more work on the jockey's death. How would you like me to help?"

"As I mentioned, Neal saw another jockey, called Ferris I think, hand Juan a coffee that morning, before he got on the horse. Is there any way you can convince the powers-that-be that there should be an autopsy?"

"I know the Chief Coroner personally. Is it okay with you if I or my assistant, Ramona, talks to Neal?"

"Of course." I'm relieved to get some useful help with something.

"Assuming Neal tells me the same story about what he witnessed, as well as the matter of the coffee, I will advise the coroner that the death should have been reported to her because it occurred suddenly and unexpectedly. Then she'll investigate."

"That's what we need. Given that this might take some time, I wonder if you could find out if there's a link between this jockey, Ferris, and Dominic?"

"The Coroner will ask for the assistance of the police, so it shouldn't need us to find out who's behind the death."

"I know, but Dominic seems to be a common thread in everything that's happened, except for my mother, of course." I manage a half-smile. "I told Tammy that I suspect he could be the person behind my horses being stolen. They're both great racehorses, and he could have plans to use them as ringers, which would be a good fit for his gambling business. And Dominic helped Frank set up his stables and Tammy told me he boasted to Frank about his race-fixing. And that Frank told Tammy he was going to look into it."

"You mentioned this earlier. It appears that Dominic is a common thread here, but that doesn't mean that he killed the jockey, stole your horses and murdered Frank. It could all be coincidence. He could be innocent, except for his illegal gambling business. His business could be the common thread. It's not inevitable that he's a murderer."

"I get that. And I admit that the note left on my truck wasn't professional at all, not likely to be his work. But he's still the only person who might have a motive in both murders that I can think of right now."

"That's valid." William smiles at me, and I feel as if I'm being wrapped in warm, reassuring comfort. He's come a long way since I first met him. His friendship, loyalty, understanding and forgiveness mean that I almost trust him as much as I do Kelly. I glance down at the dog, who smiles at me with her dark brown eyes, and looks at me as if she adores me. I hope she knows I adore her.

Soon after William leaves, Murray turns up unannounced. I still haven't moved from the kitchen table. Not much is going to get done unless I do. But perhaps it will. I plan to grill Murray about his visit, since I still can't make sense of it.

He puts a bag of freshly baked cheese croissants down on the table.

"I thought you might need some carbs. And I brought tea. I know you can make it, but I got it anyway."

"That's nice. Thanks. I seem to be in a bit of a slump this morning." I bring Murray up to speed, including the phone call from the RCMP.

"Chuck won't be the only suspect," he says. "Remember, I was there around the time of his death as well."

"I want to know exactly what you were doing there. I don't buy this thing about reconciliation, and, from what Tammy said, Frank wasn't happy to see you and your visit wasn't a long one."

"That's true. It was difficult. He was mad because his disappearing act didn't work and he was getting bothered by people from his past, as he put it. And I'm sure he was still trying to run away from the pain of Louisa's death."

"You said all that before. But you're his brother. I can't believe he'd be that angry about seeing you, despite your past. His reaction must have been something to do with why you were there."

"I don't want to tell you."

"I need to know, and I have a right to know. I want to find out the truth for all our sakes. Tell me."

"Part of my reason for going was to ask for money."

"Murray! Why?"

"Not for me. I was pleading a case on your behalf."

"What would you do that for? You have no right to do that. Frank lived up to all his financial obligations included in our marriage contract."

"I know he did. But we now know he had or has several millions, at least ten, in off-shore accounts. You have a right to some of that money. And you lost your job, and things seem tight here, and I thought he should help you out. After all, he was your husband."

"Murray, that's crazy. I'm dumbfounded. I'm not at all happy that you did this." That is an understatement. I'm furious. My face is reddening and beads of sweat are growing above my upper lip.

"I'd hoped he'd see reason; that he'd want to come back and be reconciled with all of us. But he pointed out that he'd faked his death, so it wouldn't be plain sailing for him. I told him I'd graduated from the rehabilitation program and he said he'd heard, and that he was glad and happy for me, but I should know better than to ask for money, especially when money has been a bone of contention between us. I reminded him I was asking for your sake, not mine. But he said he was adamant he would not discuss money with anyone, least of all me. Things escalated, and he said I was a pariah and always had been. Those were his words. Then he got really riled and said that he would have to leave Louisa's Acres and probably even leave the States because everyone knew he was there and were seeking him out, and he was as mad as hell. Then he told me to get out and never come back."

"But you went back on the day of his death."

"I did. I was upset that we'd parted on such horrible terms. I've always been distressed by our poor relationship. But it has always been poor, since you want the truth. If anything has ever been said to the contrary, it isn't correct."

"So, how did the next visit go?"

"I got out of the car and walked into the barn. I assumed I would find Frank in his office, as I had the day before. But, I'm sorry Meg, Frank and Chuck were in the aisle between the stalls, near to the office, and they were arguing. It's an enormous building and I don't think either of them caught sight of me. I was about eighty feet away, at least. But it was definitely Chuck. I was shocked. Their voices echoed and resounded in the large, cavernous space, and I heard some words before I beat a hasty retreat. They were having a heated discussion about money and I heard your name mentioned."

"The world has gone mad. Why were both you and Chuck pestering my husband about money for me, when it's none of your business, either of you?" My anger is frothing and foaming inside me, but there is also a sinking feeling. What Murray has said, if true, implicates Chuck and is consistent with what Tammy told me. It's not good.

I'm relieved when Murray leaves, although I find the wherewithal to thank him for telling me the truth. Because I think he has told me the truth, unfortunately. I should have asked him if he's told the police.

Despite the cold, and the wispy whirls of snow in the air, I put on a jacket, take a croissant and my lukewarm tea, and sit on the verandah with Kelly. This will have to serve as lunch. I feel numb, not from the biting air, but from the bombardment of things that are happening. Things I wish I could resolve quickly and satisfactorily. I'm being pulled in different directions.

Kelly growls a low, rumbling warning as a black SUV turns into our driveway, its oversized wheels crunching the gravel as it nears the house. It reveals nothing of its insides through the sinister dark glass. Kelly barks with her hackles raised as two men, dressed in black to match their transport, walk with deliberate steps towards me. Now what? I stay put.

"Can I help you?"

"As a matter of fact, you can. Meg Sheppard, right?" The man who's speaking sits on the chair next to me with a patronizing grin on his face. The other man stands in front of us with his hands clasped and his legs splayed apart, as if to prevent me from leaving. I'm holding Kelly by the collar as she continues to alternate between barking and growling. Neither of us like these men. I don't respond. It's fine with me if they have to shout because of the noise she's making.

"You can help us and help yourself. Nice dog you have there. I expect he's special to you. I expect you'd miss him."

"Her."

"Her. Doesn't make any difference to us, does it, Drake?"

"No difference." Drake's face doesn't appear to move as he speaks. His wide shoulders and square head make me think of a wrestler. He must be the heavy. The man sitting next to me has a slimmer, less bulky build, with a hard, angular face which has no sparkle of warmth or glimmer of humanity. Perhaps he's a robot. That thought helps me to keep calm.

"My boss, I think you know him, Mr. Dominic Marcel, he's given me an important message to give to you. I don't know what it means, but I know you'll know what it means. He says back off. Back off." He raises his voice to a squeaky shriek to emphasize the point and to be sure he's heard over Kelly's growling. She's given up on the barking, but she won't stop telling these men in black that they're not wanted and she believes they're bad guys. She's right.

"You can tell Dominic," I say.

"Mr Marcel to you."

"You can tell Dominic that I don't know what he means. Does he mean the murder of my husband, Frank Sheppard? He might have known him as Fred Simpson in Kentucky? Dominic did business with him and I think there was a falling-out, you could call it. The police are treating Frank's death as a homicide. I'm sure they'll contact Dominic soon, if they haven't already. That's out of my hands. Or does Dominic mean the murder of Juan, the jockey? Someone has contacted the coroner and there's going to be an investigation. This one's out of my hands too. Or does he mean the theft of my beloved racehorses? They could be destined to be ringers. This is the only one that I could back off from, but I won't." The man sitting next to me has let his mouth drop open as I talked, and the man in front of me fidgets.

"Mr. Marcel won't be pleased to hear this." The man next to me gathers himself together. He stands up but I don't raise my eyes to meet his. I pat Kelly while still holding onto her collar. "You'll be hearing from us again, and next time it won't be a social visit."

"No, it won't," the large man in front of me says as they both leave the verandah and climb back into their black hole. I'm shaking. It took a lot of inner strength to deal with those bullies, but they weren't as tough or threatening as they needed to be. Dominic won't be happy.

A croissant won't replenish the energy I just used up. I need something more substantial. I let go of Kelly's collar, rub her ears, and we both go inside.

7

Whinnies

I give Kelly two large dog biscuits, and I make a sandwich, using a bun I found in the freezer and a chunk of cheddar. I take one bite and almost choke on it as my mother comes through the kitchen door. It feels as if a boa constrictor is tightening its grip around my neck as she sits down in front of me, ruffling her brown permed hair with her fingers.

"I expect you wonder what I've been doing?"

I don't answer.

"Well, I've been looking into this Chuck, Charles you've been hanging around with."

"You have no right to do that."

"I'm your mother. It's natural for me to take an interest in the man you're having a relationship with."

"It's certainly not natural for you. And it's none of your business." The sandwich looks even less appetizing as my resentment grows:

yet another person interfering in my personal affairs. But I can't stop a crumb of curiosity from creeping into my thoughts.

"I found out Chuck's secret. He inherited a sugar cane plantation in Barbados, but lost all his money. That's why he needs your money, that's why he's after it. I think it's disgusting that his family is in the plantation business. Do you know what horrors go on in those places?"

"What a ridiculous lie. I've heard more than enough from you. Time for you to go."

"No, no, not yet. I think I should do the decent thing and tell you what I've told the police." She sighs, and she contorts her face into what I guess she thinks is a show of pity. I try to swallow a mouthful of my unappealing sandwich. I need the strength, but my mouth has gone dry and the boa constrictor hasn't loosened his grip. Kelly growls. She must know what I'm thinking and feeling.

"I told the police, you know, the Kentucky State Police. Nice man I talked to. I told them that Charles or Chuck wanted your husband, Frank, out of the way so that he could marry you. Charles asked Frank to divorce you, but he wouldn't, so that's why he had to kill him. Of course, you know this, don't you darling?"

I've never felt such utter contempt for anyone as I feel for my mother at this moment. My rage is driving surges of adrenalin through my body, and for a split second, I think I might strangle her. But I don't. I scream and yell and tell her what a nasty, horrible, lying bitch she is, amongst other much more vicious comments. I don't stop my rampage until I have a coughing fit. The large bite of sandwich is still not completely swallowed. Perhaps I'll choke to death right here and now, and that will be the end of this nightmare.

"Oh, don't carry on so, darling." I think I might have rattled her a bit with my noisy, out-of-character, abusive tantrum. I pick up where I left off, and resume my furious tirade of name-calling and oaths. I stoop down and yell in her face. She is flustered, a little. That helps me to collect myself.

"It's beyond me how a mother can be so absolutely callous, cruel, and calculating as you. I don't want you in my house a moment longer. I'm calling the police."

"Do you think that I have never done anything for you?"

"I don't think it, I know it."

"Ah, but I've done a very big thing for you, you know. Something huge."

I don't take the bait. I pick up my phone to call the police.

"I'll go. No need to call the police, darling. But I want you to know that I killed Stan, just for you. For you."

"You're lying. I don't believe you killed Stan. Let's say you did, well, how did it help me? I had left years before he died. You should have killed him two weeks after he moved into the house. Get out."

She agrees to sit on the verandah until the taxi arrives. I feel exhausted, pummelled and frustrated. She seems calm, cool and collected.

I toss my sandwich in the garbage and get a brandy. I think about what my mother said. Why is she so bound and determined to get rid of Chuck? And did she really call the police? I have to contact Chuck. I text him yet again, but this time I tell him it's urgent and that he could be arrested. I think that will get his attention, and then I call him and I'm relieved, beyond belief, when he answers. Although, in my surprise at hearing his soft voice at last, I hesitate. He sounds drowsy and lethargic.

"Are you there?" Chuck asks.

"Yes, I'm here. Are you okay?"

"I'm at the writers' conference. What's so urgent?" I hear a tremble in his voice, a wavering, as if that's not what he wanted to say.

"I'm worried, Chuck. It's about Frank's murder."

"What? How and when?" His voice has become full of tension and agitated.

"I sent you a text a while ago. He was shot. The police are treating it as a homicide. You're a suspect. Why the hell did you go down to see him?"

"I'm a suspect in his murder?" It's almost as if I can feel him quaking through my mobile.

"The trouble is, you were heard arguing with him, in his stables, at about the spot where he was found dead, and the words 'money' and 'Meg' were said, according to a witness. And, what I'm very concerned about is that the police have been told. Why were you there?"

"This is impossible to talk about on the phone."

"Well, try. I want to help you, but I won't be able to if you don't tell me what's going on."

"I don't know how to say this. Our relationship hasn't been the greatest for a while." His voice is trembling again. "And I went down to see Frank because I thought the reason for our challenges was that Frank is, or was, still alive. You had a husband. I thought you felt loyalty to your husband. I thought you were clinging on to the relationship even though he'd faked his death. I wanted Frank to face up to his responsibility to you, and officially divorce you. He was the one who raised the issue of money. He accused me of being another person after his money, and that it was all I was interested in. I was shocked at how rude he was to me, and how angry he was."

"You had no right to talk to Frank about a divorce." I'm fuming. "What were you thinking? That was my business." And since Frank was officially dead at that time, Chuck's actions verge on insanity.

"I knew I couldn't explain this well. I was trying to mend our relationship."

"You should have talked to me. Frank has nothing to do with anything."

"So, you're saying our relationship is wanting, not because of Frank, but because you don't love me, that it's my fault?"

"That's not it." But a tiny part of my heart and a large part of my brain agree with him. He has been absent a lot, he hasn't talked with me, and he's asked my husband to divorce me behind my back. But a large part of my heart and small part of my brain tell me I should have made more of an effort to grow the relationship with him. He didn't talk to me, but I didn't talk to him either.

"What is it then?"

"We should have communicated more. I should have told you about my past. I think you overheard something the other day when you were here. In a nutshell, I was sexually abused by my stepfather over several years, until I left the house. My mother did nothing about it. And you should have talked to me about your absences and what you're doing. But, you're right, it's not easy to talk about this stuff on the phone."

"I suspected something when I overheard you two at the farm, and I got out of there. We'll talk when I'm back home."

"I hope you make it here. You may soon be jailed for a murder you didn't commit. Help me so I can help you."

"I've told you all that I know."

I ask Chuck if he saw anyone else visiting that day. And the only person he saw was someone who looked Mediterranean in complexion and rather short. Chuck wondered if he was or had been a jockey.

"I think I can guess who that was, and that's very helpful. Try to remember what he was wearing, and any details of what he looked like, and email me, so I can follow up. And tell the police if they get hold of you." I feel like I've been on a roller-coaster of emotions, and the energy has been sapped out of me. "When will you come home?"

"Tomorrow."

I put my mobile down and think about Chuck's lack of reaction to my revealing the raw truth of my past, albeit with a few abrupt words. Did I expect some compassion, some empathy? There was nothing. Is that how someone who loves you and cares about you responds to something like that?

I divert my thoughts to what he said about his visit to see Frank. Murray had told the truth, then, about what Chuck said, and Tammy told me that the argument was overheard by some of the barn staff. But no-one mentioned hearing a gunshot, and the body was found by Tammy when Frank didn't show up at the house. Frank must have been shot after all the staff left.

It's good news that Dominic probably visited on the same day. I've not met him, so I don't know exactly what he looks like, but the description of a person with a Mediterranean complexion and the height of a jockey makes me hopeful that it could be him. I can feel a layer of tension peel off, as if I'm being released from a cocoon and might soon be able to fly.

I'm looking forward to tomorrow, but I'm also apprehensive because I'm even less optimistic that Chuck and I can salvage our relationship, such as it was. I make another sandwich and sit in the kitchen, listening to the clock tick. Tomorrow I won't even notice its incessant ticking when Chuck is here, and we're talking at last. The phone breaks the near-silence. It's Tammy.

"I thought you'd want to know about the autopsy results on Frank. I hate talking about this. We know that the bullet which killed Frank didn't come from his gun, and now they say that the angle it went in means someone else must have shot him for sure."

"I'm sorry you're having to deal with all this."

"I'm surprised they're not contacting you instead of me, but I suppose I'm here and you're in another country."

"I expect so. Did they say anything else?"

"No, not that I can remember. I can still get a bit muddled, but if I do remember something, I'll let you know. One strange thing happened. Annabella called me and wanted to get all the details. But as she was talking, some of my muddle cleared and I remembered another person came here on the day that Frank died. Simeon!"

"What would Annabella's agent be doing there? That makes no sense. Are you sure?"

"I'm sure. I know what he looks like. I met him often enough when I was in Paris. I saw more of him than of Annabella, who is a bit of a diva."

"No wonder Frank was getting angry. He had at least three people, Murray, Chuck and Simeon and possibly Dominic as well."

"I didn't see Dominic. Why do you think he was here?"

"Chuck said he saw a Mediterranean-looking man who had the stature of a jockey, so Dominic immediately came to mind."

"That would have been Simeon, not Dominic."

"Really? Can you remember when he was there?"

"Oh, gee, let me think. It wasn't early, but I can't remember."

"Let me know if anything comes back to you. And what could he want with Frank?"

"I guess he must have been here because Annabella asked him to see Frank. It's sure odd that he didn't come and visit me for a chat."

"I'm going to talk to Annabella. I'll let you know if I find out anything."

I can't help feeling disappointed that the person Chuck saw was more likely to have been Simeon than Dominic. But, if I want to get to the truth, I'd better not let my biases and wishful thinking take over. Why on Earth was Simeon at Louisa's Acres?

* * *

Neal calls me on my mobile.

"Have you found Speed and Rose yet?" The sound of their names sends a feeling of dread surging through my body, sapping my small energy reserves. I've done virtually nothing to get them back. I don't know where to start.

"No. I hope you've got something."

"It won't help you, but I've checked with all the sources I can think of, and I've dug deep, and word is that Dominic is not responsible. He didn't take them and he doesn't have them, I'm pretty sure."

"Oh. I don't know what to do now. That was my only lead."

"I'm sorry. Don't know what to suggest. But I'll keep my ears to the ground."

"Thanks."

It seems my theory that Dominic is responsible for Frank's murder, my horses being stolen and Juan's death, is going up in a puff of smoke. The hardest one to let go of is Juan's death. I just can't imagine that he's not responsible, somehow. There's too strong of a connection and certainly a motive.

* * *

It's time to put the horses in, and as I peer into the two empty stalls which should be filled by Rose and Speed, I feel the void. I have let them down. What are they doing now? A wave of panic starts in my stomach and runs through my body and mind as I remember the ultimatum in the note. I have to deliver $1million or my wonderful, innocent horses will be sent to the slaughterhouse. At least, that's what I assume would be the outcome. I shudder. I have to make them my top priority and find them, somehow. After all, Chuck is on his way home, so perhaps solving Frank's murder is not as urgent at the moment.

Kelly walks ahead of me on the path back to the house. The sky is clear at last, but we're turning away from the setting sun and we'll lose all of its waning warmth soon. There's a tingle in the air which holds the promise of frost. Kelly whines, looks at me, turns to face south, whines louder, comes to me and jumps up and yaps, and looks south again. I don't know what she's telling me, but she's agitated and wants me to do something. She cocks her head as if listening to something, then whines and looks at me with such pleading that I walk towards her and she keeps going, through the field and across to the road and then down the edge of the road. I stay close behind her. She stops now and then to listen. Then I hear something. A whinny! I start to jog and she picks up the pace ahead of me. Kelly leads me to the dilapidated barn on the property where Joanna and her husband live. I recognize the whinny; it belongs to Speed.

We walk into the barn, find a light switch and I'm horrified by what I see, albeit dimly lit by a couple of incandescent bulbs which are covered in fly dirt, cobwebs and dust. Rose and Speed are in make-shift stalls with no sign of feed buckets, some hay which looks more like straw, empty water buckets caked in dirt, and no bedding on the dirt floor. They look lethargic, and there's not a trace of the beautiful sheen they had on their coats when I last saw them. They are caked in muck, their eyes have lost their sparkle, and they have at least some abrasions, but I can't see well enough to tell how serious their injuries are.

I can't leave them in this hell-hole a second longer. With trembling hands, I find some baling-twine dumped in a corner, and create a couple of lead-reins. The stench of ammonia from their urine hits me as I walk into each stall and tie one of the make-shift lead-reins to each of their halters, which are still in one piece, although scuffed and dirty. The smell tells me they must have had some water at least, and the dry, hard, pale manure suggests they had some poor-quality feed. They are both quiet and co-operative but eager to leave their stalls, so I tie Speed's lead-rein to a post as I grab hold of Rose's and then pick up Speed's. I've never led them both together, and it would be impossible when they're full of energy and vibrant with the joys of life. They seem to sense that they need to do just as I say, and perhaps they don't have the strength to do anything different.

I wonder how we're going to get past the house without being seen or heard. Darkness is making its slow descent but horses' hooves, when shoed, can make a lot of noise, and I wouldn't trust them not to whinny again. I take a risk and walk away from the house, with a horse on either side of me and Kelly in front. I think I remember a gap in the fencing that leads onto the next property, and then I can get out onto the road from that neighbour's driveway, which runs under a canopy of tall pine trees.

We find the gap and the horses follow calmly behind me. I talk to them the whole time in furtive whispers. Rose nuzzles me a couple of times with her nose and Speed walks just a little behind so I can feel his warm breath on my neck. We get through the gap and then we make a noisy trip down the gravel driveway to the road.

My whole body is shaking by the time we finally walk into our barn. I put them into their stalls. I give them a fifth of a bucket of water each. I'm concerned about the potential for colic, so I plan to introduce food and water in small amounts and regularly. I text Neal and Linda to let them know that I've found Rose and Speed at a neighbour's place and tell him I think they'll be okay, but they need a lot of tender loving care.

Linda phones me almost as soon as the text is sent.

"I'd love to help. Can I come?" Linda asks.

"We would all love that. Thanks. But haven't you got a job for the winter?"

"No. I'm not working at the track in Florida this year. And not found anything here yet."

"Can you come tomorrow morning?"

"Sure. I'll be there. I'll bring my stuff."

I look at the horses more carefully in the better lighting and decide I should call the veterinarian. In the meantime, I give them both a light brushing down as I check them over, doing my best not to disturb them as they nibble on the good quality, sweet-smelling, green hay. Then I put some more water into their buckets to replace the fifth that's all gone. By the time the vet arrives, they're both lying down, which is unusual for them at this time of evening.

* * *

The vet is thorough, kind and patient with me and with the horses. She gives them each a shot of penicillin and hands me a bottle of antibiotic powder which I'll need to add to their feed once a day. I have antiseptic wash for the various cuts and abrasions, none of which need stitches. Some of the larger wounds look red and raw, but they are not deep and are probably mostly due to the inadequacy of the bedding on the concrete floor. Their feet need a good clean and to be medicated because there are signs of fungus along the sides of the frog under the front feet of each horse. That would be because they were standing in urine-soaked mud and muck. They're dehydrated, but not seriously so. What I'm doing, the vet says, is fine. There's no sign of colic at the moment, but grain should be reintroduced slowly. Hay is good. She suggests letting them out in a small paddock for only half-an-hour on the first day, and then gradually building up the time as they feel better and regain their strength. I comment to her that it's distressing to see how quickly horses can go downhill. She tells me they're lucky I found them when I did, because a couple more days could have brought much more serious consequences.

"They're in good hands," she says, as she backs her SUV away from the barn.

I turn to Kelly. "You saved their lives, Kelly. I would never have heard their whinnies from here, and you told me in no uncertain terms that I needed to follow you. You are one special dog." I hope she understands at least part of what I'm saying. She seems pleased with herself, with her silky tail wagging and her dark eyes smiling at me. I'm going to phone Joanna, but not before I have something to eat. I'm trembling from the combination of physical exertion, emotional stress, and lack of food. And Kelly deserves a special treat.

8

Linda

Kelly's gnawing on a big chew I found in the cupboard. She's the hero again. She so often is. Does everyone realize how wonderful animals are? But they're vulnerable. The state of my horses after only a few days of near-neglect is evidence of their reliance on us humans. I let them down.

I pick up the landline phone and call Joanna's number, hoping that she, and not her husband, answers.

"Yes," Joanna says.

"I've just rescued my horses from your barn. Tell me why I shouldn't call the police." I say it calmly and without raising my voice.

"It was nothing to do with me. It was all Ewert. He had this stupid plan. He wouldn't listen to me and I had to go along with it. I can hear his car in the driveway. He'll be right pissed when he finds out. I won't tell him you called." She sounds as if she's gasping for breath and hangs up. I'm worried about her. I don't know what Ewert is like. I hope he's nothing like my stepfather was.

I have a sudden urge to employ a security guard for the horses tonight. I text Neal, apologizing for it being a bit late, because I know people who work at the racetrack are early to rise, often four a.m. or earlier, and early to bed. Hopefully, he's up a bit later when he's not training racehorses. He gets back to me quickly with the name of the security company he uses when he needs to protect a valuable horse about to run in a stakes race: to help ensure that no-one can tamper with the horse beforehand.

The security company can send someone out in half-an-hour, which is better than I expected. I ask them to provide the service for 24 hours, and then I'll review. Kelly and I are out at the barn again, armed with a folding chair, a small table, and a lamp I took from one of the bedside tables. I'll ask him to do a tour of the outside of the house and the barn from time to time. I feel more settled now that I have that arranged.

But I won't be able to sleep since I anticipate seeing Chuck tomorrow and am apprehensive about our conversation. I should tell him about my past, which will be harrowing for me, resulting in the inevitable return of painful flashbacks. They most often take the form of nightmares and don't haunt me during the day as they did years ago. And I don't hate myself quite as much, but I still feel unworthy of love. Am I able to show love? I still have serious problems with relationships, especially intimate ones. I would need a very special, patient and understanding man. Something tells me that Chuck isn't this person. I feel it in my bones. Also, I've let him drift too far away.

Having stirred up feelings from the past, I fear the nightmares returning. So, in an odd sort of way, I'm glad that I'm planning on giving Speed and Rose regular, small quantities of water throughout the night. Since I'll be awake most of the time, I might as well sit in the barn myself, guarding the horses. But it's warmer in here, and I can make tea when I want it. So, I flip through old racing magazines as I sit on my bed, propped up with a couple of pillows, with Kelly lying beside me who is, I'm sure, dreaming of rescuing horses.

The morning takes a long time to dawn, but it's here at last. The window's closed and most of the birds have left for the winter, so I'm not greeted by a dawn chorus. But the sun has begun to emerge over the horizon, and the farm looks as if it's covered in shimmering silver glitter as its rays are caught and bounced back by the frost crystals. I go downstairs to get a fresh cup of tea and some coffee for whomever is on security duty in the barn. I imagine they've changed shifts since I was last out there.

I'm startled by some heavy knocking on the door and nearly drop the mugs, which I've just retrieved from the cupboard. The security guard is standing with Joanna on the doorstep.

"Do you know this woman?"

"Yes. I suppose you can come in Joanna." I thank the security guard as Joanna follows me into the kitchen. Her eyes are red, her face flushed and she's shivering.

"Ewert made me spend the night in the barn because he says it's all my fault that you found the horses."

"You can tell him that Kelly found the horses, if that makes any difference. You had a bad night too."

"You must be furious and upset."

"I'm too tired to feel anything at the moment except sad, and worried about the horses."

We're interrupted by another loud knock on the door. The security guard has Linda in tow.

"Linda, I'm so glad to see you. Thanks for coming. We'll go to the barn as soon as I have my stuff on."

"I love Speed and Rose. I want to help."

I ask Joanna to make coffee for the security guard. I ask Linda to take Kelly out into the paddock while I throw on my barn clothes. I look presentable, even though I've been up most of the night. I'm one of those lucky ones who doesn't have to wear make-up, and my long black hair is always shiny even when I only give it a quick brush-through.

Joanna hangs back as we enter the barn. Linda gasps when she sees the horses. The last time she saw them they had gleaming coats, bright eyes and lots of energy. I gave them a light brush last evening, but they still look ragged and unkempt and have lost weight. Their ribs are showing even more than expected of a racehorse in training. Racehorses are trim and fit, just as human athletes are, but Speed and Rose look like sad apologies for thoroughbreds. And this deterioration only took a few days.

"How could anyone do this?" Linda asks. Both horses whinny and walk towards their stall doors. I can see an improvement in their eyes, which means we might have combatted the dehydration, and they've eaten a reasonable amount of hay. I hope they feel better.

"It's a good job you didn't see them yesterday. They've turned a corner overnight. What they need now is some good grooming and wound management, as well as hoof cleaning, and I think I'm going to give them a vitamin supplement I have. And, of course, they're on antibiotics."

"I'm here to do whatever I can for these guys." Linda is snuggling with Rose and Speed is watching. "I brought a bag of carrots in case you need extra."

"That's good. The moisture will be good as well as the sugar. Great." I feel a sense of relief because I trust Linda to do a fantastic job of caring for the horses. "How long can you stay?"

"I can help for as long as you want. I've nothing else planned."

"I'll pay you the same daily rate as you'd get at the track with a bit extra. Okay?"

"I didn't expect to be paid, but I won't say no. Thanks."

"Joanna, we need to talk." I lead the way back to the house, leaving Linda with the horses and the security guard sipping his coffee with Kelly at his feet. She must think she should be helping with guarding the place. Kelly isn't the best guard dog, but she has saved me from some nasty scrapes in the past.

"Joanna, you've some explaining to do." I should kick her out, but my curiosity has got the better of me. I hand her a mug of coffee and get my tea at last. I forgot to offer Linda anything. I'll take her something when we've finished talking.

Joanna erupts into tears. I hand her a box of tissues.

"Joanna, that won't help. I want to know what's been going on, and crying is just going to make me angry. I'm the one who should be crying."

She sniffles, blows her nose, takes another tissue and dabs her eyes. The mascara has painted faint dark streaks part way down her cheeks. "It was all Ewert's idea. But it's not his fault. He's involved with a man called Dominic somebody. He does something with him on gambling." She sobs again, and rips a tissue out of the box. Cooper chooses this moment to jump on the table and roll on his back, purring. He obviously has no clue what's going on and has no idea that this is a terrible moment to be asking for attention. And he's the worst for obeying the rules, but I can't get angry with him. I pick him up, give him a quick stroke, and put him on the floor.

"A man called Dominic is involved. How?"

"Ewert told me that Dominic hired him to take your horses. Ewert had planned to hide them in a barn somewhere else, but he thought he'd get the money for looking after them if he kept them at our place. He said Dominic would pay in cash."

"Has Dominic been to see the horses?"

"No. Ewert has been trying to get hold of him. Out of town or something. Ewert wasn't sure where they were supposed to go after our place."

"I'm sure Dominic would have been appalled to see them in the condition they're in now."

"I'd better get back. Ewert will be home soon."

"Should you go back there?"

"Yes." Her grey eyes look smaller, surrounded by puffiness, but something about them reminds me of someone else. She takes a couple more tissues, and I put the thought out of my mind. I'm relieved when she leaves, but am left perplexed as well as angry about Ewert's scheme.

* * *

Juan's wife, Susana, calls me on the landline phone. She lets me know that she's just heard that Juan was poisoned and the police are investigating. I must thank William for making the case for an autopsy. Just as I'm about to text him, he knocks on the door, with the security guard hovering behind him. Kelly knows who it is before I do.

"You look tired, Meg." I update him on Kelly's discovery of the horses, and their rescue. We agree we'll go to see them once we've had a chance to talk. I give him the latest on Frank's murder, including the fact that the police have been told that Chuck had an argument with Frank, and my disappointment that Dominic wasn't seen at Louisa's Acres as far as I know. The three people who were, I tell him, are Murray, Chuck and Simeon, Annabella's agent. I tell him I must follow up with Annabella, since I can't imagine what Simeon was doing there.

"I agree we need to find out why Simeon was there," William says, as he measures coffee grounds into the filter. I have a fresh mug of steaming tea, and Kelly is warming my feet.

"I don't think I thanked you for doing whatever you did to get that autopsy on the jockey."

"Just a few phone calls and a couple of emails. It'll be worth it if they catch the person who did it." Dark brown aromatic liquid is pouring into the glass carafe. I like the smell of coffee, but I don't enjoy the taste.

"It has to be Dominic behind it. I just can't think of anyone else with a motive."

"Have you talked to the jockey who gave Juan the coffee? Do you know anything about him?" William turns and looks at me. His deep dark brown irises contrast with the white of his eyes, but their intensity doesn't reflect the softness of his expression.

"No. I just know that he's part of Dominic's race-fixing ring. I get your point. I've been jumping to conclusions, and have assumed Dominic is responsible for Frank's murder, the theft of my horses and the poisoning of Juan. I need to have a more open mind."

"It's a mistake the police sometimes make. They convince themselves that someone is guilty and then go about trying to prove it. Some innocent people have ended up in jail because of it."

"It's hard when you're involved personally. It's harder to have an open mind."

"Especially when you're trying to prove that Chuck is innocent, as in the case of Frank's murder."

"I have to assume he's innocent. I just can't think otherwise." But a little, niggling slither of doubt pricks me. What if my mother is right? That Chuck demanded that Frank divorce me so that he was out of the way, so Chuck and I could be married. And, he might blame Frank for the challenges in our relationship, because I was still married to him and, in his mind, having trouble letting go and moving on. But something about this theory doesn't ring true with me. Chuck has never talked about marriage or even hinted at it, and he's been at the farm more and more infrequently.

"You're shivering, Meg. Are you all right?"

"I'm fine. It's all just a bit overwhelming." I notice the carafe is full. "Do me a favour and take a mug of coffee out to Linda in the barn."

"Of course." Kelly follows him. They soon return.

"How's your mother doing?" William asks. I haven't revealed to him how poisonous my relationship with her is.

"I've almost forgotten about her. I haven't seen her today." And I don't want to. "Chuck hasn't arrived yet."

"He's coming back today? That's good news."

But my intuition is raising doubts because I've heard nothing from him since our phone chat yesterday, even though I've texted him twice to ask what his travel plans are. I don't like the ominous silence, and I wonder if Chuck is coming back at all.

"Meg, you look like you could do with some rest. I'm going to leave now. I'll see you later."

"Sorry, I'm not good company at the moment. I think I'm exhausted."

"Don't do what I did and try to bury your worries and sorrows with drugs. I know you won't. You have more resilience than I do. It might help to focus on one thing you can tackle."

"I know. I'm just going through a low patch. I'll pick myself up."

"Is there something I can do?"

"I'm just wondering if you could find out something about the jockey who handed Juan the coffee, as you mentioned? I'm going to focus on Chuck. I'm worried."

"I'll see what I can do. In the circumstances, Chuck deserves your full attention, I agree."

After William leaves, I take my tea into the family room, and lie back on the recliner, but my eyes are wide open and every muscle in my body feels tense. Despite my reluctance, I know I won't feel better until I solve the riddle of Frank's murder. I have to find out who killed him and why.

I want to talk to Annabella, so I email Simeon. I wish I could call her myself, but the accepted practice is for her to call me.

The long-awaited text from Chuck arrives, but it's not good. He tells me he's at the border, but has been told he may not cross into Canada because he's a suspect in a murder and will be taken in for questioning. He will soon be on his way back to Kentucky. He asks for my help. I reply that I'll do everything I can to get him home. But what, exactly, can I do? What if the police believe he's guilty and are determined to prove it?

I must believe in his innocence and must do something to help. I stroke Kelly's silky head and gaze into her shiny brown eyes, looking for inspiration.

I pick up my mobile and call Murray. Perhaps he'll remember more about what happened that day in the stables.

"Meg. I was going to call you." His speech sounds a little less slurred than I remember from last time we spoke. I tell him about Chuck being a suspect and being detained.

"I hope I didn't make matters worse," Murray says.

"How do you mean?"

"I got a call from the police. They questioned my whereabouts and came on hard. I got nervous. I told the police that I'd heard Chuck arguing with Frank. I'm sorry Meg."

"You argued with Frank too. Did you tell the police that?"

"No, because that happened the day before his death. And I didn't talk to him after his argument with Chuck."

"But you were there that day, and the police believe you didn't kill Frank, but believe that Chuck did."

"I don't know if it's fair to say that they believe Chuck is the murderer. Fortunately for me, they seem to believe that I didn't kill Frank."

"But I don't know if I can believe you."

"That's pretty low, Meg. I'm not lying to you."

"Even though it sounds as if you're drinking again?" I shouldn't have said that. But I'm angry with him. He's made things worse for Chuck.

"I'm surprised you haven't mentioned that before." I hear an edge of bitterness in his voice. "I'm not drinking. I had a minor stroke which affected my speech, but I'm almost back to normal now. If you want to check my story out, you can call the day hospital. I've almost finished my sessions of speech therapy."

"Oh, I'm sorry, Murray." I don't know what else to say. I should have kept my mouth shut. I shouldn't have jumped to that conclusion. When Murray was drinking, I don't remember him ever slurring his speech or having difficulty with speaking.

"I honestly did go to Kentucky for you. I wish I hadn't. It was the wrong thing to do. But I was angry. I was mad that Frank had multi-millions and didn't give you your fair share. I wasn't as mad about him not giving me some of that money as I was about him not treating you right. You losing your job made me get angrier about it." Murray had a temper when he was drinking, and I'd assumed it was an effect of the alcohol. But perhaps he's also rather hot-headed when he's sober.

"But, as I said, he lived up to our marriage contract."

"But he didn't reveal his true worth when you signed that."

"We're not going to get anywhere with this conversation, Murray. Is there anything else you can think of that might help Chuck? That's what really matters to me at the moment."

"I can't right now. But if I do think of anything at all, I'll let you know, I promise."

I'm almost relieved when we end our chat. It wasn't the helpful conversation I was hoping for. The landline phone makes me jump as its ring reverberates round the house.

"This is Dominic Marcel. I think you know who I am." His voice is high-pitched and almost feminine-sounding, which doesn't fit my image of him as a tough, ruthless kind of guy.

"What do you want?"

"I want you to back off."

"I don't know what you mean. Your thugs visited me, but they weren't very informative. They just threatened."

"I'm sure you know what I'm talking about."

"No, I truly don't. There's my husband's murder in Kentucky. I think you knew him as Fred Simpson. You set him up with racehorses. Then there's the theft of my horses. Ewert someone or other said he stole them on your behalf. And then there's the murder of Juan, the jockey, who's part of your race-fixing business. So, is it all the above? Or just one or two?" My face is hot and my hands are sweating. I'm angry.

"Bullshit. It's all bullshit." His voice almost cracks. He's angry too.

"What do you mean it's all bullshit?" I'm shaking, and hope it isn't showing in my voice. Kelly is agitated and looking up at me with a questioning look in her eyes.

"I'll tell you, goddam it. I'm not the bad guy you think I am. I heard about Fred, and I've been asked questions. I've proved that I was nowhere near Kentucky when Fred was shot. I just helped him get horses, that's all. And, before you ask, none of my thugs, as you call them, were anywhere near there either. And I don't know anyone called Ewert. I don't need some nobody stealing horses for me. And the jockey. That would be a dumb-ass thing to do. Yeah, he didn't want to play the game anymore. Any of these guys who drop out of the game know damn well that they're in serious trouble if they rat on their pals, so they don't. And he hadn't. I would know."

"So, why the visit from the thugs?"

"Because you're stirring up trouble. I'm a good businessman, running a harmless gambling business operation, which a lot of people enjoy. Don't need some princess poking her nose in."

"Your gambling business is illegal, and despite what you might think, I'm pretty sure the police are investigating."

"Yeah, but they haven't got evidence."

"Well, I don't either, so you can call your thugs off."

"They're not thugs. They're nice guys with families. They just keep things on track for me."

"Well, call those nice guys off. I don't want to see them again."

"Only if you keep out of my business. You watch out for yourself. I'll look after myself."

And he hangs up. I don't know if I can believe a word he's said, but I'm inclined to think he might have been telling the truth. Perhaps I should talk to Joanna. If he's telling the truth about Ewert, perhaps I can believe the rest of what he told me.

The phone rings again almost as soon as I've hung up.

"Meg, how nice it is to talk to you." It's Annabella with her soft Italian accent. I enjoy hearing her speak.

"Annabella, thanks for calling me so quickly."

"Simeon says that Chuck is a suspect in Frank's murder. I am sorry."

"News travels fast. Yes, I'm worried about him."

"Tammy told Simeon that Chuck visited Frank in Kentucky, at the stables."

"Yes."

"Simeon heard Chuck was in Frank's office where he keeps his gun."

"Oh?" I haven't heard this before. "Simeon was at the stables too. What was he doing there?"

"I still had a couple of Frank's things which he had forgotten. As you know, he left in a hurry. That is why I asked Simeon to find him. Then I asked him to deliver them to Frank personally."

"What were these things?"

"A watch. I thought it might have sentimental value. And it looked expensive, of course. And a picture of Louisa in a beautiful frame. And a ring." Annabella is lying. Frank never wore a watch. He found they irritated his skin, whatever kind of watch strap he used. And he didn't like to wear jewelry of any kind, including wedding rings. I'm not as certain about the picture of Louisa, but his favourite one still sits on his desk and her haunting eyes watch me whenever I'm in his office. I find it disconcerting, but can't bring myself to put it away. I suppose it's possible he could have had another one. But Annabella is lying.

"That was good of Simeon to make the long trip to do that. You must have forgiven Frank for leaving you."

"Perhaps." She laughs. A soft, muffled laugh which sounds forced.

9

Gunshot

After my conversation with Annabella, I sit at the kitchen table, thinking. Cooper is weaving around my legs, rubbing against me and meowing. He's trying to tell me something. I pick him up and his meows morph into purrs which are much louder than can possibly be produced by such a small creature. He's warm, soft and loving, but he wants something. He has plenty of food, and shares the water bowl with Kelly quite happily, so it must be his treats. As soon as I reach for the packet, I know I have it right. Kelly then asks for a chew by going to the cupboard where they're kept, and sitting, while looking up at me with pleading eyes. So, she gets her chew. The only one not happy around here is me. I make a fresh mug of tea and find some chocolate at the back of the cupboard. I'll have a treat too.

Back to thinking. Perhaps the caffeine will help me focus. Annabella is lying. Why? The only conclusion I come to is that Simeon must be the killer, and I wouldn't be at all surprised if

Annabella put him up to it. I remember she told me that Frank's leaving made her Italian blood boil. She lost her best sponsor as well as her lover. I wonder what hold Annabella has over Simeon that she could persuade him to kill Frank? My skin crawls at the thought of Annabella somehow compelling Simeon to commit murder. I've come to enjoy talking with Annabella, hearing her soft Italian voice. I feel as if we have a kind of kinship, since Frank deserted us both.

The only consolation is that I now have a lead with points away from Chuck. But I need something more definitive before I contact the police. I must go down to Kentucky and talk to the barn staff before they all disappear once the horses have left. I want to dig deeper.

I've barely seen Linda. Kelly and I go to the barn with the biting wind in our faces and clouds overhead, which threaten snow. Linda has convinced me we don't need the security guard anymore. She's going to be here for all the daylight hours, and we've installed padlocks and a crude alarm which will go off if the barn doors are opened at night. I find her dusting off the stall doors with a broom.

"I like to keep busy," she says as she leans the broom against the feed room door. "I hope you'll notice a difference in Rose and Speed. I've given them a good groom, and treated the scrapes and cuts."

We walk towards their stalls, and I can't believe my eyes. Linda's somehow brought some shine back into their coats, despite the fact that they're already growing longer winter hair. I can see that all the wounds have been cleaned and medicated. Their hooves have been oiled.

"I think they should have their shoes off and their hooves should be trimmed. If that's okay, I can call the farrier," she says.

"That would be great, Linda. I'm amazed at what wonders you've done. I hope you can continue here for a while. It really would be helpful. I'm thinking of going down to Kentucky again, and I'm going to be pretty busy for a bit."

"I'd love to keep working here. And I can stay at the house, if you like, while you're away and look after your dog and cat. My mother can manage for a few days without me."

"Are you sure? I know your mother isn't well."

"Yeah, I'm sure. I'll go home a few times in the day, to make sure she's eating and get her into bed, if that's okay."

"Of course. As many times as you want. I'll make sure you get money for gas too. And I won't hear any arguments."

"That's nice. Thanks. I could let the horses out tomorrow for an hour in the morning, while I clean their stalls, and an hour in the afternoon as well. Is that okay?"

"Sounds like a sensible plan, as long as we don't have a winter storm. I don't like the way the wind's picking up and the clouds look ominous to me."

"Don't worry. I won't put them out in bad weather. I'll call the farrier tomorrow. Do you want the vet to do a recheck?"

"No, not unless you see something. They're on antibiotics, so I think they'll be okay, especially with the tender loving care you're giving them."

"Hope so." Linda strokes Rose's long face as she munches on hay with her head over the stall door.

* * *

I feel an unwelcome twinge of guilt as I settle into bed and open my book. I haven't seen or heard from my mother for two days and haven't attempted to contact her. But I can't find it in my heart to forgive her. It would be easier if she didn't lie so much, and I'm still angry about her implication that Chuck murdered Frank and also her accusation that Chuck stole the horses. But I'll contact her tomorrow to see how she is.

* * *

It's probably because I was thinking about my mother, that nightmares woke me up twice in the night. They had a similar theme and were close to my reality. I was back at home and my stepfather came into my room. He loomed over me like a terrifying bird of prey. His eyes were a flaming red and his breath was hot and foul. I felt helpless and afraid, with no-one to rescue me. It felt so real that I'm having trouble erasing the image from my mind, and I feel far from refreshed this morning.

I let Kelly out of the kitchen door into five inches of wet snow. She has to be encouraged to venture more than five feet from the house. I can see Linda's little blue car, which looks too vulnerable to be allowed on the treacherous roads. The lights are on in the barn and it's nice to know that the horses are being so well-cared for. They'll be wallowing in all the attention. Kelly is soon back in the kitchen, shaking herself in a disgruntled kind of way, trying to make a point. She's not much of a winter dog.

Almost immediately after I close the door, a loud knocking startles us both, and Kelly barks, but I can see it's Joanna.

"I didn't expect to see you back here after what happened," I said.

"Can I come in? I must talk to you." Her angular face looks even more gaunt and is red from the cold, and her blond hair looks dull and unbrushed. Her eyes are puffy. Those eyes: I now know who they remind me of.

"Okay." We sit at the kitchen table, after she's deposited wet snow all over the mat.

"I worry about Ewert. He gets himself into messes. And taking your horses is one of the worst."

"It could have been disastrous."

"Ewert has a gambling problem. He can't get into the casino anymore and they know him at the racetrack. He found out about Dominic's gambling business and got involved. He happened to hear Dominic talking to a couple of guys about ratcheting the business up a notch by getting a couple of ringers. Ewert found out what ringers are, but I don't think he got the whole picture. He didn't realize that a ringer has to look exactly like a particular, poorly performing racehorse, so that it could be substituted for it. Then the ringer would win at long odds, making a lot of money for the bettors. I've got that right, haven't I?"

"Yes."

"Ewert was desperate to get into Dominic's good books because he owes him a lot of money. He thought the ransom note would be great, because he planned to take your money, as well as give your horses to Dominic. But it all went wrong." Joanna slumps with her head in her hands. "It was stupid."

"It was more than stupid. It was illegal and potentially life-threatening, and not only to the horses." I mull over what she's just said and watch her tears dampen her fingers. "But Dominic Marcel told me he doesn't know anyone called Ewert."

She snaps her head up. "You believe some scoundrel like Dominic, rather than me?"

"That's not what I said." I'm puzzled by her aggressive reaction. "Go on. I assume there's a lot more to this story."

"Oh." Joanna looks taken aback, but doesn't hesitate for more than a second. "Have you guessed then?" She looks at me with those grey eyes. "I'm Louisa's sister. And that's why Ewert wanted to live here. When he found out that you were widowed, he assumed you'd been left a pot of money. Louisa boasted to me that Frank was very wealthy, knowing that Ewert had next-to-nothing. Ewert resented the fact that Frank didn't leave me a cent in his will. And Louisa didn't either, but she didn't have much of her own money, although Ewert thinks she did. And Ewert resents your wealth, the lovely home, racehorses and your fancy lifestyle, and thinks we should be living like this."

There's a bang on the kitchen door, which makes the mugs in the cupboard jump and Kelly growl. The door flies open, revealing a man with a greying, scraggy beard, and small beady eyes which flit from side to side as he stands on the threshold. His grey track pants are too long, and noticeably wet from walking in the snow. But what grabs my attention is the gun in his unsteady hand. I assume he's Ewert. I've not met him before. He points the gun, which wobbles violently and seems to go off of its own volition. He turns and runs, making grunting noises. The racket of the gun going off in such close quarters has upset Kelly, who's quaking under the table. My ears are ringing and feel as if they've gone numb. Then I see blood. Joanna is still sitting at the table. She's clutching her thigh.

"You've been shot. What the hell is going on, Joanna? I'll call an ambulance."

"No! Don't! Ewert didn't mean it."

"He shot you!"

Linda bursts in, her rotund body bouncing as she lunges through the open door.

"What happened? Who's hurt?" She sees the blood seeping through Joanna's jeans and shudders.

"It's just a scratch," Joanna says.

I explain to Linda as best I can, and suggest she sits down for a bit, but she insists on going back out to the horses.

"Meg, Ewert wouldn't shoot me. He probably didn't mean to shoot at all."

"What the hell was he doing, then?"

"I don't know. He's desperate, I suppose."

I'm grovelling under the table so that I can check Kelly out. There's a bullet hole in the floor about a foot in front of her nose. She's petrified and won't move. As I lie sprawled out beside her, I call the vet and get an emergency appointment for an hour's time. Kelly needs sedatives, I'm sure. Despite all my stroking and soothing talk, her eyes are big circles with large black pupils, and she's panting.

"How badly injured are you? Is it really just a scratch?" I ask.

"I'm fine. How's Kelly?"

"She's in shock. I'm hoping that sedatives will help. I wish the vet would come here, but I'll have to go to the clinic in Vannersville."

"Ewert isn't well." I hear Joanna sniff. "He suffers from PTSD as well as having this awful gambling problem. And he won't get help. But he doesn't see it like I do. He's ashamed of the PTSD. It makes him feel inadequate and weak. And with the gambling, he thinks that next time he'll win big. There's always a next time."

"Sounds like Ewert needs a lot of help. Why do you stay with him?"

"Because I love him, and he needs me. He hasn't got anyone else."

"But he's out of control. He could kill you."

"No, he won't do that. And I'm sure he didn't want to hurt Kelly. He has outbursts and does rash things, but I can calm him down and get him to stop."

"I'll have to get the security company back. I can't have him coming around here with a gun."

"I'll talk to him. I promise he won't come here again." Joanna puts her head on her arms, which are crossed on top of the table. The blood is still oozing through her ripped jeans. She's sobbing and her whole body is rocking. I don't know whether to encourage her to talk more about Ewert, or to change the subject. Partly out of curiosity, I decide on the former.

"How did Ewert get PTSD?"

Joanna lifts her head, gets up to find a couple of tissues and sits down again, with her chair at an angle so that she can see me and Kelly under the table.

"He was a journalist. Nothing fancy, just freelance. He wanted to do an in-depth piece on human smuggling from Africa to Europe." She has tears running down her cheeks, but keeps on talking. "The short version is that he was taken hostage. His captors thought that the Canadian Government would be willing to pay a lot of money to have him set free, but they didn't realize that he was working on his own, that our government doesn't pay ransom, and his family isn't wealthy. That caused a lot of tension, and Ewert seized the opportunity to escape while his captors were having a violent argument. But he's never been the same since." She puts her head in her hands again, and her voice is muffled. "He started gambling not long after he came out of hospital. At first, I thought it was good. It took his mind off things. It was like a diversion. But it's now an addiction."

"This is terrible. I don't think I could live with someone who's so damaged."

"I love him, Meg. And I want to help make him better. That's what I want more than anything. He never smiles any more. I haven't heard him laugh." She dissolves into heart-breaking sobs.

"Once Chuck is back, I'll see if there's anything I can do to help." I wish I had something more supportive to say. I suggest she stays at the farm for at least a couple of days, but she insists on going back to Ewert and says she'll be fine.

* * *

As I drive Kelly to the vet, I contemplate Joanna's unwavering devotion to her unbalanced husband, and also how people can be diabolically cruel when money is involved. It's likely that Frank's murder had something to do with money, Juan's death probably did too, and the theft of my horses certainly did. And Ewert has been permanently damaged by his experience at the hands of his greedy captors.

But there's something about Joanna's story that doesn't make total sense to me, although I can't quite put my finger on it. Perhaps it's related to her role in taking Rose and Speed.

* * *

Kelly looks brighter by the time we reach the clinic. Nevertheless, the vet prescribes sedatives and advises me to keep her in a quiet place, and gives me some dog food which is apparently easy to digest but consumes a lot of money. I will do anything to help Kelly get better. She deserves the best.

At home, I put her bed under the kitchen table because that's where she goes when she's stressed or worried, even though the bullet hole is there to remind us both of what happened. And I put the water bowl close by. She refuses one of her favourite biscuits, but I leave it beside her and hope that she'll change her mind. She doesn't touch the pricey dog food, so I give her a little of her regular food in a separate bowl. I call Linda on her mobile phone and let her know I won't be leaving the house, not even to visit the barn, until Kelly is feeling better. We chat about Ewert and I sense Linda is nervous, so I call the security company again to get a guard as soon as possible, and let them know that there could be an armed threat. It's hard not to call the police, but Joanna's story stops me.

I get a mug of tea and sit on the floor with Kelly, but I wonder if she'd rather be left in peace. I get up, deciding to check emails and text messages, hoping for some news of Chuck, which I missed. Nothing.

There's a knock at the door. It's too soon for the security guard, so I'm leery of who it might be.

"You've locked the door," William says as I open it. The wet snow is melting fast, making a slushy puddle by the entrance to the kitchen. The drainage needs to be fixed.

"Come in, you'll get wet feet standing there."

"I thought you'd like to know what's happening in the case of the jockey's death."

"I would. But I'll give you an update on what's been happening here first." As I get him up-to-speed, I make some coffee for him and Linda. It's the middle of the afternoon and I haven't offered

Linda anything yet today, and I haven't eaten. When I tell William about the shooting and show him the bullet hole, he is adamant about calling the police. It takes quite a while to persuade him not to. He points out that it wasn't clear who Ewert was intending to shoot, and that I could have been the target. After all, why would he shoot his wife in my kitchen, in front of a witness, rather than shoot her in their own kitchen? He stresses that, in his opinion, I should lay charges. Someone could get killed next time and it could be me.

I give him the whole story about Ewert, as Joanna told it, but I don't manage to convince myself that we're safe, let alone assuring William. He's relieved to hear that I've rehired the security company and turns his attention to Kelly. He sits down on the floor to talk with her and pat her head, but she doesn't move. He puts a light hand on my shoulder as he passes me to get to the coffee machine, which stopped dripping some time ago. He takes a mug of coffee out to the barn. We both know that Linda won't come in and join us.

I'm relieved when he changes the subject on his return.

"Perhaps you know that there are plans for an official inquiry into illegal gambling as well as race-fixing at the racetrack?" he asks. "And that there's an ongoing criminal investigation as well?"

"No, I haven't heard that. But I haven't been listening to the radio or reading the papers."

"And I talked to the jockey, Ferris, who handed Juan the coffee that morning, as you suggested. Ferris admits he knew there was something in it, but claims that he didn't know any more than that. He told me he was acting under the direction of Dominic Marcel, and that the intent was to scare Juan and nothing more. He said he would never have agreed to give Juan the coffee if he thought it would lead to his death. But I think Ferris is rattled, and it's because he now realizes that his actions could be considered as aiding and abetting in a possible murder, if not worse."

Kelly gets up and puts her head on William's lap. I'm heartened by this definitive sign of acceptance and approval. I agree with Kelly, William is a good person. And it's a relief to see her brighter and no longer cowering under the table.

"That's interesting." I pick up Kelly's biscuit and hand it to her, and she starts to eat it. "I think I forgot to tell you about the conversation I had with Dominic. So much seems to have happened since we last chatted. He phoned me. I was taken aback. He told me to back off. I played dumb and said that I didn't know what I was supposed to be backing off from. As you know, I'd convinced myself that he had something to do with Frank's murder, Juan's death and the theft of my horses. He said it was all bullshit and was obviously angry. He's worried that I'm drawing attention to his harmless gambling business, as he put it."

"Perhaps he's telling the truth. Although my chat with Ferris has created serious doubts in my mind about his innocence in the Juan case."

"I have to admit that Dominic might not be Frank's murderer or be the person who stole my horses, though."

"But, going back to his presumably lucrative illegal gambling business: given the possibility he was involved in Juan's murder, you might be in some danger. He probably thinks that you were the one who informed the Racing Commission, which has led to the inquiry and the criminal investigation."

"I should talk to him again. I remember I told the police that Dominic had revealed to Frank that he ran a race-fixing business, and that this angered Frank. And I know they made note of it, telling me that Dominic was known to them."

"The police will investigate because his gambling business, assuming that it exists, would be illegal, and I'm confident that the police would have advised the Racing Commission, hence the inquiry. But that doesn't mean that Dominic won't put the blame for his downfall squarely on your shoulders. I'm glad you've got a security guard coming."

"He'll be here this evening."

"I'd like to stay until he comes. Not that I could do much, but just being here might help."

"That would be nice. Thanks. I can't think of what we can eat, though. And Linda should have something as well." Food seems to be at the bottom of my priority list. It doesn't help that I am a reluctant, and therefore infrequent, shopper.

"Don't worry. I'll dig up something. I'd like to be helpful."

"Thanks. I don't feel like doing anything at the moment."

While William is rummaging in the fridge and digging into the cupboards, the phone rings. It's the police again. The even-toned, deep-voiced man asks me questions, which he says are routine, about my whereabouts at the time of Frank's murder. I ask him if there have been any developments in the investigation and he replies that there have. The good news is that Chuck is not the only one being investigated by the Kentucky State Police. He wouldn't tell me any more, except that they think they've found the murder weapon. A gun was found in an overgrown ditch just a short distance from the stables. And it's being tested for fingerprints.

As William boils some rice and heats some thick soup, adding a few frozen peas, I tell him what the police officer said.

"I'm relieved that, so far, they haven't asked questions about Frank's faked death and if I was involved. As you know, I wasn't, but it makes me uneasy. After all, I knew he was still alive, although I didn't find out till one year after his staged accident."

"Their focus is on his murder. I'm glad that they have more than one suspect. They'll want to narrow it down soon. Hopefully, they'll release Chuck then."

"I need to find out who the other person is. My guess is that it's Simeon. Murray would have let me know if he was under suspicion, so I don't think it's him. And I don't believe Annabella's story about why Simeon needed to visit Frank. It was all lies. She said Simeon was delivering some of Frank's things which he left behind, but it didn't ring true at all."

"Sounds like it could be Simeon, then."

"I haven't heard from Chuck for what seems like an eternity."

"He's probably in custody. He might not have access to a phone or be permitted any calls at the moment."

"It must be a living hell."

"It wouldn't be any fun, that's for sure." He has sweat on his forehead as he reaches for some plates. I get the cutlery and some water for the three of us, hoping Linda can be persuaded to join us for once.

"He'll need a lawyer. William, can you connect him with someone?"

"I can try."

Linda should have gone home by now, but I know she hasn't. She's told me several times that she's happiest when she's with horses, and it doesn't seem to matter what she's doing. She helped to unload the hay we had delivered earlier today, and she's organized a delivery of wood-shavings for tomorrow. I still puzzle over how she can have such a round body when she works so very hard.

William has made a presentable meal out of what he could find, and Linda is eating with us and seems to be enjoying it. She doesn't say much, but does mention that she tires of cooking for her mother, who is very finicky and often complains. I don't know what her mother will be eating tonight and suggest that she should take some of William's concoction home. She says she might just do that.

10

Fingerprints

Everyone has left the house. It's eerily still and quiet, except for Kelly's breathing and the ticking of the clock. The security guard wasn't sure where to position himself, because he has to be concerned about the occupants of the house as well as of the barn. The compromise is that he has parked his car near the side of the house where he can watch the barn and the kitchen door, and is visible from the driveway. He asks me to put on all the outdoor lights, some of which light up the verandah at the front of the house. I'm not sure that any of this will deter Ewert if he wants to attack, but I stay silent.

* * *

I wake with a start. The phone is ringing. I'm on the recliner in the family room and Kelly is at my feet. I have no recollection of getting here, including what time it was, and am in the clothes I wore yesterday. It's about seven in the morning. I'm usually awake before this. It's the police on the phone, and as soon as I hear the voice, I know I won't like what he has to say.

The only fingerprints on the gun they found in the ditch are Chuck's. I insist that there must be some mistake, but I know that it's pointless. I ask if I can talk to Chuck and, much to my surprise, he says he'll see if something can be arranged.

I sit in a foggy mess of thoughts, and niggling doubts return to nibble at the edges of my consciousness. Is it possible I've been deluded, and that Chuck did kill Frank? My mother's poisonous words resurface and make my head ache. The trouble is that she guessed it right when she told the Kentucky State Police that Chuck wanted Frank to divorce me. Nevertheless, I can't understand why Chuck or Murray went down to Kentucky, and as for Simeon, that makes even less sense. From the perspective of the mood I'm in at the moment, I see each of them as a suspect, and it makes me feel sick.

I let Kelly out of the kitchen door, who's showing signs of being her normal self again. She has more resilience than I've given her credit for. As I stumble over to the kettle, and then grab a couple of aspirins, I tell myself that I need to follow Kelly's example, and get going again.

The door bursts open and my mother walks in on the arm of the security guard with what I assume is a triumphant smile, revealing her stained, uneven teeth. The uniformed man advises me he ascertained that she is, indeed, my mother. But what if I don't want to see her? I don't go down that road, since I haven't told him she's not welcome. She has two brown paper bags in her hand and puts them ceremoniously on the table as if they're rare treasures.

"I got the taxi to go to Tim's and bought us breakfast." She hesitates and looks down at Kelly. "I thought you might want something to eat." She moves to the table and puts her brown jacket over the back of a chair. "I want to say something." She hesitates again and strokes Cooper, who's leapt onto the chair where she was about to sit. "I'm sorry." She picks Cooper up and puts him down next to Kelly under the table and sits down. She looks different. The devilish sparkle has fizzled from her eyes, her hair is frizzy, and her powdered face is pale.

"I'm making tea," is all I can say. I don't know how to react to this person. Something has changed, drastically. But I'm wary and keep my guard up. She's had a lot of practice at acting and pretense, not to mention lying, so this could be a new strategy to cause me more hurt and anguish. But I'm not sure.

We eat the breakfast sandwiches and hash browns in silence. I must be starving, because I demolish mine in half the time that it takes my mother to eat hers.

"I have to make some phone calls," I say as I pick up my mobile. "You can sit in the family room if you like."

"Okey dokey." She gets up with no argument and no taunting. It's strange and unnerving. Cooper follows her. He has taken a liking to her this morning.

"There are some good books in there." I have no clue what she likes to read.

I email Simeon, asking when would be a good time to call him. And then I leave a message for Dominic stating we need to meet, and then call Tammy.

"It's so nice to hear from you, Meg," she says. "It's getting lonely here. The police have still got a section of the stables marked off with that yellow tape, but they're not here much and just about all the horses have gone, as well as the workers." She tells me that the farm has been leased to new occupants who'll be arriving in a couple of weeks. Tammy still doesn't know where she'll be going.

"I'd like to make another trip down, just a short one, before everyone leaves." I explain that I'm anxious because Chuck is the prime suspect, and I must do all I can to help him.

I hang up and reflect on how I feel. I think of Joanna and her love for Ewert, despite all of his challenges, and her determination to help him. She's a good example. I wish I felt as sure and confident of the love between Chuck and me. I'm questioning a little more each day if we ever did love one another. Regardless of these painful thoughts, he can't be guilty of Frank's murder, and I should help him.

Much to my surprise, Dominic returns my call and we set up a time to meet later this morning at a sports bar in Vannersville.

I tell Kelly to sit with my mother, who's dozed off in the recliner, so that I can visit Linda in the barn.

The horses' coats are shining, including Eagle's and Bullet's. She's looking after all four of them as if they're royalty, and it makes me smile.

"Meg, even though the melting snow is slippery, I'd like to get them out. I'll give them some tranq so they can be in the paddock for a bit."

"That's fine. By the way, I'm going to Kentucky tomorrow. Is that going to work for you?"

"No problem."

"I have an idea. My mother is at a loose end, and I know that your mother is sick. Do you think your mother would like some company while you're here? I thought we could try it for an hour today and if it works, my mother could visit her regularly for the rest of her stay. I haven't asked her yet, mind you."

"That'd be good. Mom gets lonely."

My mother agrees readily and seems almost grateful for the suggestion. I can't get used to this new person. Long may it last.

* * *

Dominic is easy to spot in the sports bar, partly because there's only a spattering of people clustered in dark corners, and partly because he's the only person who is both short and Mediterranean-looking. His jockey days must be well behind him because he has a square appearance and the start of a potbelly, so I guess he's tripled his weight since his race-riding days. He greets me with his high-pitched voice and a chubby, sweaty hand. His half-smile reveals pearl-white, even teeth. I wonder if they're false. Perhaps he lost the real ones in a fall off a horse, but I'm not here to chat with him about his racing adventures.

I order sparkling water, and he orders a single-malt Scotch and starts the conversation.

"So, you ratted, didn't you?" He leans back in the chair, and perches his Scotch on his stomach, which appears larger when he's at a forty-five-degree angle.

Looking at him, I see no reason not to be direct with this man. I don't feel I have anything to hide. And he doesn't frighten me.

"When the police called me to tell me that Chuck, my partner, is a suspect in Frank's murder, they asked questions and I told them that Frank was involved with you, and that you'd told Frank that you run a race-fixing business. They just said they'd be checking out all leads. That's it."

"Who told you that? Who told you what I was supposed to have said to Frank?"

"I'm not telling you that."

"I'll guess. That mixed-up, foolish, American girl, Tammy, that's who. She doesn't know what she's talking about." He takes a gulp of his whisky. "I asked you, nicely, to back off, and you didn't. Now there's going to be an inquiry. I blame you. You're the one rocking my world. It was going just fine till you came along with your pal Billy."

"William. It was bound to happen, once the death of the jockey, Juan, was deemed suspicious."

"And your poking around led to that."

"Perhaps it did, in part. But people asked me to help. I didn't instigate it. It would have happened anyway."

"You should mind your own business. But I'm not here to argue about it. I'm here to talk about Juan." His tone is softer, and it unnerves me more than when he's accusatory and vaguely threatening. After all, that's how I expect him to behave. "Since you're so good at snooping, I want you to find out what happened."

I hesitate. I can't quite figure this man out.

"Okay", I say, slowly.

"I did not, and I repeat, just in case you didn't hear me when I told you on the phone, I had nothing to do with Juan's death. But, since they're saying poison was involved, it looks bad. This is where you come in. You owe me one. So, I want you to find out who poisoned Juan."

I don't agree that I owe him one, but I'm intrigued.

"Why?"

"I want to avoid the spotlight. I don't want the police snooping around."

"What's in it for me?" I'm puzzled. After all, the police are already investigating.

But perhaps I can work this situation to my advantage.

"Me out of your life, that's what." He's perilously close to tipping his chair over backwards as he downs the rest of his Scotch. And then he leans forwards, breathing hot, liquor-laden air in my face. "And I can't give you names, because I wouldn't know, would I?"

"I get it. But I'd like something more from you. Chuck, my partner, is the prime suspect in Frank's murder. Can you ask anyone you can think of, and I'm sure you have lots of connections like horse shippers, and so on, if they saw anyone or heard anything at Frank's stables around the time of his death?"

"I suppose I can do that." He gets up and goes, without further comment, leaving the bill for me to pay.

I didn't find him intimidating, and he wasn't particularly forceful, which makes me wonder if he's guilty of anything more than running his illegal gambling business. And I'm puzzled by his asking me to find out who's responsible for Juan's death, because he knows the police will continue snooping around, as he put it, gathering evidence about his illicit business, regardless of who killed Juan. Perhaps it's all a smoke screen and there's something I'm not seeing.

* * *

Tammy wraps me in her long arms and doesn't seem to want to let me go.

"Oh, it's great to see you." She releases me from her embrace, and I can breathe again. "I'm sure sad to hear that Chuck is the prime suspect."

"It's not good. I'm hoping that someone will remember something, or that I'll unearth evidence that'll help. I'm going to visit Chuck. I need to find out how his fingerprints got on the gun they found in the ditch."

"That sounds bad."

"It does, but there must be an explanation. Wouldn't the killer have worn gloves?"

"You'd sure think so."

Since I'm staying for the night, Tammy has prepared one of the large bedrooms. I unpack the few things I've brought with me, and then join her for salad, cheese and crackers, and wine.

"You should like this wine. Frank selected it." Tammy says. "I've almost finished the wine he had stored in the cellar. And it'll be a good thing when it's all gone. Help me drink some." She pours me a large glass of merlot.

"Frank never drank, that I knew of."

"He told me he didn't want alcohol any place where his brother could find it and didn't want Murray ever to see him having a drink."

"That makes sense." But Frank didn't tell me this. I just accepted that he didn't drink. So many things we should have talked about, and that I should have known. "You've been under a lot of stress, Tammy."

"Suppose I have. I could've done with some support from my goddam family, but they're too busy with their own lives, I guess."

"They probably don't understand what you're going through." I take a sip of the deep ruby-red wine, which is as smooth as silk as it swills over my tongue. Frank must have known his wines better than I knew him.

"Anyhow, what do you want to do tomorrow? We should get things figured out."

"I'll set up the visit to Chuck first, then work around that. I'll see if I can do that now, before we eat. Then I want to talk to any of the stable hands who are still somewhere in the vicinity."

"I can give you two names and numbers. Bart and Zack are still around."

"Good. By the way, did you tell Simeon that Chuck was in Frank's office?"

"No. I don't recall telling Simeon anything. I'm pretty certain I haven't talked to him since I've been here. I know I can be muddled because of all that's happened, but I'm sure I would have remembered Simeon. Why do you ask?"

"Because that's what Annabella told me."

"That's odd. Why would she say that? Perhaps I have forgotten. I told you I'm a tad muddled."

* * *

My visit with Chuck was set up for early in this morning. He looks like a shadow of himself with his gaunt face, dark circles under his eyes and sullen expression. Even his soft, brown curls look as if they've lost their bounce. He slumps over, with his face nearly touching the cold steel table. He's thinner, and as I register this, I recall how he looked in the spring. He's been losing weight for a few months, not just for a few days.

He looks ill, and I ache inside, thinking of his suffering. But neither of us wants to dwell on how he's doing, so it doesn't take me long to get to the question I most want answered.

"How did your fingerprints get on the gun?"

He lifts his head and looks at me for a second, with blood-shot eyes. "I messed up. I was stupid. I went back to see Frank again in the evening." I have to be patient. Chuck's speech is ponderous and difficult to make out when he folds forward, but he's talking, that's the main thing. "Frank was dead, and a gun was lying there, in front of me. I picked it up without thinking. Then I realized my fingerprints would be on it."

"Could you have wiped them off?"

"I panicked. All I could think of was that I should get rid of it. I reckoned I must have been the first one to find him dead, but there was no-one around to back up my story."

"Why did you go back to visit him again?"

"I hated to leave him on such bad terms."

"You weren't going to raise divorce or money again then?"

"No. Of course not. I thought I could smooth things over with him. I'd left him so angry with me that I thought you'd hear about it."

Perhaps he's being genuine, but I feel frustrated with him. Something has changed in Chuck, and it makes me feel as if I don't know this man. And it doesn't help that what he's telling me sounds rather bizarre.

"You threw the gun into a ditch. That doesn't sound like a well-thought-out plan."

"I wasn't thinking clearly. I told you, I panicked. I just wanted to get rid of it."

"There must have been two guns at the scene, because they found Frank's gun and it had been fired as well, but the bullet didn't match the one found in his body."

"I just saw this one, the one I tossed into the ditch. I never thought that there could be two. What can I tell you? I freaked out. I've never had to deal with anything like this before." His voice has a sharpness to it, as if he's angry with my questions. He looks up at me with eyes which have lost their sparkle. "Being here is a nightmare in hell. Being suspected of something you didn't do has to be one of the most terrifying things, and I'm helpless to do anything about it." My frustration evaporates and is replaced with compassion and concern. He's frightened.

"William is doing what he can to find a decent lawyer for you." I'm sure my voice faltered, wavered as I told him that. It sounds pathetic, under the circumstances. "Can you remember anything else that happened when you were in the stables?"

"No. I've been wracking my brains, trying to find some forgotten piece, but there's nothing other than what I've already told you about the Mediterranean-looking guy who looked about the height of a jockey." He sounds exhausted and defeated, as well as somewhat irritated.

"Keep thinking. Keep going over everything in your mind. Any small detail might help. I'm going to do my best to find out the truth."

"I could end up on Death Row."

"You're innocent, so let's focus on finding who killed Frank so you don't have to go to trial in the first place." I try to sound optimistic and upbeat, and hope he doesn't hear the quiver in my voice.

I leave him looking forlorn and dejected, and I'm digging into my resolve to build up the optimism I tried to infuse him with. But I'm not doing a good job. Not only am I alarmed about his being accused of Frank's murder, I'm also distressed about his apparent poor health and annoyed at myself for not registering the changes in Chuck over the past months.

* * *

"You look like you've seen a ghost," Tammy says as I walk into her kitchen. "Sit down and have something. How about some hot chocolate?" I mumble something which is interpreted as being acceptance of the offer and realize that I'm shivering. It's a bone-chilling December day outside, but I had my winter jacket which keeps me warm in Ontario, so I should have been okay.

The hot chocolate warms me up and helps me to collect myself so that I can tell Tammy all that Chuck said. She listens without comment, as we sit perched on the high chairs at her granite counter by the large window. The dull grey day reflects my mood.

Tammy touches my hand with her long fingers, as if brushing me with a feather. "You believe that he's innocent, don't you?"

"Yes, I do."

"I'm sure you'll find the guy who did it. That's why I asked for your help. I know you'll be able to find out the truth."

Her confidence in me doesn't help. I don't want this responsibility solely on my shoulders. I should at least follow up with Foreign Affairs to make sure they're aware of Chuck's situation and find out what they are doing and what they plan to do.

"By the way, Bart and Zack are working here today," she says. "They asked if you could meet with them in Frank's office. They told me they don't think they can help, but you never know."

I walk down the sweeping asphalt driveway towards the enormous stone barn. The large oak doors are ajar, and I walk inside. It's dimly lit, but I can make out someone near the other end, as well as a couple of horses who are watching me with interest. There's no sign of yellow police tape.

"Hi, I'm Bart. You must be Meg Sheppard. Sorry for your loss. I understand Fred was your husband." Bart is forward and friendly, which puts me at ease.

"Thank you. It was a shock to hear he'd been shot." We walk towards Frank's office. It feels empty and cold, and it's dustier and messier than when I was here last. I shiver.

"The damp can get to you," Bart says as we sit down on a couple of chairs in the corner. I explain what I'm doing and ask him if there's anything at all that he can remember from around the time of Frank's death, but he can only recall Murray arriving and Chuck leaving. Chuck went at about the time Bart left, and Frank was definitely alive then. But Chuck told me he returned, so none of this helps.

I meet with Zack, who is large in stature and has the booming voice and firm handshake to go with it.

"I know less than Bart. You need to talk to Jimmy. He knows more about what went on. Here's his number. I'm sure he'll chat with you. He's a swell guy."

I'm not sorry to leave the near-empty, near-desolate stables. Noises echo and reverberate against the walls of the empty stalls, and cobwebs laden with dust are already taking over. It has the aura of a mausoleum. I'm relieved that Jimmy wants to meet in the donut shop in town, just a couple of miles away, and that he can make it this morning.

Jimmy seems reluctant to speak at first, so I give him a detailed run-down, explaining what I'm doing and why. He warms up as he drinks his coffee and tucks into a jelly donut. I ask him who he saw and when, and what transpired between each of them and Frank.

"You call him 'Frank', but he went by the name 'Fred Simpson' when he was here."

"I know, he's the same person."

"Okay. Right. Three guys visited him on that day. I remember because Fred didn't have visitors at the stables other than people involved in his horse business, and they'd meet in the office, not out in the stables. Fred didn't handle the horses himself. He dealt with the business. It was up to me to care for the horses."

"So, these three guys weren't business contacts? Did any of his usual business people also visit on the day of Frank's, I mean Fred's, death?"

"No business people. The first guy had whopping feet and a red face. He visited before that accursed day. He called Fred 'Frank', like you. Fred wasn't pleased to see him. They had angry words. I heard 'money' mentioned more than once. He came into the stables again, on the day that Fred was shot, but I didn't see him with Fred. As I walked towards him, he turned and left. Fred was having an argument with someone else in the aisle, so I guess that's why he went before seeing Fred."

"And do you know who this second person was?"

"No. But the description I gave the police matched a photo they showed me. He had curly brown hair, large eyes, in low forties and about six feet. He and Fred were yelling at each other in the aisle like banshees. Fred did most of the shouting. I reckon it was about money. The other guy looked kinda odd. His behaviour was erratic."

"And then there was another visitor?"

"That guy had a foreign accent, was tanned, short and carried a small backpack. He looked nervous and kinda uptight as he walked through the barn. He argued with Fred in his office. It was muffled, so I didn't catch it."

"Did you tell the police about this third visitor?"

"No. They didn't ask me. They were interested in the first two."

"When did this third visitor leave?"

"I didn't see him go, but Fred was alive when I left. I knocked on his office door and signaled I was going. He was alone, and he waved at me, but no words. I kinda wondered because he liked to check with me about the horses before I left. I guess that visitor got under his skin."

"You aren't aware of any other visitors?"

"No."

I learned nothing new, which is disappointing. But the conversation has me considering the possibility that there was a fourth visitor. It could have been one of the three returning, just as Chuck did, or it could be another person, the killer.

11

Simeon

Tammy has prepared sandwiches and fresh-squeezed orange juice.

"There was Frank's gun, which was fired but isn't the one that was used to kill him, and then there was another gun," I say, as I savour roasted vegetable and goat cheese flavours. I haven't enjoyed such a delicious lunch for a long time. "Assuming the killer is someone from Frank's past, whom I've yet to think of, I'm wondering how a non-American could get hold of a gun here, quickly."

"I don't know, Meg, but I guess there's a way. It's about knowing the right guy, I reckon."

"Perhaps Dominic Marcel would have some ideas."

"You have it in for him, don't you!" It's nice to see her smile.

"Hey, I don't any more, not really. But he's got connections, let's put it that way."

I help Tammy clear the lunch things and then she makes tea for me and coffee for herself. I receive a text message from Linda as I sit down with my mug. My mother has had a fall at Linda's mother's house and is in hospital, although Linda doesn't think it's serious. I reply that I'm about to leave Kentucky and will be back as soon as possible.

It's not easy to leave Chuck behind, wondering if he's destined for Death Row in the State Penitentiary. As I drive back home from the airport, I feel lonelier than I've ever felt before, and angry with myself. Perhaps if our relationship had been stronger and had more love in it, Chuck would never have visited Frank. Despite my remorse and my regret, I'm still annoyed with both him and Murray for interfering. They each say they went down to meet Frank because of me. They shouldn't have.

Linda meets me at the kitchen door. Kelly jumps up and licks my face, which is strictly forbidden, but I pretend not to notice. She's running around, liable to knock a chair over, obviously feeling much better. We all go to the barn, Linda grabbing her down vest on the way. The icy wind is cutting through the jacket I wore for my Kentucky trip.

"Your mom suddenly started to behave weird, so my mom says. Mom got scared and called me."

"What did my mother do?"

"She told Mom she was dizzy and had a headache, and she wouldn't sit still. I quickly straightened things out here, and was leaving, and I got another call from my mom. She said your mom had fallen in the bathroom but she was conscious. I called an ambulance, so she's in the hospital."

"Sorry about this, Linda. Is your mom alright?"

"No-one's fault. She's fine now that I've promised her I'll be there soon. Hope your mom's okay."

"It could have been great if it had worked out. I'll go to the hospital when I've washed and changed. You go home."

"I've done everything. Kelly's been fed too."

"That's fantastic. She seems to be back to her old self. Thanks for everything you've done while I've been away."

"It's been fine. I've made friends with one of the security guards who does the evening shift, so I might come back and chat to him later if that's okay." She looked at the floor and mumbled most of the words. But I could make them out.

"That's absolutely fine. You're welcome here when you're working and when you're not. See you later, then."

* * *

My mother has aged ten years. Her face is wan and drawn, her skin looks fragile, the fine wrinkles more pronounced. She recognizes me, which is a good sign. We have a bizarre conversation since all she can talk about is her desire to go back to England. It's almost as if she's panicking. I find out that they plan to do scans and other tests the next day, so I tell her I'll be back sometime tomorrow, probably later on. I make sure that the nurses have my contact information.

When I get home with Kelly sitting on the seat beside me in the truck, I find William's car in the driveway. I hope he has some helpful news.

As soon as I see him, I ask him whether he's found a lawyer for Chuck. He says he has, but it wasn't as easy as he'd thought it would be.

"Why not?" I ask as we sit at the kitchen table.

"I completed a background check on Charles Alexander Murphy. I hope you won't take offence at that, but I didn't want my colleague to get any surprises. I wanted to know more about the person I was referring."

I don't say anything, but the way William looks at me makes me quake like an aspen.

"Interesting what I found out. Nothing terrible, but it's interesting." He hands me a folder which I hadn't noticed he was holding.

He stays still, like a carved statue, as I read through the several pages, some hand-written in a scrawl which I have difficulty deciphering.

"I can't believe this," I say.

"It is rather odd, I agree."

"But what's oddest to me is that my mother told me what I assumed was an outrageous lie, that Chuck inherited a sugarcane plantation in Barbados, but lost all his money. She accused him of wanting my money. Well, Frank's money. Also, she said something about the horrors of the plantation business. She wanted me to know because she'd been talking to the police about Chuck, which I thought was disgusting, as well as interfering."

"That wouldn't be helpful, under the circumstances." He points to a couple of pieces of paper in the folder. "As you see from these newspaper articles, he's been working at reviving the plantation, but his business plans must be wanting. He's lost his shirt and is in danger of losing the Murphy Plantation altogether."

"So, when he was away, he was most likely in Barbados, dealing with this business, at least some of the time. I had no clue. I was completely in the dark."

"He must have had his reasons for not telling you."

"The cynical side of me tells me he didn't want me to know, because he needed Frank's money. When Chuck went to Kentucky, he asked Frank for money, claiming it was for me. He asked him to divorce me, for the sake of our relationship, so he says."

"That raises an interesting question. Since Frank had been declared legally dead here in Canada, I'm not sure, even though I'm a lawyer, if a divorce was necessary. Here, you were, in the eyes of the law, a widow."

"I hate that word. But you make a good point. That makes me even more sceptical about why Chuck was in Kentucky. But, if he did ask Frank to divorce me, then presumably, the next step would have been our marriage: Chuck assuming that Frank, in a new will, left his millions to me, which he hasn't. He'd then dispose of Frank. And then, if I refused to give him the funds from my inheritance that he wanted for his plantation scheme, I would have been next. That's downright scary." Even as I say this, I just can't bring myself to believe it, and Chuck has never mentioned marriage to me.

"In my opinion, none of this is feasible. It would take a seriously desperate and depraved man to carry out that plan."

"I'm glad that's what you think. But I wish Chuck had talked to me about the plantation thing."

"Communication is good, usually."

"One conclusion that emerges from this is that I think this whole business confirms Chuck's innocence. If he murdered Frank that day in the barn, he would have been killing the goose which had yet to lay the golden egg."

"Agreed. And, as I mentioned earlier, I think I've found a proficient lawyer who's willing to take Chuck's case on. He's seen all the material in this folder, by the way. You'll have to foot the bill, though."

"Oh, I suppose I will."

William points out that they haven't laid charges yet, but will have to within a matter of hours, or release him.

As we each sip on mugs of hot chocolate, I tell William about my meeting with Dominic.

"Do you have any suspects for Juan's death, now that Dominic Marcel appears to be ruled out?" William asks.

"Not really. At the moment, I can only think of another jockey."

"I bet it's hard for you to focus on this when you have so many things on your mind."

"You mean Chuck and the plantation and his behaviour, and my mother? Yes, it's very hard. But I have to do this. Dominic could be helpful in solving Frank's murder, so I want to do my bit and find out who killed Juan."

"I hope he can be trusted to keep his side of the bargain."

"I'm counting on him to do some digging with his connections in Kentucky to find out if there was a fourth visitor." As I'm saying this to William, I realize how much of a long-shot it is. If none of the workers or Tammy saw or heard anything, then what hope is there of Dominic unearthing something, through his contacts, to help identify the mystery fourth person?

"How are you going to find out if another jockey is the culprit in Juan's death?"

"I'm going to start with Susana, Juan's wife, and ask her who the jockeys were who he worked with. Dominic wouldn't give me names, to protect himself I suppose, although the inquiry is bound to uncover all his connections."

"Perhaps. But he's wise to play things close to his chest right now."

"And I want to ask him if a foreigner can buy a gun in Kentucky."

"That's easy. The answer would be 'yes'. The purchase would no doubt not comply with the rules and regulations, but it could be got."

"I want specifics, though, on how and who, because it might lead to the mystery fourth visitor."

"What if there wasn't a fourth visitor?"

"Then one of Murray, Simeon or Chuck must have come back. And I know Chuck came back once. But I'm now convinced, more than ever, that he's not the murderer. Other than the mystery fourth visitor, who I hope exists, there is no probable suspect other than Simeon."

"What about Tammy?"

"She was the one who asked me to help solve Frank's murder. She called me and said she was convinced it wasn't suicide."

"Ah."

"You have a point. I shouldn't dismiss her. But I'm not aware of a motive. She gave me the impression that she's now hard-up, and doesn't expect to benefit financially from Frank's death."

"She could be financially stretched until things are settled. Do you know if there was a written contract between her and Frank?"

"She didn't mention one. I don't want to ask her. Would you be able to find out?"

"I'll try."

"She must be a bloody good actor if she's involved in Frank's death. I've been taken in by her, hook, line and sinker."

"I'm not saying she is, necessarily."

"I know. You're right, though, we should check her out."

William raises the subject of the humane society and my dismissal.

"I had an opportunity to talk to one of the Board Members when I was at a fundraising event a couple of days ago. She told me that the Board finally ousted the President and that there is an Interim President."

"Oh."

"And she suggested you talk to the Interim President. I think she's reaching out to you on the Board's behalf."

"Perhaps. But they could contact me directly, couldn't they? Anyway, I'm not willing or able to deal with that right now. If they're really interested in talking to me, they'll connect with me somehow."

"Okay. Just the messenger."

Linda bursts through the door, breathless and red in the face.

"Sorry. Didn't mean to interrupt." She's flustered and shuffles from one foot to the other, wringing her red hands.

"Is there a problem, Linda?"

"I forgot to tell you that someone called Simeon phoned when you weren't here. He wouldn't leave a message. But I wanted to tell you 'cause he sounded upset."

"I suppose he didn't tell you where he was calling from?"

"He might have said London, but I'm not sure."

"Thanks, Linda. There's no need to be concerned. I'll connect with him by email." Linda gives the impression that she has one foot outside and wants to leave. "Drop in before you go home, Linda," I say as she closes the door behind her.

William leaves soon after Linda's quick visit. I email Simeon and tell him to phone me tomorrow at about noon, London time. I'll make sure that I'm in the house.

Linda pops her head round the kitchen door as if she's checking the place out. I think she's just making sure I'm alone.

"Linda, how are things going?"

"Good."

"I'm sorry about the incident with my mother. I hope your mother is okay."

"My mom's fine. She's worried about your mom, though. She thinks she's real sick."

"She might be. She's always been different and I've not had a close relationship with her, but I have to say that her behaviour has been more bizarre than I can remember."

"I think it was your mom's dizzy spells that scared my mom. But my mom's okay now."

"Are things alright in the barn?"

"Yes. I was talking to Austin, you know, the security guard. He's got the evening shift."

"I'm not sure what to do about the security company. Perhaps Joanna is right and Ewert won't come here again."

"You said Ewert has PTSD, right?"

"Yes, that's right. He also has a gambling problem."

"Austin told me he used to be a cop, but his partner got shot dead in front of him in a drug bust that went wrong. He has PTSD."

"That's horrible."

"Yeah. It's bad. But I wanted to tell you 'cause he's found a program that's helped a lot. It's a mix of extreme exercise, like boot-camp, and therapy, counselling, I think he said. Austin is raving about it. He's thinking of setting up his own program."

"That sounds interesting."

"Austin might talk to Ewert if I ask him."

"I'll ask Joanna and then hopefully give you his phone number. And, I wanted to talk to you because I'm feeling bad about asking you to work here all this time. I'm sure there are other things you'd like to do in your time off from the track."

"I'm enjoying it. But I meant to tell you that Neal is going to Florida to train and race some horses for a part of the winter. He asked me if he thought you'd like Rose to go."

"And I expect he wants you to go?"

"Yeah, he does. But I won't leave my mom."

"That's another reason that I wouldn't want Rose to go, if you weren't going to be there to look after her. Also, I wonder about the various bugs and parasites down there. I'm not sure how valid my worries are, but still, I'd rather not risk it. And the long journey could be stressful for her. The other thing, and perhaps most important, is that I think Rose deserves a good, long rest before next racing season. I'll let Neal know."

"Okay. Can I stay working here for a bit longer?"

"I'd like that, thanks Linda. I saw the horses outside in the paddock today and they looked great."

"I had them out today for a bit longer because tomorrow they say we'll get another ice-storm."

"Just what we need."

* * *

I wish I'd told Simeon to phone earlier. It seems like a long wait until seven in the morning, and I have too many things mulling around in my mind for me to sleep properly. Kelly and I both have a fitful night listening to the increasing roar of an incoming windstorm. The gusts have me envisioning felled trees and lost barn roofs. We're dozing at about six o'clock, when there's a loud knocking on the kitchen door. I leap out of bed. Kelly barks and charges downstairs. I follow as I tie my robe around me and stumble after her.

Kelly's not impressed with the two strangers, but I usher her out of the door, past a security guard I've not met, who's standing in front of a short man with a Mediterranean look about him. I guess he's Simeon, and I'm right. He looks windswept and chilled.

"What are you doing here?" I must be easy to find. First my mother, now Simeon. I let him inside. He looks ashen and his clothes are wrinkled, he's unshaven, and his eyes are red.

"I was lucky. I got a ticket on the overnight flight from Heathrow. I have to talk to you. I thought it best to come."

"We could have talked on the phone. It's a long way and a lot of expense just to have a chat."

"I'm in big trouble. And I believe you're the only person who's able to find out what really happened. The truth is being twisted and turned. It's bad for me."

"I'm going to make tea. Would you like coffee?"

"That would be good. I couldn't eat or drink on the plane. My stomach churned the whole time."

"I expect you're dehydrated." I get him some water. "And I'll get you something to eat in a minute. So, tell me what's going on."

"You know I'm Annabella's agent, and her assistant, too. And you know that Frank's sponsorship was super-important to Annabella's career. She was just starting to get somewhere, but she needed to travel to auditions, which is expensive, and she needed to have coaching from the best, which is also expensive."

"Yes."

"When Frank left her, she was distraught and furious. I've never seen her so upset. She asked me to find out where he'd gone. It wasn't difficult, because I knew that he'd left with Tammy, and I kept in contact with her, and found out that he'd leased a horse place in Kentucky." He attempts to stifle a yawn with every ounce of strength he has left after his long journey, but the warm air from his lungs erupts and flows into the room. I can only just constrain the urge to do the same.

"I know you found out where he was."

"At first, Annabella told me to demand the rest of the sponsorship money from Frank that he'd promised her. But that went nowhere. So, she told me to blackmail him. She said he wants to be dead, so tell him you're going to tell everyone he's alive and where he is. It made me sick."

"So why did you do it?"

"I'm a fool, that's why. I thought Annabella and I had something special between us. I did lots of extra things for Annabella, because I wanted her to need me. I was sure that, one day, she'd realize she loved me, and that we were meant for each other. I would have done anything for her."

"Love can do that." I'd like to believe this. He looks down at his coffee, and I'm sure that I see his bottom lip quiver. "How did you feel about her relationship with Frank?"

"I could tell that she loved Frank. She couldn't believe it when Frank let her down and left her, just like that. It was a terrible shock."

"It doesn't sound like Frank was fair with her. It seems he promised a lot and then didn't honour his promises, which is not the Frank I knew, by the way."

"I think Frank was sick in the heart. He seemed stressed, unhappy, perhaps even depressed. I could tell he didn't love Annabella, but I think he wanted to."

"Mm. I reckon that was how he felt about me at one time, too. But that's another story. What happened when you approached Frank with the blackmail scheme?"

"He laughed in my face. He asked me if I realized how many people already knew he was alive. He said he was thinking of putting up a billboard on the freeway with his picture and the words 'Frank is alive' on it. He used some explicit language and then said that he should never have given Annabella any money, that he never wanted to see me or Annabella ever again. He said that I was scum and told me to get the hell out, and he said to tell Annabella to get a real job. That shook me, because I thought he genuinely loved opera, and at least cared for Annabella."

"What did you tell Annabella?"

"I just told her it didn't work, and that he'd said there were several other people who already knew he was alive. She had a tantrum. She threw her water bottle at the window, which burst and made a mess and then stormed out of the room, slamming the door behind her."

"I suppose that was the end of that."

"No, it wasn't. That's nothing to what came next. And this is why I'm here."

"Oh."

"Annabella ranted and raved about how Frank had treated her, that he shouldn't have dumped her, that he owed her, that he'd broken promises and therefore her career wasn't going anywhere, and her blood was boiling. She often said that. Despite all this, silly love-sick me wanted to help her. I hated to see her so distraught."

"What next?"

"She told me to put some pressure on Frank. I didn't want to see him ever again, but she was so upset that I did go back to Kentucky to meet with him once more. But as soon as Frank saw my face, he yelled at me to get out with such vehemence that I didn't have it in me to confront him, even for Annabella's sake. When I got back, Annabella told me that Frank was dead, and the police had called and she had no choice but to tell them I was blackmailing Frank, and that I'd met with him the day he died. An arrow pierced my heart, and it almost stopped beating. My rose-coloured glasses shattered, and I realized I could never win her love. After she told me this, she disappeared, and missed two rehearsals for the only performance contract she's had in two years. And, thanks to her, I must be the prime suspect in Frank's murder. It's a miracle that I was allowed to get on a plane and come here without a hassle. So, I'm desperate and I thought you'd be able to help. I know you're trying to find out the truth."

"I can't understand Annabella reporting you to the police."

"Her pride and her future were ripped apart by Frank, and it made her very, very angry. She demands loyalty."

"But she hasn't been loyal to you."

"But she expected my one hundred percent commitment and dedication to her, which I was happy to give. It's my doing. I got myself into this mess by becoming more than an agent, and I fell in love."

"You're not the prime suspect. Chuck, my partner, is at the moment. He went back a second time to the stables, but he told me he found Frank already dead. He picked up the gun that was lying in the aisle and panicked, and threw it in a ditch."

"I don't think he did it."

"Why?"

"Because, I was just walking down the driveway, trying to keep out of sight, when I saw a tall person, I mean taller than me, wearing a wide-brimmed hat, go into the stables by the side door. I heard two shots. I was too afraid to go back in, and too afraid to tell the police because I was there for the wrong reasons, and I don't think they'd believe me."

"Do you have any idea who it could have been?"

"No. And that's the only description I have."

"I'll see if I can find out more somehow. You think you'll be under suspicion because of Annabella's report on the blackmailing, but Chuck's fingerprints were found on the murder weapon. I think you're less likely to be seriously considered than Chuck. After all, fingerprints are powerful evidence."

"Perhaps."

"I'm not sure what to do next, but I'll think of something."

12

Hospital

Since Simeon wants to lie low, I book him into the large hotel near the airport. It's easy to fly under the radar there, in the impersonal, busy comings and goings. It's a bit more of a drive than to the Vannersville Inn, but he's more likely to go unnoticed.

I can see that he's tense, tired, saddened and anxious. I can't do a lot about those things, but he admits that he's also starving. I make a cheese omelette and prepare some toast and more fresh coffee. I apologize for the unsophisticated menu, but he seems to be genuinely grateful and his appetite has returned enough for him to eat it all. I tell him to get some rest at the hotel, and that we'll talk some more after lunch.

As soon as he's left, I call Tammy and tell her that Simeon is here. She has trouble understanding why he would travel across the Atlantic to Vannersville. Her voice is filled with both suspicion and concern. Tammy's reaction to Simeon being here increases the size of the question mark in my mind about his coming.

I ask her if she can recall mention of a person wearing a wide-brimmed hat, since Simeon saw a person matching this description enter the stables.

"No, I can't. It sounds crazy to me." Tammy is clearly irritated by the suggestion, and this niggles at me.

"Why does it sound crazy?"

"It's downright odd. My guess is that he's created this guy to turn the attention away from himself."

"But it's not on him. Chuck is the prime suspect."

"But you think Chuck's innocent. And I believe you. So, it looks like Simeon is the most likely suspect."

"Oh. I didn't know that's what you think."

"Well, I do. And I've been going over what happened that day and I'm pretty sure I saw Simeon leaving the stables. I can't be sure he was the last person to see Frank, but I think he was."

"You didn't tell me this before."

"I've been muddled. It's difficult, Meg. You, of all people, should understand."

"Yes, okay. Thanks." Now I'm the one feeling confused. Both Annabella and Tammy think Simeon is the murderer, but he's come all the way here for refuge and swears he's innocent.

In the silence of the house, I can hear the wind howling outside, and a few large branches lie, broken, on the frozen ground near the barn. But the building looks fine as far as I can see from the kitchen window.

Dominic isn't picking up his phone, and I don't want to leave a message. I'm disappointed that he hasn't got back to me with any leads, and I want to ask him where someone could get a gun. A fleeting thought flits through my mind, but I can't imagine Dominic fitting the description of a person taller than Simeon. I'd guess they're about the same height. And I can't think of anyone who wears a wide-brimmed hat. The mystery person, if he exists, must be someone new to me.

The power goes out. A tree must have come down on the hydro lines somewhere. I fumble around in the cupboard for my bright flashlight, with the help of Cooper who hangs onto my sleeve, upside down, biting my hand playfully. I can still use my phone and my mobile, so I make some calls to see if I can track down any of the jockeys who were in Dominic's race-fixing business with Juan. I want to keep my side of the bargain with Dominic, so that he follows up with his contacts who visited Louisa's Acres around the time of Frank's murder. I'm counting on Jimmy having missed seeing someone who visited Frank that day, perhaps the person wearing a wide-brimmed hat. But my heart sinks as I admit to myself that it's a long-shot.

Susana, Juan's wife, is the most helpful. She gives me the names of four jockeys who Juan had often mentioned, not including Ferris (the one who apparently gave Juan the poisoned coffee). I find out from one of them that two have left for the States to race during the winter, but two are still here and are willing to meet with me. Ferris is still here, but the phone number I have is no longer in service. I'm sure Dominic will know how to get hold of Ferris when I want to talk with him.

* * *

I'm surprised that the two jockeys are eager to talk with me, and together. Perhaps they have some useful information. We meet in a small, unimposing coffee shop in an uninspiring strip mall, but it's quiet and there are booths at the back where we can talk without being overheard or interrupted. I'm not one for dwelling on preliminaries, and it seems they want to get straight to the point of our meeting, just as I do.

"We've chatted, Benito and me. And we think the same way."

"Yeah." Benito is sitting next to Hurley. He turns towards his colleague and nods.

"We'd like to tell you what we know," Hurley says as he leans back into the corner of the booth. I'm sure neither of them can reach the floor with their feet. They each have small statures, both in height and bone-structure.

"I appreciate you meeting with me. All I know is that the coffee that was given to Juan by Ferris was poisoned, and that Juan was part of a race-fixing scheme run by Dominic Marcel as part of his gambling business."

Hurley pulls himself upright, away from the corner of the booth, and Benito leans forward with his hands clasped in front of him. They each have a large mug of black coffee, but not much has been drunk. My tea wasn't made with boiling water and smells mostly of chlorine, so I'm not drinking it.

"We want to tell you we were real shook up about Juan. We know riding racehorses is dangerous, but we don't expect to get poisoned, and we don't reckon on getting killed when we're not racing."

"That's right, Hurley."

"Benito and I don't mind telling you, we're scared. We're scared 'cause we don't know who did this." They don't appear to be particularly scared, and if that's all they're going to tell me, this will be a very disappointing meeting.

"Oh." I push my mug of grey tea aside. "You must have more to say than that, though?" I'm hoping.

"Yeah," Benito says.

"Yeah. We think you might be after the wrong guy. And you said you know about his gambling business," Hurley says.

"Yeah. But Dominic's not a bad man."

"Like Benito said, he's not a bad man. Yeah, race-fixing is bad, but you have to make a buck somehow. And making money at racing is getting harder. You would know, being an owner. If you listen to the bitching at the track, the feeling is that people who don't know shit about racing are making decisions that are destroying the business."

"I don't see what that's got to do with Dominic," I say. I can't help feeling impatient. I don't need a lecture on how the government has pulled the rug out from underneath the industry, and how the new administration is mucking things up. I'm well aware of that.

"It has, in a way. Dominic said it got too tough to make it as a trainer. Less horses. And it's tougher for jockeys in Canada too."

I could mention that Dominic lost his trainer's licence at Canadian and US tracks, but decide not to go there.

"So, you think Dominic is justified in running his gambling business, including race-fixing?" I ask.

Hurley looks at Benito.

"Yeah," Benito says.

"Yeah. Anyhow, what we want to tell you is that Dominic is not a murderer. He wouldn't kill one of us jockeys, not for anything."

"How can you be so sure?" I ask, wondering if I'm wasting my time and theirs.

"Because he treats us like we're his nephews or something, like family. He helps us and our families out if things go bad for us," Benito says as he wraps his small hands round the white mug of black coffee, cold by now.

"But Ferris, who gave Juan the coffee, is a control freak," Hurley says. "Ferris was mad that Juan wanted out. He told me he was afraid that Juan would talk and that would mean an end to our race-fixing gig and we'd be short a bunch of dough. I told him Juan wouldn't talk."

"The money is important to Ferris, I know that much," says Benito.

"Dominic wasn't that upset about Juan pulling out. He reckons any of us who talks will get themselves into trouble too, because they were part of it, and weren't forced or anything. So, he doesn't worry about it."

"Dominic a murderer? I just can't see it," Benito says.

* * *

Back at the farm, I'm relieved that the power is back on and put a piece of bread into the toaster as I contemplate my next step. I want to meet with Ferris, but don't have his contact information. I'm sure that Dominic will be able to set the meeting up, so I call him and explain why I want to meet with Ferris, without mentioning Hurley and Benito. Dominic is quick to agree and thinks he'll have it arranged within a couple of days, but surprises me by saying he wants to be there, too.

He tells me he has some contacts asking questions in Kentucky and expects to hear something back soon. I let him know that someone saw a person at the stables, wearing a wide-brimmed hat, and that it would be useful to get more information.

The piece of toast has gone cold and lifeless, and the same will happen to me if I don't get some nourishment. So, on a whim, I call Simeon and suggest we have a bite to eat in the hotel café, and then I'll go from there to the hospital to see my mother.

It's easy to find Simeon in the concrete and glass café, since no-one else is here. It's cavernous and cold, crammed with heavy metal chairs surrounding tables draped in black-and-white checkered tablecloths. Nothing about it begs one to stay, but it works well for us. We have the privacy we want.

While Simeon has more colour to his face and brighter, clearer eyes, his slight frame is slumped and he looks dejected.

"The more I think about Annabella telling the police I was blackmailing Frank, the more devastated I feel. I loved her, and I, the idiot that I am, thought she felt something for me. But I was a pawn to her, to be played so that she could get what she wanted, which was money. I'm sure revenge was involved too, with Frank. She was really mad at him for letting her down."

"I don't understand why she told the police you were blackmailing Frank, especially since you attempted to blackmail him at Annabella's behest and she knew you weren't getting anywhere."

"Instead of being grateful for me going to Kentucky, she was mad at me for not getting the money out of Frank. She blamed me. I told you, she expects one hundred percent loyalty, and nothing less will do. And she's a passionate woman. She feels things strongly and reacts strongly."

I think I believe Simeon. It's an odd story, but the truth can be bizarre sometimes. After we've eaten, I suggest Simeon get some more rest and tell him to be patient, and that we'll get to the truth, eventually.

* * *

I find my mother propped up in bed looking almost as pale as the white sheet which is tucked under her arms. Her permed hair is frizzy, and I think I can see a trace of fear in her eyes. Her demeanour is different. I can tell by the appealing way she looks at me as I walk towards the bed. I ask her what happened.

"I suddenly lost my balance. It's as if the floor moved, and I fell so quickly I didn't have time to save myself." Her voice is quivering, and there are tears in her eyes.

"Have they done any tests?"

"They've done a scan, and they found a tumour on my brain."

I'm not sure if I believe her. I can't break down the wall of distrust that stands between me and this woman.

"What does the Doctor say?"

"You've come at the right time, because he's supposed to come and see me about now. He'll probably be late. They always are, aren't they?"

"I'll ask at the nurses' station. Be right back." They tell me he'll be here in about ten minutes, and that there's a small kitchenette where visitors can make coffee or tea, so I make some tea for both of us.

"I thought you'd left," my mother says, as she takes the Styrofoam cup of tea with a shaky hand.

"I should have told you I was making tea. The Doctor will be here any minute."

The Doctor walks in and, in a brusque manner, tells me that my mother has a brain tumour, and that it could be benign or it could be malignant. He doesn't appear to realize that my mother can talk. It's almost as if she's already dead. I shift my eyes to my mother in a futile attempt to have the Doctor address her directly, instead of through me. There are several questions, some of which I have to ask my mother because I don't know the answer. I don't know why I don't tell him, point blank, to talk to my mother directly.

He advises that my mother should return to England as soon as possible, so she can receive whatever treatment is indicated, under the National Health Service. I'm concerned about her travelling. He says he'll write a letter that she can carry with her in case of any complications or questions, but that she should be okay to travel. He'll prescribe some medication which will help with some symptoms for now. He has mastered the art of detachment. The cold, almost callous, way in which he expresses the possible prognoses, gives me goosebumps. My mother bursts into tears as he leaves. I'm relieved to see the back of him. I wish Dr. Milton was here, then this would have been an entirely different experience.

For the first time that I can remember, I put my arm round my mother and do my best to console her. My distrust has evaporated. She's been telling the truth. She stops crying and asks for the tea I set down on the bedside table, which is out of reach. I pull the chair close to the side of the bed and watch as she sips the tea. No words fill the air between us. I feel the gulf of emptiness, of nothingness that has been our relationship.

"Thank you for coming," she says as she hands me the cup. The tea tastes of plastic, and I put my cup down with her empty one.

"That's okay."

"I don't know what to say. I suppose I've known something was wrong for a while. But I've been too scared to face up to it, or do anything about it. I think some of my behaviour was affected by the tumour, but most of it was bravado. I was putting on a show for myself, more than anything."

"Why did you come?"

"I wanted to say I was sorry, but it all went wrong. I was, am, too afraid of everything: of you, of not feeling well, of being alone (even though Stan was a brute), of old age, but perhaps I won't get old so no need to worry about that anymore." She makes an attempt at a smile which barely lifts the sagging corners of her mouth.

"You didn't come just to say sorry, though, did you? I think you were going to ask me for money."

"Perhaps. Maybe."

"Why?"

"I'm not a very nice person, you know that. I was jealous that you had a wealthy husband who left you a whole pile of money, and my husband, the cad, left me next to nothing. I don't know why I thought you should give me money, or why on earth I thought you would give me any. I think I felt vulnerable or something like that. I thought money would solve a lot of my problems, but it can't fix the past, it can't make me a better person, and it can't bring me my life back."

"What happened to Stan?"

"He's dead, that's all that matters. I wish I'd never met him. I don't want to talk about him. I can't take away the pain. Nothing I can say will do that. But I am sorry about what happened."

"It helps a bit to know that you're sorry."

"I know it was bloody awful. But talking about it will only bring back unbearable memories for both of us. I'm hoping this tumour will erase my memories of Stan. I sure hope so."

"Let's talk about what you're going to do next."

"I'll leave for England as soon as I can make the arrangements. I'm sure they'll discharge me tomorrow once they've got the prescriptions and the letter from that bloody doctor. I'll change my reservation for a flight the day after. I want to go back to the Inn tomorrow. I have my things there."

"Okay. I could help you change your flight if you like, and I can drive you to the airport."

"Thank you. I don't deserve that. But that would be nice. I'm scared about what could happen. I don't trust my brain anymore. I meant to ask you how your Chuck is doing? I think I made matters worse."

"Probably. He's still the prime suspect in the murder of Frank. I think you knew that. I'm trying to find out who the real murderer is."

"If you love him, and if he loves you, don't let him go. True love is very special. Your father and I were truly in love. It was wonderful to be loved. I miss him terribly." She sobs as I squeeze her hand. I've never heard her mention how she felt about my father before. I've just heard lies and stories which made no sense.

"I'm going to do everything I can to get Chuck back."

"Good."

* * *

I'm not pleased with myself as I drive home. It's like turning a big ship around at sea as I attempt to reform my image of my mother. I've only known her to be uncaring, cold, and detached. The woman I was just with is so different. I've not had a meaningful conversation with her ever before. How much is this momentous change due to her remorse and quest for healing in our relationship, and how much is due to her tumour? I can't help wondering this as I drive up towards the house.

Kelly is keeping Linda company as she scrubs the feed buckets in the chilly wind outside the barn. I can see steam rising.

"I hope you don't mind, Meg. I got some hot water from the house. The buckets needed cleaning."

"You're amazing. Thanks. How is everyone?"

"I'm going to bring them all in soon because there's a bitter wind, and they're getting restless."

I can see Eagle and Bullet standing in a run-in shed in one paddock, but Rose and Speed are pacing up and down the fence-line closest to the barn, making it quite clear that they'd rather be in their stalls. They're just beginning to grow their longer winter coats, whereas Eagle and Bullet have a head-start and they have more fat on them than the racehorses. They don't feel the bite of the strong wind that's rattling the barn roof as much as the trim athletes do. Kelly comes with me to check out Rose and Speed, but nothing we can say to them will make them quit their agitated pacing.

"I'll help you bring them in now, Linda, if you like. They're not going to settle down. I'll just get my barn boots on."

13

Annabella

With the horses settled in their stalls and Linda on her way home, Kelly and I walk into the house, taking a rush of crisp, cold air in with us. Cooper swats at Kelly's nose with his paw, which I assume is some kind of greeting because the dog gives the cat a lick on his ear. As Kelly turns towards me, her wagging tail is too much for Cooper to resist. The kitten sits on his haunches and biffs at the moving, silky target and gets his claws stuck. The dog looks round, wondering what's weighing her tail down, and I disentangle them. It's just as well that Kelly is such a kind and tolerant dog. Cooper bats his stuffed mouse around the kitchen instead.

An unexpected knock at the door stops all of us in our tracks. I decided earlier in the day that, since there has been no sign of Ewert ever since the shooting, that the security guard isn't necessary. With expenses mounting up, I decided that Linda's help is more important at the moment.

Joanna, not her husband, is on the doorstep.

"How's the wound?" I beckon her to come in and sit down at the kitchen table.

"It's much better, thanks."

"How are things going?"

"Ewert has hardly said a word since he came here. I know he didn't mean to shoot. It's eating away at him inside. Is Kelly okay?"

"She's much better. I'm glad you came, because I was planning on giving you information on a program that's helped someone else, an ex-cop, who has PTSD. His name is Austin. He was one of the security guards assigned here, and he's willing to talk to Ewert. He's thinking of setting up his own program here in Vannersville and could probably do with some help, you never know. I have the info written down somewhere."

"We need something, some small strand of hope to hang on to. Things have got pretty bad." She rings her hands and then rubs her thighs.

"Here's Austin's contact information." Joanna looks morose. She's hanging her head and ignoring Cooper, who's weaving around her legs, leaving traces of cat hair.

"Ewert told me a bit more about Dominic. I think he's frightened of him. Dominic can be a charmer when he wants to be, but if you cross him, watch out."

"That's not what I heard from the jockeys who are directly involved with him in his race-fixing thing. I met with two of them and they made out that he treats his jockeys like nephews and helps them out if things get bad."

"I'm just telling you what Ewert believes."

"Okay."

Joanna shuffles on the chair and stares down at the table. I wonder if the wound is aggravating her more than she wants to let on, or if something else is unsettling her.

"I didn't come here just for a chat," she says. Her face is flushed, and her eyes are brimming with a trace of tears as she raises her head and looks at me. I cringe. I know what's coming.

"We're broke. We can't afford the rent on that apology for a house and we've just been handed an eviction notice. We have to leave by the end of the month."

"You're asking me for money."

"Ewert said I should ask you. I didn't want to." She swipes the back of her hand across her face, sniffing. "Ewert said you'd give us something because Frank was my brother-in-law."

"I won't give you money that will feed into Ewert's gambling addiction. I'm willing to consider paying one month's rent, to give you a chance to get things sorted out."

"Aren't you the stuck-up bitch!" She stands up, leans over with her face almost touching mine, and screams at me. "We're practically your family, and you won't help us out. Just sitting in your luxury, with Frank's millions, watching us starve."

Kelly barks and has her hackles up. She doesn't like the tone of Joanna's voice any more than I do. I've not seen Joanna lose her temper before. I stand up and she spits in my face. I walk to the kitchen door and open it and tell her that neither she nor Ewert are permitted to set foot on the property again. I contact the security company. This time I ask for a monthly renewable contract. I just have to spend the money.

And I call William.

* * *

Kelly and I watch out for William as we sit on the verandah in the cold crisp air, our faces surrounded by our misty breaths, hardly moving a muscle. Kelly knows we're waiting for someone and knows who it is as soon as William turns into the driveway. He's arrived before the security guard has shown up.

"What are you doing sitting out in the cold?" William asks as he walks towards me with the dog licking his gloved hand. "I know the sky's clear but it's not dark enough yet for star-gazing."

We walk round the house to the kitchen door and peel off our coats. William has brought tea for me and coffee for him, as well as two soups.

"I had a feeling you might not have eaten much today." He places the Styrofoam bowls on the table with the plastic spoons. His thoughtfulness almost makes me cry.

After Joanna's outburst, a sudden sense of loneliness took hold. As I washed my face, feelings of worthlessness swept over me. I felt like a fragile shell tossed up onto the beach by the sea, likely to be crumbled into a million pieces. It's as if William has picked up the shell, believing that it has some value, and is worth preserving.

"Thank you," is all I can say. We consume our soup without another word. The badly needed nourishment settles my stomach as well as my mind. As we reheat our drinks, the security guard arrives. William raises an eyebrow like a question mark as I explain the situation to the new guard who hasn't been here before.

We move to the family room with Kelly and Cooper close on our heels, and I update William on all that's happened. He's a good listener. He says nothing, but I know he's paying attention. Perhaps that's something to do with his training as a lawyer.

"I wish you'd been willing to report Ewert to the police. This whole matter could be escalating. Would you at least let me look into getting an injunction against Ewert and Joanna?"

"I don't know. I'm not sure that it would stop Ewert from coming here and shooting me."

"You have a point. Wise move to get the security company back. That's probably more effective." He purses his lips, as if he has a foul taste in his mouth. I think he's concerned for my safety.

My mobile's vibrations tingle my fingers as I grab it. I was about to turn it off, but Dominic Marcel's face is staring out at me with a half-smile, and my curiosity gets the better of me.

"Hi, Dominic."

"Hi. You asked me to do some poking around. Right?" His tone sounds ominous.

"Yes."

"Then there's someone with some info, but I'm guessing you won't like what he has to say. Want to talk with him?"

"I do."

"The guy's called Marvin. He's a farrier working in Kentucky and he overheard a conversation in Fred Simpson's barn. I got this lead from a shipper I talked to that Marvin blabbered to. By the way, don't let on that you're called Meg. I told him you're to be called Mrs. Sheppard."

I thank him and take down the contact information. He wouldn't give me any more details.

"Why do I have a sinking feeling about this, William?"

"Because, as you told me, Dominic thinks you won't like what you're going to hear. But there's no point speculating. Why don't you call him now?"

"I suppose it's not too late. I know I'm hesitating. Ignorance is bliss sometimes."

I get through to Marvin without a hitch and he assures me it's a good time to talk.

"I've gotta assume Fred didn't know I was working on a horse in the stall next to his office. I was bent over just about all the time, so when he and this guy walked past, they wouldn't have seen me, I guess. Dominic says you're trying to find out what happened to Fred. Well, what I heard might help you out."

"Good, thanks."

"My guess would be that Fred had asked this guy called Chuck to meet with him, because he acted like he was expecting him and as soon as he showed up, he let into him. He asked about this guy's relationship with someone called Meg. Fred accused the guy of being after Meg's money. I couldn't catch all of it, even though they were just about shouting at each other, especially Fred. I did get that Fred wanted this Chuck to leave Meg. He said that he didn't believe that the guy loved her. It was real interesting when Chuck said he would leave Meg if Fred gave him enough money to turn around what sounded like a plantation. That bit gotta be wrong. Fred laughed at him. It was a raucous laugh. I didn't like the sound of it at all. My horse got fidgety. He didn't like it either. They moved into the aisle, as if Fred was trying to get rid of him. I heard Fred clearly when he said that he would tell this Meg person what that guy Chuck had just said if he didn't leave her. There was a bit more yelling as they moved down the aisle, but that's all I can tell you."

"Thank you, Marvin." I inhale too quickly and almost choke as I put my mobile down. William moves to the sofa to be nearer to me, but doesn't say a word. I can hear him breathing and a waft of spicy aftershave tingles my nose. I try to be distracted, to pretend I hadn't heard what Marvin told me, that it was a dream. But it doesn't work.

We sit in silence. I contemplate what is the most upsetting thing: the likelihood that Chuck killed my husband Frank, or the revelation that he doesn't love me. It seems as if Frank had more concern for me than Chuck does. But they've both been deceitful: Frank in faking his death and Chuck in hiding his plantation ownership and perhaps more. I tell William everything that I can recall about the conversation. I wish I'd used speaker-phone, it would have saved me that pain.

"William, my feelings about this are confusing me." He doesn't move or say anything. Even though I'm in a state of despondency, I notice he doesn't offer me a hand, a hug, or any physical contact. I suppose that's a lawyer for you.

"What do you mean?"

"I think I'm more upset that this information, if it's correct, points to Chuck being Frank's killer than I am about the suggestion, more than suggestion, that he doesn't love me."

"It's possible that Marvin misheard."

"Somehow I don't think so."

"Is there anyone who would want you to believe this about Chuck? Who would want to lie about Chuck?"

"A couple of days ago, I would have wondered if my mother could orchestrate something like this. She had it in for Chuck. But her last words to me were something like if I love him and he loves me I shouldn't let him go."

"The key issue being if he loves you and you love him." William stands up. "Sorry, I shouldn't have said that. It's none of my business. And I should probably be going."

"I know I've taken up a lot of you time, but I'd really like it if you could stay longer. I don't mind admitting that I'm shaken, and I'd enjoy your company."

He hesitates. I wish I could put on the pleading look that Kelly uses successfully with me. I look at him with wide, imploring eyes instead.

"Okay. I'll get something for us to drink."

* * *

Last evening William helped me to get a plan worked out in my head. I have too many balls in the air and don't want to drop any. I'll visit my mother once she returns to the hotel later today, and I'll see her off safely to England whenever she plans to leave. And I'll get her banking information so that I can send her some money.

Everyone is after money.

I'll get hold of Chuck, somehow, and confront him with what I've heard. I need to listen to his side of the story.

I'll connect with Dominic and ask him about the arrangements to meet with the jockey Ferris who was the one who handed Juan the coffee, since I haven't heard from him yet.

And I'll tell Simeon to come out here to the farm in a taxi.

And I plan to give Murray an update since he hasn't called. I don't feel like talking to Tammy today, so I'll postpone that for a day or two.

William offered to help, but he seemed agitated yesterday evening. So, I said I'd be fine. He might pop in this evening, he said, but he sounded half-hearted about it. I can't figure him out at the moment and I admit I'm disappointed. I find so much comfort in his company.

Linda bursts into the kitchen, red in the face and puffing, just as I finish my check-list for the day.

"I think you like tea. I got some. And I got a muffin. I think you like muffins."

"Linda, thank you. That is so thoughtful of you. Let me pay you."

"No. It's nothing. I'm going to the barn. Kelly can come." She rushes out as if her life depends on it.

I call after her, "She'd love to. Thanks. Thanks for everything." Something tells me that her friend Austin must be on security duty for the day shift.

The landline phone rings, jolting me out of my warm and fuzzy feelings for Linda, and back to hard reality.

"Oh, Meg, how nice to hear your voice," Annabella says.

"It's nice to hear your voice too." I'm not being entirely truthful. I'm scanning my memorized checklist and want to get on with it.

"How's Chuck? It is difficult for you both."

"Yes, it's bad."

"I thought you would want to know that I have found out that my trusted agent has betrayed me. He tried to blackmail Frank."

"He told me. He said you'd asked him to do it."

"What a fantasy. That man is dreaming."

"Simeon said you'd disappeared."

"Nonsense. Not true. What a liar he is! It is hard to believe he is so bad. He has worked for me for years and I trusted him. I was not feeling well. He knows that."

"Hope you're feeling better."

"No. I feel bad for another reason. I wonder if Simeon killed Frank."

"Why do you think that he might have?"

"It is hard to think this way, but I do wonder. I wanted to tell you because of Chuck. So, bad news for me might be good news for you."

"Yes, I suppose so. By the way, there is some speculation that there was a fourth visitor to the barn. Someone taller than Simeon, wearing a wide-brimmed hat. The murderer could be someone entirely different."

"That is unexpected news. That could be good news for both of us." But Annabella's voice has a trace of a tremble and she hangs up after a couple of words of farewell.

I sip some of the tea and eat pieces of the moist muffin. Trust Linda to buy a carrot one. It has to have some link to horses. This thought brightens me a bit and, for a moment, I reflect on how kind-hearted she is. Just having her around is helping me in so many ways, even though we don't interact a lot. I used to think Chuck was warm-hearted, honest, and trustworthy. But that was several months ago. As I look back, I can see that things changed soon after he moved to the farm.

But these thoughts won't get me anywhere. I need to find out who killed my husband and who killed the jockey.

I text Dominic and ask when I can call him. Two minutes later we're chatting and he tells me that the meeting will be set up soon. He sounds keen, perhaps because he wants to be sure that he doesn't get landed with a murder rap.

Simeon is on his way in a taxi. I'm not sure what I'm going to do with him. I hope he's had some breakfast because I've no food in the house. I've nearly finished the muffin.

As if William has read my mind, he opens the kitchen door and brings in about eight bags of groceries. The working-out he's been doing is obviously paying dividends because they seem to be almost weightless in his hands.

"I took a guess at what you like." He puts the bags down on the kitchen table and Cooper immediately jumps up there to check them out. William puts him down gently and gives him a couple of strokes as the kitten tries to biff him with his paws. William is another kind person in my life and I don't know what I give back to him. I thank him and put the groceries away while he goes back out to the car. I wonder if he's going to leave without saying goodbye. He seems quiet and more reserved than I'm used to. Another curious thought: I remember him saying that he wouldn't come till later in the day.

"I have news. A couple of days ago, it would have been a reason for celebration, but today I'm not so sure." William hands me my second tea of the day, which he's retrieved from the car and sits down at the table with his coffee. I close the fridge and sit down opposite him. As he looks down at his drink, struggling with the flap in the lid, I notice how shiny his balding head is. If I could see my reflection, I bet my mouth is sagging at the corners and there's puffiness under my eyes. He looks up and his eyes are bloodshot. I hope he's okay.

"The lawyer I lined up in Kentucky phoned me first thing to let me know Chuck has been released. Apparently, the bullet fired from the gun which has Chuck's fingerprints on it, is not the one which killed Frank. It entered one of the barn posts. They seem to be hellishly slow down there with their forensics."

"Wow. I'm glad to hear he didn't murder Frank."

"It's not clear to me if they intend to lay some other charge. But I suspect that there's insufficient evidence to link him to the crime, at the moment."

We sit in silence for a couple of minutes, and I try to turn my thoughts away from Chuck. I let Cooper distract me as he plays with the receipt, which reminds me I need to pay William for the groceries, but he won't accept any money.

"I have some news, too. I had a curious call from Annabella." I update William on the conversation, admitting that I'm surprised that she's accusing Simeon of murder.

"What do you make of all this?" William asks.

"I'm going back over all the suspects and motives. I believe it must have to do with money. Chuck seems to be the most desperate for money, but it seems he's not the person who pulled the trigger after all." I take a gulp of tea. "The only suspect I can think of is the mysterious person in the wide-brimmed hat."

"So, who else wants money? Everyone, I suppose." William looks down at his coffee again. He's not his usual self.

"Annabella. She was furious with Frank for leaving her. I think she was mad, mostly because of the loss of the sponsorship he'd committed to. But her attempts to get money out of Frank failed. And, if she's to be believed, she was not behind the plan to blackmail Frank. Simeon acted on his own. But I can envisage her wearing a wide-brimmed hat. Isn't that the sort of thing divas wear?" I lift the corners of my mouth in a half-smile. But William is looking down at Cooper, who's found his way onto his lap.

Tammy's face appears on my mobile.

"Oh, Meg. You've got to help me." Tammy sounds as if she's hyper-ventilating.

"What's happened? Before you tell me, drink some water. Try to calm your breathing."

"Okay. Okay."

"Are you still there?"

"I'm a tad better. Just hearing your voice helps."

"I'm going to put my phone on speaker because I have a good friend with me who's helping."

"Okay."

"What's happened?"

"Annabella just called. She accused me of murdering Frank. She says she can prove it. You know I didn't do it. I wouldn't have."

"Wow. I just talked with her and she accused Simeon of killing Frank. But then I told her that someone had seen a person, taller than Simeon, wearing a wide-brimmed hat, enter the barn."

"Gee, she thinks it was me! I can't believe she'd do this to me after all we've been through." Tammy doesn't attempt to dampen her sniffling. I'm wondering if she'll be able to continue our conversation.

"Tammy, what do you mean 'all you've been through'?"

"I thought you'd have guessed." Tammy blew her nose. "Annabella asked me to work with her to get money from Frank for both of us. She convinced me I deserved something because I was his new partner, and that she deserved what she said he'd promised her. Oh, God, I wish I hadn't listened. Now he's dead!" She breaks down into sobs. I feel mercenary. I really want to know the whole story.

"Tammy."

"Sorry. I'm upset."

"I know this is difficult. But I want to help you and unearth the truth. So, please tell me everything you know." In between more sobs and nose-blowing, Tammy tells us that Annabella asked her to contact her as soon as she and Frank found somewhere to stay in the States. Simeon set up a telephone call between the two women, during which Annabella told Tammy what they should do to get their just desserts. Annabella said that Simeon would do all the dirty work. He would approach Frank and ask him for money. After all, Frank wanted to be dead. He had gone to great lengths to fake his death. It must have been very important to him that he should disappear, and so it would be easy to get money out of him in return for keeping quiet. And besides, he had millions and could spare some.

"But we know that didn't work," I say.

"Frank said that too many people already knew he was alive."

"Annabella told you what happened then?"

"She said that Simeon needed to try harder and sent him back here. I thought that was a stupid idea. I got nervous. Annabella was so determined. She believed Frank was stinking rich. She was angry."

"Were you angry?"

"No. I thought I was lucky to be living with him and in this beautiful place. I hadn't known him for very long, so wasn't expecting a lot. I should have had the guts to say no to Annabella, and perhaps Frank would still be alive."

"Do you think she could have murdered Frank?"

"She sure was mad, but I can't imagine her pulling the trigger. I can see her throwing things and yelling. She's good at that."

"Where were you when Frank was shot?"

"I was alone in the house. I don't have an alibi, if that's what you mean." Tammy sobs again. "I lose Frank and, if that isn't bad enough, I might lose my freedom. I can't bear it. This has to be a nightmare." It sounds as if Tammy is retching.

I do my best to console Tammy and tell her we'll do what we can to find out what happened. I'm concerned about her as I end the call.

"What do you think of all that, William?"

"My assessment of people isn't always right, but I'd say that Tammy didn't kill Frank."

"Annabella sounds like our most likely suspect then."

"Perhaps."

"What do you mean 'perhaps'?"

"I don't know, really. It's just not obvious that's all."

"I desperately want to know who wore that wide-brimmed hat." I can imagine Annabella wearing one.

14

A Letter

Someone knocks forcefully on the kitchen door. It's a new security guard with Simeon standing behind him. I usher Simeon in. His Mediterranean complexion has a sickly pallor, as if he's been kept in a dark place for too long. But it doesn't take much time for some of the colour to return as I relate the essence of Tammy's telephone call, especially the fact that Annabella is now accusing Tammy of killing Frank.

"I'm relieved for myself, yes, but I'm now worried for Tammy." Simeon looks at me and then at William, his dark eyes like saucers. Kelly slinks away from him and puts her head on William's lap. He strokes her absent mindedly.

"Do you think Annabella could be capable of murdering Frank?" William asks Simeon.

"No, I don't. But she did disappear, as I mentioned."

I give Simeon the facts as I know them, about the date and the time of day, which was the evening, probably close to five o'clock.

"She couldn't have made it to Kentucky by then." Simeon says. William is busy making coffee and scrambling some eggs. He says he can manage that much even though he's not a great cook. I'm grateful for any help with food, since I invariably go without and regret it later when my energy level hits rock-bottom. "She phoned me late morning to make sure I'd got to Kentucky, and that I was going to meet with Frank. It would have been near tea-time in England. I'm pretty sure she was there. I could hear the orchestra tuning up in the background. They were about to have their first run-through. But I heard nothing from her after that. She disappeared and I know the Maestro was in a rage."

"But she wouldn't have had time to get to Kentucky to see Frank before he'd been killed."

"No. She could have left after I texted her, with trembling fingers, that I'd not had any luck with Frank. But she wouldn't have reached Kentucky until the next day."

William produces three plates of scrambled eggs and toast, along with coffee for him and Simeon, and a steaming mug of tea for me. I'm not hungry, but I know I should eat, and I'm grateful for William's thoughtfulness.

"I wonder," says William, "if we should ask Annabella outright?"

"Just what I was thinking," I say. "Simeon, can you get hold of her? I don't have her contact information."

"I can." He sounds reluctant. "But I'd rather give you her number so you can call her yourself."

"Of course." I shouldn't have asked him. Their relationship must surely be poisoned by Annabella's suspicions and accusations.

As William takes his plate to the dishwasher, Simeon wonders out-loud if Annabella will speak with us. But I connect with her successfully and ask if she's willing to be on speaker phone. I don't mention that Simeon is in the room. I should have.

William offers to put his lawyerly hat on.

"Annabella, this is William Porter. As you might already know, I'm a lawyer and I'm assisting Meg Sheppard with her inquiries regarding her husband's tragic murder in Kentucky."

"This is Meg, Annabella. Thanks for taking this call."

"Why do you want to talk to me?" I detect a wobble in her voice, not the confident, powerful voice I've heard in the past.

"We want to clarify something. Where were you at the time of Frank's murder?"

"I was in the hospital. You can check the records. I stayed for a couple of days. I suppose you want the details. You will not be satisfied without them. I tell you just because I do not want to be accused of being a killer. I am not. I was in the hospital for alcohol poisoning. I was distraught about how the rehearsal went, and I drank too much. I give you permission to talk to the doctors, if you wish."

"I'm sorry to hear that you were sick. But why have you accused Tammy of being the killer?" I ask.

"Because she must have been the killer. It is simple. You told me that Simeon did not kill Frank, I was not there, so who else is there? Who had reason to get mad enough with him to shoot him? Tammy."

After the call ends, the three of us sit around the table in silence for a moment.

"I just can't believe Tammy would kill him. I don't think she could have put on that whole act on the phone," I say. "And she would have had to put on an act each time I visited; let alone the fact that she was the one who contacted me in the first place to help her find out who murdered Frank. I just can't believe it's her."

"Who are we left with?" asks William.

"Just in case you're wondering," Simeon says, with a shaky voice and watery eyes, "Annabella had a drinking problem before I met her. She said it was under control, but I think her story is probably true, about drinking too much after the rehearsal, that is."

"I think so too. What do you think, Meg?" asks William.

"I agree, and I wasn't even going to check with the hospital. But this whole business is making me more cynical by the day."

"I'll check with the hospital," Simeon says.

I fiddle with my food, but, feeling guilty about not eating what William prepared, I make an effort and eventually consume nearly all of it while the three of us sit in silence. Cooper laps at the bowl of water and Kelly lies at William's feet.

"I don't know who to suspect any more. I don't have a likely scenario in my mind," I say.

There's a knock at the door, and William opens it. Linda hands him my mail from the box at the end of the driveway. She disappears before I have a chance to thank her for picking it up. William puts four envelopes on the table in front of me, and my hand visibly shakes as I reach for the envelope which has Frank's hand-writing on it. There's no mistaking it. Receiving a letter from a dead person, my husband, makes my skin crawl and my heart ache. No-one says anything as I open the letter. They can see that I'm distressed and, as I read a few lines, the paper trembles like an aspen leaf. I put the letter down and hold my head in my hands.

"William, it's from Frank. Can you read it aloud? I just can't read it."

"Of course, if you're certain you want to share it with us."

"Yes." I figure I'm going to need a lot of support to deal with what Frank says in the letter, whatever it is.

"Here goes," William says. He sits up straight and assumes his lawyerly voice and reads the letter, with clear diction and ponderous precision. "*My Dear Meg: I am aware that you know I survived the crash (the whole world seems to know), but I'm not writing to you about the debacle of my attempt to disappear by faking my own death. I'm not writing to apologize, although you might think, perhaps rightly, that I treated you abysmally.*

One reason I'm writing is to assure you you mean a lot to me. I have not found the warm companionship you offered with anyone else. Despite the cruel, unimaginable abuse you suffered in your past, you were loyal, and honoured our contract. You are a good person and don't deserve to suffer any more in your life.

And this leads me to the second reason I'm writing. It concerns Chuck. You need to know that your friend, or should I say partner, Charles Alexander Murphy, is not what he appears. I feel at least partly responsible because I brought him into your life believing that he's essentially a decent kind of guy. I know more about him than I told you, and for that I hope you'll forgive me. I wanted to help him because he was desperate, but I now know it was a mistake.

When I saw him in the backstretch and offered him the gardening job at the farm, he looked terrible. He didn't want to talk about it then. But I've done some digging. I found out that he inherited a plantation in the Caribbean. The history of the Murphy Plantation is documented on the web (check it out!). It's about 200 acres and has a 12,000 square-foot house. Not all that large as plantations go. Briefly, it was badly damaged in the 19th century slave uprising. It was eventually restored, and the Murphy family managed the business remotely from Ireland. But things didn't go well. The business collapsed, and the property deteriorated, becoming a virtual ruin. Then Chuck inherited it about three years ago and invested everything he had into it, with the aim of putting it back into operation. He'd planned to marry a wealthy woman called Dania Lichfield, but she called the wedding off immediately after he revealed his plans to reactivate the plantation. The break-up sent him into a dejected state, which led to him losing his job, which made matters worse.

But I understand he hasn't given up on his dream despite all that has happened and the serious debt that he's in.

The point I want to make is that he is desperate for funds. You might wonder why I know he's so desperate. The clincher is that Chuck has just visited me here in Kentucky, and he had the audacity to ask me for money. I asked him why he was so much in need since I understood he had a profitable writing career. He told me he's not been able to focus on his writing because of the plantation business. One thing led to another, and I told him I didn't think he loved you or respected you (forgive me for being presumptuous) and that he should do the honourable and decent thing and leave you. You won't like what he said. He told me he would leave you if I gave him enough money to get his plantation operational, in other words, a lot of money. I thought his request so preposterous I couldn't help laughing. I think he's insane. I told him I would tell you about our conversation if he didn't leave you. But he just went beet red and told me that I'd be sorry. I have to say I've never seen him act in such an aggressive manner. He's not the Chuck I once knew.

I'm writing this because I care enough about you and the farm to alert you. Please beware of this man. I'm sure that he's scheming to get your money as I write this. (It seems likely to me he assumes I left you a small fortune when I "died").

Not only am I concerned for you, I don't wish the money that is meant for you to get into his hands for the purposes of running a plantation. And, what's more, I find the history of the plantations to be abhorrent and reprehensible, and I assume you feel the same way.

I'm writing this letter rather than using any other form of communication because by the time you receive this, I'll be gone. This time it will be to a permanent hiding place where no-one can reach me. I don't think this will surprise you or perhaps even upset you. But I thought I should let you know. My need to say a final goodbye has nothing to do with you. It has all to do with my inability to cope with my loss of Louisa (at least I can openly say that now). And that won't surprise you either. By the time you receive this letter you'll know that I've gone. Perhaps the police will contact you. You can show them the enclosed affidavit which states that you had nothing to do with my earlier disappearance, that I was the only person responsible for faking my death and that no-one else should be held culpable."

William puts the letter down, grabs a tissue and wipes the beads of sweat off his brow. He hands me the letter, and as I take it, I feel his hot hand brush against mine.

"There are some other personal comments which follow which I won't read out-loud." William gets up and pours a sparkling water for each of us. "It occurs to me he must have put this in the mailbox almost immediately after his meeting with Chuck, just before..."

"There's a rural mailbox at the end of the driveway. I noticed it when I was there." I pick up the letter, and, as I read, I feel a headache coming on. Frank tells me how much he cares about me and how much he misses me, but he doesn't tell me why he chose such drastic action: faking his death. And he repeats that this time he'll disappear permanently. That certainly turned out to be true. He must have decided on this during his altercation with Chuck. I wipe unwelcome tears off my cheeks and fold up the letter.

"Meg, do you believe Frank?" William asks. He leans towards me, his intense, dark eyes rimmed by traces of moisture. I sense his concern for me, and curiously, his compassion gives me some strength. Simeon slowly lowers his head and rests it on his crossed arms, which are on the table.

"Yes." I slump in my chair. William suggests all of us should move to the family room so I can relax in a recliner. We all traipse out of the kitchen, followed by Kelly as well as Cooper, who I notice is leaving a trail of dirty paw-prints from some misadventure which none of us noticed.

Kelly sits at the side of the recliner, resting her silky head on the arm, her shiny, dark eyes wider than usual. The poor dog knows there's something wrong and I stroke her ears to reassure her. Whereas Cooper is licking his paws and purring, oblivious to the tension tugging at everyone around him.

I break the strained silence, belatedly adding to my earlier response to William.

"We can check some of this out. But why would Frank lie to me? What's the point?"

"That's valid," William says. "But I like to double-check. It's astounding how things can get twisted, people can be misunderstood, information misinterpreted. It happens all the time."

"Frank said there's info on the history of the Murphy Plantation online."

"I'll look into it," William says, as he opens up the laptop that's sitting on the coffee table. He turns to Simeon, who looks as white as the flakes of snow which have just started to fall past the window, despite his Mediterranean blood. "You're very quiet. Are you okay?"

"Not really," Simeon says as he stretches his short legs out in front of him and hugs his body with his arms. "I'm just finding it overwhelming I guess."

"We all are," I say as I tip the recliner back. I hear the laptop's keys clicking as William searches for information.

"I know this is out of line, but I just have to ask," Simeon says. "He refers to terrible abuse you suffered, Meg. I can't believe anyone would want to hurt someone like you." His voice sounds strained.

Before I can say anything, William responds as he continues to focus on the computer screen and click with the mouse. "I agree, Simeon. Meg suffered unspeakable abuse by her stepfather."

"William! How do you know?" I'm not sure if I should be angry or relieved. I sit upright as the recliner folds up on itself with a sudden clang.

"Oh, Meg." William's face is ashen. "I apologize. I'm so sorry. I should not have said anything without your permission. As a lawyer I know how to keep confidences, and I made a mistake. I hope you accept my apology."

"William, don't be ridiculous. Frank said it in his letter. Simeon heard it. That's not what I mean. I mean, how the hell did you know my stepfather was my abuser? I thought Frank was the only one who knew until I told Chuck a couple of days ago."

"Your mother."

"My mother! I don't mean to scream, but, my mother! How?"

"Okay. Here goes. You'd made arrangements for your mother to go to Linda's place so that Linda's mother would have some company I believe. And perhaps to give your mother something to occupy her." I nod and cough, as if I'm choking on the incredulity of it all. "I don't know if you were aware, but Linda said she'd take your mother to her place at lunch-time on the first day. It was arranged that your mother would come here, and Linda would drive her to her mother's. I think Linda's early start in the morning made it infeasible for your mother to go to the house first thing. She didn't want to go when Linda wasn't there. I came here late that morning to check on things. I know you didn't ask me to, but I wanted to assure myself that Linda was here, that the security guard was on duty and that nothing was awry. After all, your horses were stolen the previous time you were away. Your mother arrived just as I was about to leave. I told her I was a friend and for some reason the floodgates opened. She poured out her story of the loss of your father, her marriage to Stan, how he'd abused you and she'd not done anything to protect you. Her remorse and grief came pouring out. It was overwhelming for both of us. But I just listened. I'm good at that when I have to be. I like to think it helped her to talk because I have a feeling it's been bottled up inside. She said she finally said 'sorry' to you, but she felt it was pathetic to apologize for something so life-altering as sexual abuse. She cried. She then said she has recurrent headaches and is scared. But asked me not to say anything. I kept this confidence, as you know, until now."

Simeon rocks on the sofa, hugging his knees into his chest.

"Simeon, pull yourself together. That won't help Meg." William says. "Can you make tea?" Simeon nods. He looks wan, despite his

French heritage. "Well, go out into the kitchen and get us all some delicious mugs of tea. And give Kelly a treat. They're under the sink."

"You were rather abrupt with Simeon, William. He was accused of murder by someone he loves or loved, and was frightened enough to come across the Atlantic in search of help."

"Perhaps. But you're the one I'm concerned about. You're trembling. I hope I haven't made matters worse."

"No. I'm just shocked that my mother told you. As far as I know, in the past, she's denied anything happened. She's blocked it all out." I notice Kelly has stayed with us, probably because she knows I'm upset.

"Do you mind that I know?"

"No, I don't think so. I think I'm relieved. But I'm so ashamed."

"As far as I'm concerned, it won't affect our friendship. You'd be completely mistaken if you thought that for even a second."

"Thank you. That means a lot to me. A great deal." I can feel those blasted tears on the verge of tumbling down my face.

"I have some understanding of the effects of abuse on the psyche. Sometimes victims feel they are not lovable, or perhaps that they don't deserve to be loved. Sometimes victims have trouble with intimate relationships, and even resist being touched."

The tears emerge, trickle down my burning hot cheeks, and drip onto my jeans. I can't make them stop, but at least my crying is silent. William hands me a couple of tissues from the box on the coffee table.

"I must say this, although I know it can't make any real difference. You are lovable and you deserve to be loved. And that's the truth." William returns to the computer as if he's just made a comment about the weather. I watch him. There was something in the way he said those words that sparked an unfamiliar glimmer of hope inside me.

Kelly knows the rule that all dog food and cat food should be eaten in the kitchen, but won't go out to Simeon to get her treat, despite encouragement. Cooper saunters in with a swagger, as if he's the ruler of the 'farmdom', a small piece of ham dangling from his mouth. The cat's unabashed behaviour helps me in my supreme effort to stop the tears.

"I had to give the cat something," Simeon says. "I couldn't find his treats, so I gave him some ham I found." He places a tray on the coffee table, nearly knocking the laptop flying. He's found some chocolate cookies to go with the mugs of tea, and a biscuit for Kelly, which I hand to her, ignoring the rule.

"Thanks." I can barely stop the tears welling up again.

"Meg," William says. "Would you rather we left? Don't give the answer you think you ought to give. Be honest."

"I'd rather you both stayed. You are both being kind. And I could do with some help to make sense of this mess."

"Okay," William says as he stares at the computer screen. "What Frank said about the plantation seems to be correct. And I've been able to find out more about Chuck's involvement from an editorial that was published in the local newspaper there. The Murphy family is not held in high esteem because the plantation, in the past, was run with an iron fist. It's thought that this is why it was a target in the slave uprising. The Editor expresses surprise that Mr. Murphy would want anything to do with the property since it has a history of cruelty, poor management and failure. He states he hopes, for the sake of the community, that Mr. Murphy is made of different stuff than his ancestors, and that he'll be able to make a go of it. But he ends the piece with a comment that things haven't worked well for Mr. Murphy so far. It's known that he's in debt, owes some of the staff their wages for the past two months, is behind in paying suppliers, knows nothing about sugar cane production and, most damaging, he doesn't appear to have made any effort to educate himself and has only come to the island four times."

"It seems surreal," I say.

"Have a cookie. I bought them when I got those groceries the other day, so I know they're fresh. It's amazing how one of those can change your perspective on life." William smiles as he passes the plate to me, and I take one.

"While I was making tea, I emailed someone I know who works in the hospital where Annabella would have gone," Simeon says. "She'll let me know for sure. She's a good friend."

"That's great."

"What would you like us to do next, Meg?" asks William.

"I would like to know if Chuck still owns his condo. He told me he kept it. The other thing that's bothering me is that he told me he donated the $50,000 left to him by Frank, to the Vannersville Children's Centre, and there was a newspaper article with a photograph of the cheque presentation. This doesn't fit with his desperate desire for money for the plantation."

"Easy to check out both of those. Have you got another computer? I'm sure Simeon would like to help."

I direct Simeon to Frank's office to collect the other laptop and give him the information on Chuck's condominium.

William searches the annual reports including the financial statements, as well as the lists of donors, all posted online, for the previous three years, for Vannersville Children's Centre, and tells me that there is no trace of the donation. He speculates that the check must have bounced, and that Chuck made the donation in a futile attempt to gain favour with Dania, his ex-fiancée.

"This gets more surreal by the minute," I say. I'm regaining my composure. "I'm having another one of those cookies. I think they must have magical powers, because I already feel better."

"Told you," William says.

"The condo was sold in the spring of this year," Simeon says.

"Just when Chuck moved in here," I say. "I suppose he thought he could stay here and save money. I've been such a fool."

"It can happen to anyone," William says. "I've been taken in by people and stuck my professional lawyer's neck out for them, and have nearly got my head cut off more than a couple of times. Don't beat yourself up."

"I've been had by Annabella," Simeon says. "So, as William says, you're not alone." Simeon has Cooper on his lap and the cat is lying upside down, thoroughly enjoying all the attention. "Can I get Cooper another piece of ham? He really liked it."

"Sure. You might as well get Kelly another biscuit while you're at it." I feel as if I've lost control of my life, my home and my animals. I might as well let go. I lie back in the recliner.

"What else can we do?" asks William.

15

Ferris

The kitchen door flies open and Linda bursts into the family room, her boots leaving a trail of barn bits and pieces. I upright my recliner with a sudden thump as William stands up, Simeon puts his hand over his mouth, Kelly barks and Cooper hides under the coffee table.

"Meg, Austin has been hurt." Linda spins around and tears out of the house.

"William, call 911. Simeon, you look after the animals. I'm going to find out what's going on." I slip on my boots and a jacket and jog out to the barn. Austin is lying on the ground just outside the open barn doors, and Linda is squatting beside him, rocking backwards and forwards with tears pouring down her face.

"William's calling 911. Where's Austin hurt?"

"I'm not badly hurt," Austin says as he raises his head. But he's shaking as if there's an earthquake erupting in his body.

"Linda, what happened?"

"I, I." Linda sobs.

"Linda, please pull yourself together for Austin's sake, so we can help him."

"Ewert, that no-good idiot, shot Austin in the leg."

"What the hell for?" I ask.

"I don't know."

I bend over Austin.

"May I look at the wound, Austin?"

"Sure. It's just a scrape." Austin's barely audible because his teeth are chattering. "I asked Ewert why he was here. He was real twitchy. I made a mistake when I reached for my mobile. I should have escorted him off the property. I shouldn't have tried to contact you first." He swallowed and took a deep, shuddery breath. "I guess he thought I was reaching for my gun, and I let my guard down."

"Ewert needs to be locked up," Linda says.

"The likelihood of that is pretty high, I would say." I rip the pant leg apart so that I can see the wound.

"Why is Austin shaking so much?" Linda asks, as she crouches down beside me.

"Shock, I think. You told me he suffers from PTSD. I'd guess that being shot would be about one of the worst things that could happen to someone trying to recover from seeing his partner shot. But I don't think the wound is deep. It's much the same as Joanna's scrape. It's bleeding, of course. Grab a horse bandage and I'll wrap it." Linda stands up. "And get a horse blanket as well. I'm concerned he's getting cold. And a saddle pad." Linda reappears, dragging a heavy horse blanket, and holding a bandage as well as a saddle pad, just as William runs out of the house.

"The ambulance is on its way," William says. "How's Austin?"

I give William an update as I wrap Austin's leg. William and Linda put the horse blanket on him. I fold up the saddle pad and place it under Austin's head.

"Where did Ewert go?" I ask.

"I saw him and Joanna running down the driveway," Austin says.

"So, Joanna was here too," I say.

"She came out of the barn," Austin says.

"What the hell was she doing in the barn?" Linda's face is flushed and her voice is high-pitched. "I didn't see either of them. How did they get here without us noticing?"

"You were out at the back of the barn unloading bags of wood-shavings, and I was with you, when I should have been here." Austin groans, as if the effort of talking is too much. "When I heard something, I came out front."

"Never mind that now," I say. "I'll try to find out what on Earth was going on here. You focus on getting better, Austin."

We're all visibly relieved when the ambulance growls up the driveway, tailed by a police car. A fire engine parks on the road. I'm impressed with the 911 response, especially since the farm is well out of town.

* * *

"Back to my earlier question, what can we do to help?" asks William, as we stand in front of the barn in sudden, frigid stillness.

Linda has left to be with Austin in the hospital. Another security guard is on the way and is expected within twenty minutes.

"I'm going to talk to Joanna. I'm going down to their house."

"I'm coming with you." William says.

"From the tone of your voice, I'd guess it's not debatable." A trace of a smile flickers on my face.

"You guessed right. That man is armed and dangerous."

"I'm not going down there right away, though. The police might be there."

"Okay. What else can we do?"

We enter the house. Kelly greets us with a couple of woofs, and we find Simeon on the floor playing with Cooper. After updating Simeon, we gather in the kitchen where William does his best to make something for lunch. He couldn't hide his disappointment when I told him that no restaurant or fast-food place will deliver this far out of town. Supplies are low.

I open an email from Dominic Marcel. He says he's set up a meeting with Ferris, the jockey who handed Juan the coffee, for tomorrow morning, in a private room at the sports bar, and asks me to confirm that I'll be there. He adds that he's sorry it's short notice, and that he's got some information about someone else who visited Frank on the day of his murder.

* * *

The house is quiet and empty when I put the kettle on before dawn. Daylight hours are fewer and when the sun rises its weakened rays are often obstructed by clouds. I'm wondering how Austin is doing, and pick up my mobile phone to connect with Linda. But just as I tap the first tiny key, Linda knocks on the door and opens it a crack, asking if it's okay to come in.

"I was just going to send you a message. How's Austin?"

"He's fine. You were right, it was a scratch. He's home and getting help from his therapist. I'm less uptight about him."

"I presume Ewert has been arrested."

"No. I'm sort of mad at Austin about that. He doesn't want him charged with anything."

"Why not?"

"Because he knows Ewert isn't well, and has PTSD like he does. He's already met him and chatted. Austin thinks Ewert's interested in helping with his extreme exercise program. He really wants to get going on it now."

"I'd want Ewert charged if I was Austin. Are you sure you want to help today? I didn't expect you to come."

"Yeah, I do. Thanks for asking though."

"I hope Austin is resting."

"He's decided to quit the security company. Being shot at got him thinking, and he figures security work isn't a good fit for him because of his PTSD. He's going to try to get his program idea off the ground. He's asking his father for a loan."

"That's great. Makes sense. But I sort of hoped that Austin would want to have charges laid against Ewert. I can't help being very concerned about Ewert and his gun: that's the reason I've rehired the security company."

"I can talk to Austin again, but I bet he won't change his mind about Ewert."

"No, don't bother him, at least not right now, Linda. I'm going to talk to Joanna. I think I'll go down there when I come back from my meeting later."

"Okay."

"Is something else the matter?" Linda is hesitating, and I can tell she wants to tell me something.

"I don't want to worry you, but I think you may want to see Rose. She's got discharge from her nose. It's got thicker."

"I'll come right now. We should take her temperature."

Kelly and Cooper follow us into the barn. As soon as I enter the warm, moist atmosphere filled with familiar smells, I'm welcomed with soft whinnies. I can see that Rose isn't feeling well. She's standing with her head down, looking listless. We insert the rectal thermometer and keep her still long enough to get a reading. She hates having her temperature taken and would normally make much more of a fuss.

"Her temperature is elevated. You're right, Linda. Although she's still on antibiotics, I'm going to call the vet. I'm being cautious because of all that she's been through."

"I can look after that for you. Okay?"

"That would be great." We walk towards Speed's stall to check on him, and notice he has a nasal discharge as well, although it's not thick, and he looks his usual bright-eyed self. Linda reads my mind and says she'll have the vet check him too. We agree they'll have to stay in today, which they won't like at all. Linda hooks on a lead-rein to Speed's halter. He thinks he's going outside to join Eagle and Bullet, but, sadly, he's moved to another stall so that Linda can clean his. He objects with a half-hearted rear but settles down when I toss him a flake of hay. I leave Linda to do her job, knowing that she'll phone the vet as soon as it's regular office hours.

I return to the house with Cooper leading the way and Kelly at my side. The security guard has parked his car by the house and when he sees us, he jogs towards me. He wants to know more about Ewert, what he looks like, what kind of gun he carries, who he's mad at and why, where he lives, when he's most likely to show up and other questions, nearly all of which I have no answers for. I apologize and tell him that if I get more information, I'll share it with the security company.

His questions make me realize how little I know. I have no clue what's really going on. All I know is that Ewert has PTSD, Joanna loves him, and they're desperate for money. And I'm certain that Frank's murder had something to do with money. So, perhaps they're involved? I'm running out of suspects, so I need a couple more.

Simeon emailed me from his hotel in the early hours this morning. I suppose neither of us had a good night. His friend confirmed Annabella was in the hospital. She couldn't divulge the diagnosis or treatment, but could release her admission and discharge times. The conclusion is that Annabella could not have been in Kentucky at the time of Frank's murder. He added the surprising postscript that he's leaving today because something's come up. I sent a brief reply, wishing him well.

William can't come today. He has a new court case and needs to prepare. I miss him. A small shiver travels down my spine when I think of Chuck. I've not been missing him like I think I should. But things have changed. I've learned things about Chuck that I'm having trouble forgiving him for. Deceit is something I can't ignore. I've been played for a fool, and fell for all the stories. Worst of all, when he first came to live at the farm, I thought he loved me and I thought I loved him. But my "love" pales in comparison with Joanna's love for Ewert. She has forgiven him for shooting her. I can't forgive Chuck for his deceit. And he must care more about the plantation than he does about me. It's all about Frank's money, which I don't have.

I can't dwell on this. It's not getting me anywhere. I turn my attention to getting ready for the meeting with Dominic Marcel and the jockey Ferris.

* * *

I find the sports bar closed, so I knock on the door and hope that someone opens it. It looks dark and dingy, with greasy, streaky windows and peeling paint on the frames. I knock again. Since there's no response, I walk around to the back. The stench oozing from the contents of the dumpster makes me want to hold my nose, but the bearable smell of stale beer takes over as I approach the back door. It's open, and a man dressed in a suit asks me to follow him. I'm certain he's one of the men who visited me, uninvited, at the farm.

"Meg, good, you made it. I was about to text you to say come to the back. I don't think I told you that," Dominic says. He gets up from his chair, which is one of six surrounding a large round table crammed into a small room with no windows. The glaring fluorescent light seems out of place when all other parts of the establishment are in darkness or semi-gloom.

"Ferris is waiting at the bar. I've got my two friends here, just in case there's any trouble. I know you've met them."

I nod to each of them but can't find a smile. They stand with their legs apart and their hands clasped in front of them. While I don't find them intimidating, I don't find them comforting either. Nevertheless, I'm glad I didn't pull William away from his work. He said he wanted to come with me when I met with Dominic and Ferris, but I've used up so much of his time, and he's so busy with a court case, that I didn't feel comfortable mentioning it.

Dominic commands his men to collect Ferris from the bar and asks me to sit. There's a jug of water and some glasses on the table and no sign of liquor. I choose the chair closest to the door. This has been a practice of mine for as long as I can remember. I must have easy access to the exit, in case I need it, especially when I'm meeting with men. And I can't say I trust any of them who are here.

Ferris enters the room without a word, and Dominic beckons him to sit. I presume that Dominic's men are standing outside. Ferris chooses the chair which results in the three of us being equidistant from each other. Anyone looking at this meeting would instantly recognize that this was not a friendly chit-chat. Ferris is more diminutive than I expected and looks as if he'd be happy if he could slide under the table and disappear. His dirty-blond hair is dishevelled, his face is unshaven, and small beads of sweat glisten on his brow.

Dominic opens the discussion by asking the jockey to tell us all that he knows about the incident with Juan.

"I don't know anything." Ferris' squeaky voice is barely audible.

"Don't give me that." Dominic thumps his hand on the table with such ferocity that I startle. "Do you want my friends out there to beat it out of you?"

"What's she doing here?" Ferris points a shaky finger at me while glaring at Dominic. He's not as fazed as I would have guessed.

"You tell him," Dominic says, which takes me off guard. I thought I was just here to witness the meeting. I sit up and compose myself quickly.

"A couple of people at the track asked me to look into Juan's death. They believe it was not an accident. My friend, William Porter, had a chat with you. At the time of that chat, he had reason to suspect that something had been added to Juan's coffee, which resulted in his death. You told William that you knew the coffee had something in it, but you claimed you knew no more than that. You said you were acting under Dominic's direction and that you thought the intent was to scare Juan and nothing more."

"Yeah, that's what I said." Ferris looks at Dominic, who thumps on the table again, this time with both of his fists.

"Ferris, you no good liar. You weasel. You know I had nothing to do with it. I want you to tell the truth. The truth. Now."

"You said you would look after us, protect us."

"But you're not supposed to commit murder, goddam it." Dominic stands up just as Ferris pushes past me, knocking over my chair with me on it, and charges out of the room.

I get up off the floor and rush to the open door. Dominic's men are standing on either side of the door as if nothing happened.

"You're letting him get away," I say.

"I'm not going to take the law into my own hands," Dominic says. He's sitting back in his chair.

"He'll leave the country."

"Yep."

Incredulous, I return to my chair and flop into my seat. It's one second later and I realize what really happened. But I won't pursue it. I can't burn this bridge because I need to hear what Dominic has to say about Frank's murder. He said he has some information. I ask him.

"I don't have much, but you never know with these things."

I'll take anything I can get at this point.

"A shipper I use, told me he drove past Louisa's Acres the evening Fred was murdered. He's been there several times. Anyhow, he noticed a compact car parked in the road close to the stone wall, and a person wearing a long raincoat standing outside the car, putting on a large hat."

"That could be very helpful. Can you send me the contact info for the shipper?"

"Sure. He's a good guy."

"What's his name?"

"Greg Buttons."

I'm glad to be leaving.

* * *

As I drive back to the farm, I contemplate that there's no-one to talk to at home but Kelly and Cooper. I hope William shows up this evening. I feel a need to discuss the meeting with him and I miss his company.

The security guard is patrolling the house and barn alternately, and tells me he's agitated, that he's got two young children and doesn't want to be shot. While I wonder what training he's had, I do my best to pacify him. I'd like nothing more than to be able to say he can go. I'm getting tired of the invasion of my space. But I can't, not yet.

This chat with him makes me determined to visit Joanna and Ewert, now. I grab a cookie, remembering what William said about how one can change your perspective on life, and smile.

I tell the security guard that Kelly and I are visiting a neighbour and shouldn't be more than one hour and that I'll text him if there's any change in plan.

16

Ewert

I walk down the road with Kelly close at my side. There's no need for a leash. The memory of Joanna spitting in my face gives me more reason for pause than Ewert with his gun. I can't understand why I feel this way. Perhaps it's because I saw such rage in her eyes as she screamed at me. Ewert looked bewildered and disoriented, not furious or vicious. I don't know what to make of their behaviour and have no clue why Ewert shot Austin.

Their clapboard home looks even more dilapidated than when I came here last, and the crumbling hip-roof bank-barn, which is close by, looms precariously. The front porch has collapsed at one end, the support underneath having rotted away. It's difficult to make my way to the door, stepping over broken boards and negotiating the uneven slope. I knock and don't expect anyone to answer. But, much to my surprise, Ewert opens the door, and he isn't holding a gun.

"Yes?"

"I'd like to chat with you and Joanna. May I come in?" I want to sound pleasant, not threatening. After all, I'm looking for information. Ewert hesitates and appears to look me up and down as if I'm a stranger. But then he slowly opens the door wider and walks into the house.

"Is it okay if Kelly comes in?"

"Sure." Ewert makes his way to the old, gouged, pine kitchen table. It looks as if it could be the original one installed when the house was built. The chairs are flimsy white plastic ones sold for outdoor use.

"You can sit down if you like." Ewert sounds calm and subdued.

"Thank you. Is Joanna here?"

"No."

"When will she be back?"

"Perhaps never."

"Oh, goodness. Why do you think that?"

"Because she left me a note saying she's gone and that it's for my own good," he says, as if this was not a surprise and perhaps even inevitable. He reaches for two glasses out of a cupboard which has no doors left on it, and fills them with water from the tap. The glasses are sparkling clean, but I'm not sure about the water since I don't know what kind of well they have. It's probably a shallow, dug well.

"Thanks," I say as he places a glass in front of me. "I'm sorry to hear that."

His eyes are clear and not darting about as they were when he showed up at my kitchen door with a gun in his hand.

"I could see it coming, I suppose."

I jump to conclusions and assume that her leaving is because of his PTSD and the shooting incidents. But my intuition tells me to keep quiet.

"What makes you say that?" I ask.

"Because she's unhappy, more than unhappy, I'd say sort of desperate. I don't know what she's told you, but I'll guess it's a lot different from what I would say about the whole shemozzle since she's been living a deluded existence and couldn't face the truth. Then it came crashing down on her."

"Oh."

"You've got a nice dog. I like border collies."

"Yes, she's special."

"I heard she found your horses. She deserves a medal."

"I agree." I pat her head.

"I'd like to tell you what's been going on because I hope to stay here. You must wonder what sort of person I am, since I've been on your property twice wielding a gun. And I think Joanna told you I stole your horses."

"She did."

"Don't get me wrong, I love Joanna, but she's gone off the rails. I'll start at the beginning. I'll try to give you the whole picture. You know Joanna is Frank's sister-in-law, his first wife's sister?"

"Yes."

"Joanna was obsessed with jealousy and I reckon it started a long time ago. While she's tall like Louisa was, she doesn't have Louisa's captivating beauty, and this mattered to her. I don't pretend to understand her feelings." He looks at Kelly, who's sitting next to my chair. "We got married a year before Louisa married Frank. That's when the jealousy reached fever-pitch. It's well known that Frank was extremely wealthy and powerful. Louisa was on his arm at major events and functions, photographed by the media, and introduced to all the important people. Meanwhile, I have to say that my career as a journalist was going well. I was in high demand and getting international assignments, and the pay was good. But then I was taken hostage when I was doing a piece on human smuggling from Africa to Europe. They were a bunch of bandits and didn't know the Canadian Government's policy, and didn't believe me when I told them that there would be no ransom paid; and that my family had no money. I explained I was just an ordinary guy. To cut a long story short, after a couple of months a fight broke out among my captors, because they'd got nowhere, and they literally let their guard down. I don't know where I got the strength, adrenalin I suppose. But I got out of the camp."

"So how did Joanna handle this?"

"Not well, because my doctor encouraged me to quit investigative journalism, to get therapy, and to rest. This meant a significant cut in income. So, in Joanna's eyes, we sunk even lower relative to Louisa and Frank. Her resentment of their lifestyle grew like a festering ulcer, the result of which was that Joanna became obsessed with getting rich."

"She asked me for money."

"Not surprised. That's because we have almost none. Anyway, she saw an opportunity when Louisa died. Her sister's death didn't quell her obsession for money; if anything, it fanned the flames, so to speak. About two months after Louisa's death, Joanna made her move. She was sure that Frank would fall for her and that she could convince him to part with a couple of million."

"I had no idea."

"I did, because she told me she was doing it for us. I told her she was insane, but I wasn't strong during that period. I acted like a doormat. She's a tough woman, and made me feel I couldn't manage on my own, and, to be honest, I've been afraid of losing her. And now I have." Ewert puts his head down on his arms, which are folded on the table.

"I wonder what Frank thought of her advances?"

"It was before he married you, but the way she pursued him, it was pretty relentless."

Perhaps this was another reason for Frank to marry me, to get Joanna off his back.

"Did she get anywhere?" I ask.

"The bottom line is that Joanna got no money from Frank, and gave up after you were married. But her obsession with the desire to get rich grew into desperation. It wasn't long after that, that I found out that she was gambling. It seems she got addicted to it almost instantly. I don't know exactly what she got up to all the time, but I know it was through her gambling that she met a guy called Dominic Marcel. She thought the sun shone out of his, well, never mind."

"She told me you were the one involved with Dominic and the one with the gambling problem."

"Never met the guy and hope I never do." Ewert gets up and refills his glass from the tap. I haven't touched mine. "All I know is, that after she met this guy, the little money we had evaporated. You don't need the details of our financial affairs, but I'll say that anything we had of any value has been sold. You might have guessed that, just by coming in here. Even things that were of a sentimental value to me. Gone. And nothing to show for any of it."

"She told me an elaborate story about your theft of my horses, that you were looking for ringers for Dominic."

"She admitted what she'd done when I found the horses in the barn. She said it was a golden opportunity because you'd left her in charge of receiving the horses when they were delivered to the farm. I thought she'd gone completely crazy. I was enraged, but I didn't do the right thing. I didn't because, and despite everything, I love her. I was just relieved that she hadn't said she was leaving me."

"Why the ransom note?"

"Because the ringer idea didn't work out, she said, so she needed to get money some other way. It was a mess."

"Are you going to be okay?"

"I'm not as helpless as all that. I'll pull myself together. Austin is giving me hope. He's such a great guy. He's even forgiven me for shooting him." Ewert's eyes sparkle a little as he looks at me. "But, despite all that's happened, I hope Joanna comes back."

"Why on earth did you shoot Austin?"

"I was under Joanna's spell. What more can I say? She wanted access to your barn. She was almost manic about it. She insisted I go with her, and bring the gun. We took a route across the fields, and once we got to the barn, she told me to create a diversion if anyone showed up, so that she could go inside. I don't know what the hell she was up to. I hope your horses are okay?"

"No, they're not. They have a virulent strain of the equine flu. We can't figure out how they caught it, and they're pretty sick. But I can't imagine Joanna could be responsible for that."

"There'd be no point in making your horses sick."

"I still don't understand why you shot Austin."

"I thought Austin was reaching for his gun. It terrified me. I over-reacted. It has to do with being held at gun-point in the camp. But I didn't intend to shoot him. My gun went off accidentally."

"I'm supposed to believe that?"

"I don't know how else to explain it. I was shaking like a lump of Jello. My gun went off. I'm sorry about Austin. I like the guy and he's trying to help me. Anyway, Joanna heard the shot, ran out of the barn, grabbed my arm, and we sprinted down the driveway."

"It sounds ridiculous enough to be true."

"Shooting Austin was a bit of a wake-up call for me." He looks away. "I hate that term."

"And what made you shoot at Kelly?"

"It was a plan that went wrong."

I'm about to ask for further explanation when I catch sight of a wide-brimmed hat and a long raincoat hanging by the back door. Seeing them sends a shiver down my spine.

"Do you know where Joanna was when Frank was murdered?" I ask.

"No. She wasn't here. But she rarely was. She was either gambling somewhere, or she was at your place. She didn't like gambling online much because I would get anxious and pace, and she'd get mad and say she couldn't concentrate. Anyway, sometimes she was even out all night, or sometimes most of it. She'd say she was on a roll and couldn't leave. I'm assuming it was the slots. Not sure though. She wouldn't tell me. Sorry, rambling. The short answer is I don't know where she was when Frank was shot."

"Do you know how Joanna knew Frank was alive?"

"Oh, I forgot to mention that, after Frank's accident, she saw an opportunity to pursue his brother. I think his name is Murray?"

"Yes."

"She thought he must have inherited some of Frank's fortune, but soon found out that he didn't, and that he was a rehabilitating alcoholic, and she said it seemed like his rehabilitation was using up all the funds he had. It was a big disappointment to Joanna, but Murray let it slip that Frank was alive, although he didn't know where he was. Joanna was determined to track him down, because she was still convinced that Frank had millions and she had an idea."

"Don't tell me, to blackmail him. She's not the only one to come up with that."

"To my knowledge, she didn't get anywhere with it. The bottom line is that I can't see her killing someone, and there'd be no point in her killing Frank under the circumstances. Nothing to gain."

"I can see your point."

A loud knocking interrupts our conversation, and Ewert makes his way to the front door. Kelly doesn't react because it isn't her home. But she's alert and, like me, listening. People are talking outside in rumbling voices, and I can't make out a word. A couple of minutes later, the door closes but Ewert doesn't reappear. I go to the front of the house and see Ewert in the back of a police car as it drives away. Kelly and I beat a hasty retreat to the farm.

* * *

I'm more relieved than I want to admit that William is getting out of his car as we come up the driveway. I almost feel like hugging him. I need someone to talk to about all that's happened today. And what's more, he's brought some takeout from the Italian restaurant I like.

"I haven't just got enough for you and me, I've got enough for Linda and the security guard too. The wine's just for us though."

"How thoughtful, William. That's great. By the way, I'm going to cancel the security company contract. Long story, but I don't need it."

* * *

An hour later, William is up-to-date on my visit to Ewert and, through his connections, he's been able to find out that Ewert is now the prime suspect in Frank's murder. I feel distressed about this because my bones tell me he's not guilty. There are no niggling doubts, and I can't change my conviction despite seeing the wide-brimmed hat and long raincoat.

"You're acting as if you're on pins and needles," William says, as we sit down in the family room with our half-drunk glasses of chianti.

"I'm dying to tell you about my meeting with Dominic and Ferris."

"Well, get on with it then," William says. He smiles and picks Cooper up. I can hear the cat purring. Kelly is sitting and gazing at him with what appears to me to be unabashed adoration.

I give him the details. "I think it was convenient for Dominic that I wanted to meet with Ferris because he could use the meeting to convince me that Ferris was the culprit. I think Dominic used Ferris to poison Juan. When it became know that Juan was poisoned, he made Ferris the fall-guy, to protect himself."

"You're probably right."

"I know I'm right."

"Okay. But there's not enough evidence to prove it in court. And I would guess that Ferris is nowhere to be found. What about the other two jockeys you met with who said what a great guy Dominic was, like an uncle I think you told me?"

"I now think they'd been paid by Dominic to point the finger at Ferris. It was all part of Dominic's plan to ensure that he wouldn't be implicated."

"You were saying, not so long ago, that Dominic wasn't the bad guy you thought he was." I see a twinkle in William's eye.

"I know. I've changed my mind. But I shouldn't have jumped to conclusions and presumed he stole my horses, murdered Frank and poisoned Juan."

"You said that Dominic had some information that might help in finding Frank's murderer."

"Yes. He said that a shipper called Greg Buttons has often been to Louisa's Acres, and he was driving past that evening, when Frank was shot. He happened to notice a compact car parked in the road, close to the entrance, and saw a man in a long raincoat, putting on a large hat."

"Doesn't that sound like Ewert? You saw a hat and raincoat matching those descriptions in his house. The police have their man."

"No. You know that I don't think so." I sense that he's goading me a little. That twinkle is winking at me. I grab the laptop off the coffee table and search for a shipper called Greg Buttons. I find an email address and send off a note.

And, before I have time to finish my glass of wine, he replies, confirming what Dominic said.

We hear a knock at the kitchen door, barely audible in the family room. I can tell by its tentativeness that it must be Linda. She took her Italian food home to share with her mother, but she must have come back to check on the horses.

William gets up and lets her in.

"Sorry to bother you, but I thought you'd like to know something," Linda says as she takes off her boots.

"Come and sit down for a minute. You must be tired. You've had a long day," I say as I replace the laptop onto the coffee table.

"I am a bit. But I want to do my best for Rose and Speed. They've been so sick. I borrowed a nebulizer from Neal and I've been giving them that medicine the vet gave us so that they can breathe better. It's sort of stressful that they can only breathe through their noses when they've got such awful guck."

"Do they mind having that contraption on?"

"The nebulizer? No, they soon got used to it. I bet they realize they can breathe easier afterwards. Anyway, I wanted to tell you what Austin told me."

"Is he feeling better?"

"A lot. He said that Ewert could talk with him on the phone because he hasn't been charged yet. He's being held for questioning. I think that's what he said. Anyway, Austin said that Ewert told him that the police must have searched his house, because they showed him a raincoat, a hat and a gun and asked if they were his. It freaked Ewert out because he thinks they must be connected to Frank's murder somehow, but he can't figure out how. He's pretty upset. Austin said he's asked him to get hold of his doctor."

"Meg, I'd like to help Ewert," William says. "I might be able to do something. I'm certain that it's detrimental to him, after his experience in Africa, to be locked up. And I'm inclined to agree with you when you say he's not the murderer."

I reach out and touch the back of William's warm hand and thank him. The sensation of feeling his skin, albeit only for an instant, sends a glow to my cheeks. Kelly is sitting on his feet and, yet again, gazing up at him as if he's some kind of god. I wish I knew what she's thinking. Cooper is in Linda's arms, and she's stroking him vigorously. His purrs rumble around us.

* * *

I've talked to my mother a few times on the phone, but haven't spent time with her, and I think she's got a flight booked for the day after tomorrow. So, before I did anything else this morning, I called her. I've asked her here for lunch today and have spent an hour racking my brain, to no avail. I still have no menu and no arsenal of recipes to draw on. I have no idea what she likes to eat, no clue if she has any food allergies. I should ask. I suspect she has a small appetite, so that prompts me to search for a soup recipe on the laptop. I soon find one with sweet potato as the main ingredient, with a touch of maple syrup. It sounds just right.

Kelly is looking up at me with her big brown eyes, so I tell her she can come with me for the ride to the grocery store.

17

Chuck

We arrive back at the farm with loads of groceries piled behind the seats of the truck. Kelly is sitting on the passenger seat as if she's in charge of navigation. She gives a small "woof" as I stop to open the gate. I had one installed a couple of days ago, as a disincentive to unwelcome visitors. It's a smart investment in security, but it means I have to get out of the truck twice each time I leave and each time I return. At first, I think Kelly's just glad to be home, but then I see that she's looking at a car in the driveway. I recognize it, but can't remember whose it is.

Murray is sitting on the verandah, bundled up in a well-worn sheepskin coat, his breath hanging like mist around his face. He looks stiff, and I don't think it's from the cold. I think he's tense.

Kelly trots over to him and puts her head on his lap, and he strokes her absent mindedly.

"Hi, Murray. I haven't seen you in ages," I say as I heave a few of the bags out of the truck.

"Let me help you with those. You broke down and went shopping, I see." Murray is soon off the verandah and carrying bags around to the back of the house and into the kitchen, followed by Kelly and her wagging tail.

I put most of the groceries away after I convince Linda to take some of the sandwiches I bought, since she said she isn't going home today. Her mother has a visitor who's bringing a meal for them both. I wonder what Linda would have eaten if I hadn't got something.

Murray and I settle down at the kitchen table with a plate of cookies between us.

"Murray, you look tense, as if something's bothering you."

"You're right."

"What's on your mind?"

"This." Murray reaches for his coat and pulls out a crumpled envelope from the inside pocket. "I hope it won't shock or upset you. It's from Frank and I haven't been able to deal with it. It's been in my pocket for a while."

"You got a letter as well." I should have told him.

"You had a letter from Frank? What was it about? Do you mind telling me?" His frown deepens, and it's as if his light brown eyes have darkened.

"No, I don't mind telling you. Frank enclosed an affidavit stating that he was the only one responsible for his disappearance. But the letter was to warn me about Chuck. In a nutshell, he said that Chuck is desperate for money."

"This letter is entirely different. Read it. I'll make us some tea to go with these cookies, if that's okay."

"Great idea."

The letter is about Dominic Marcel. It's ten pages long and must have taken Frank quite some time to put together. And he enclosed documents which back up his allegations.

Frank explains that he was put in touch with Dominic by a neighbour in Kentucky who'd used him to acquire a few racehorses. Dominic acted as his agent at a yearling sale and the neighbour had been pleased with the quality of the breeding as well as the conformation and disposition of the colts. Frank connected with Dominic, since he planned to fill his rented stable with racehorses.

I reckon that Dominic quickly assumed that Frank had a lot of money available, so he might have thought the relationship presented some opportunities beyond horse purchases.

Frank writes that he and Dominic developed a friendship, but Frank soon regretted it. One evening, when they were enjoying some of Frank's wine, Dominic raised the subject of gambling. Frank was curious to find out what Dominic was up to, so played along. A couple more evenings and a couple more bottles of wine, and Frank learned Dominic was running an illegal gambling business in Canada. Dominic asked Frank to consider investment. He could purchase more ringers and could entice more jockeys to join the Marcel Team, as he put it. He could expand to other racetracks.

Frank ends with a similar statement to the one he included in his letter to me, writing that he was going to a new, undiscoverable place. But he adds two additional statements. Both surprise me. He conveys his best wishes to Murray and wishes him well with his rehabilitation, which he believes is going very well. No mention of the altercation they had at Louisa's Acres. Perhaps he wrote the letter before Murray's visit. And then a plea. He implores Murray to follow up.

"That's the part that really got to me," Murray says, as we sit down and pore over the letter, sipping on tea. "I don't know why Frank thought I'd be able to do anything. He never had confidence in me in the past. He thought I was useless."

"Your alcoholism significantly affected his opinion of you. You know that. He cared a lot about you, deep down. He wanted you to get better. He wanted you to conquer your addiction and didn't want to contribute to the purchase of more booze. That's why he made those decisions about his money, including the setting up of the trust fund."

"I suppose so."

"He didn't want to give you money and feel that he was making things worse for you."

"Mm."

"Somehow, he knew, at the time he wrote the letter, that your rehabilitation was going well. He must have thought you'd be able to take this challenge on. I think it's great that he asked you to do this very important thing that he obviously cared so much about."

"I wish I hadn't gone down to Kentucky and asked him for money. I made him furious. His flushed face won't leave me. That's how I remember him."

"I agree. What I think is, he assumed that you'd lapsed back to drinking because you asked him for money again when you visited him, and that's what made him angry. And remember, your speech was somewhat slurred because of the stroke. Also, he was mad that so many people knew he was alive. He was trying to run from painful memories, as we know, but it wasn't working. And it seems to me he was his own worst enemy. One example being his naming of the farm 'Louisa's Acres', another being his leasing of a horse farm in the States." Why do I feel responsible for Murray feeling so badly? I guess it must be because he was asking Frank for money for me. But why he took it upon himself to do such a daft thing, I'll never understand.

"Meg, you know I can't handle this. That's really why I'm here. I need your help. I can't do this, even for Frank."

"You think that the stress could be too difficult, so soon after your rehab?"

"You said it. I couldn't even say it."

"Don't worry. I'm lucky, I've got William to help. And this sort of challenge is just up his alley. He has connections with the right people and will know how to ensure all this evidence gets serious review and attention."

"That's fantastic. I know I'm being selfish, but I'm relieved I don't have to deal with it. Thanks. I hope one day I'll be able to do something for you."

"Don't think about it."

Murray doesn't stay long, just long enough for me to bring him back into the loop. His face looks brighter, his forehead less furrowed, as he waves to me and Kelly and starts the car.

I haven't got long to prepare lunch for me and my mother. She wouldn't let me pick her up, saying she'd take a taxi, which is just as well since I need every minute available, especially since I'm making the soup from scratch. Cooper isn't helping. When I open any cupboard door at his level, he's inside. But he's enjoying himself so much I don't have the heart to shut him out of the kitchen. Kelly is lying under the kitchen table, watching. Whenever I talk to her, she wags her tail, which is helpful because the movement distracts the cat.

I have lunch prepared just as I hear the tuneful sound of the doorbell. Kelly leaps to her feet, scrambling on the shiny floor, as she springs towards the door, making a couple of barks. She knows what the doorbell is now. It's been put to use more often recently.

My mother, I still can't call her "Mum" or "Mom", stands on the verandah, looking thinner and paler. A little shock-wave of fear rushes through me. She's going downhill fast. I hadn't expected to notice a difference in such a short time. But perhaps it's the stress that's showing its effects, more so than the tumour.

I'm not sure what to expect when she sits down at the table. I'm not used to having any kind of decent relationship with my mother and feel uncomfortable.

She's appreciative of the meal and eats more than I expect, and makes not one complaint. Kelly sits next to her, which is a good sign. Cooper's worn out and is sleeping on the doormat with a paw in one of the overturned boots.

"Thank you, Meg. This is just the right sort of meal I needed."

"I'll make tea. Why don't you go into the family room and sit in a recliner? I'll bring it in for you."

"Sounds super. I seem to be tired for some reason."

As I walk in with the tea, she asks if I've heard from Chuck. On impulse, I tell her all about the diabolical story of the plantation and his desperation for money.

"I think I was the one who told you about the plantation. I thought it was odd. I knew he hadn't told you when you told me I was lying. And I'm now sorry I let the cat out of the bag the way I did."

"It sounded so ridiculous. And you were being difficult then."

"You're right. I know I told you that if you love him and he loves you, you shouldn't let him go. I'm now hoping you don't love him." She rests her head back and closes her eyes.

I don't answer. I just stroke Kelly, who's sitting on my feet.

"That chap called William is very nice," she says. "If I was thirty years younger I'd be interested." She giggles and hiccups, and opens her eyes.

"I heard you had a chat with him."

"The poor man heard my sob-story from beginning to end. He was so decent. A gentleman. You don't get many of those these days."

"You shouldn't have told William about what happened to me."

"No, I suppose I shouldn't have." She looks at me, perhaps to assess how strongly I feel about it. "I don't know what came over me. But it's been bottled up inside me all these years: Stan's abuse of me and his, much worse and unforgivable, abuse of you. And William was a complete stranger to me. But there was something about his sparkling, dark eyes, his calm demeanour, his smart appearance, and his warm handshake which broke down the barrier of silence I'd erected. I just started to blurt, and when I started, I couldn't stop. He was non-judgemental. He just listened. And that's what I needed. I felt better. But I know I shouldn't have said a word. Not to someone who knows you. I hope my nattering on like that doesn't cause you any grief." She closes her eyes again, her arms lying heavily on the arms of the recliner, her upper body at about a forty-five-degree angle. Her face looks pale and translucent, as if the slightest touch would leave a mark. She drifts off to sleep. Kelly and I go back to the kitchen so that I can clear up. When my mother wakes up, I'll take her back to the Vannersville Inn.

* * *

Driving back from the Inn, I mull over the difference in my mother. I'm not sure how much of the change I see in her is due to the tumour, and how much is due to her desire to reach out to me to start healing our broken relationship. I hope that it's the latter. Perhaps I'll never know.

I'm startled to find a strange, old Jeep in the driveway and my intuition puts me on guard. Sure enough, Kelly and I find Chuck sitting at the kitchen table. His brown curls have grown longer, he's unshaven and his clothes, which are usually colourful and even snazzy, look drab and ill-fitting, and there is a musty aroma hanging about him. It's as if he's been living on the streets. I wonder if it's a calculated ploy to gain my sympathy.

"Hi, Chuck. I wasn't expecting you."

"I live here. You should expect me at any time." The growling tone of his voice is so unlike the voice of the Chuck I thought I knew, I'm taken off-guard.

"You don't live here any more. Our relationship is over." As I say this, I know it's how I truly feel.

He gets up from the chair, and I step back. Kelly growls. She can sense the tension.

"What's happened to you, Chuck?" I ask. "You're not the kind, charming man I thought I knew."

"And you're not the kind, generous woman I thought I knew. Threatening to throw me out of my own home."

"It's not your home. It's where you lived for a while, but you don't own any part of it."

"I have a right to half." His eyes are shifting, almost darting around the room.

"No, you don't. Why are you like this, Chuck? Are you ill?"

"How would you be if you'd been charged with a murder you didn't commit, been detained and questioned, all the time feeling that they're just out to prove they have the right man? It's beyond anything anyone should have to contend with. And then you tell me I'm not welcome in my own home."

"I think I may have some idea what you've been through."

"I don't think so." He takes another step towards me. Kelly growls and I stand my ground, determined not to be intimidated and not to rise to the bait, but my knees wobble.

"When we talked on the phone, you said that you wanted our relationship to work," I say, hoping my voice isn't trembling like my legs are. "From what I've learned, you want it to work so that you can benefit financially. You wanted Frank to divorce me so that you could become my legal partner. I suppose the next step would be to get rid of me somehow. But what you, and many other people, don't realize is that Frank didn't leave me millions. They're in some bank in some foreign place, and, as far as I know, I have no claim to any of it. I just have enough to continue in this lifestyle. That was the business agreement that I made with Frank. And he upheld it. You're barking up the wrong tree."

"Yeah, you're right. I wanted the relationship to work, and you've only got yourself to blame for it not working. I know my rights. I know I'm owed half of the value of this property."

"You're wrong. You'll hear from my lawyer. Now you must leave. I mean it, Chuck."

He's staring at me with his green eyes, which are almost consumed by dilated black pupils, and not blinking. It's as if he's looking right through me. He stands stock still, then folds like a puppet whose strings have been cut, and collapses onto the floor. Kelly whines and I dial 911.

I yell out to the barn, and Linda comes running. I know that she's trained in CPR and I haven't. She gets to work fast. Sweat is pouring off her and dripping onto Chuck's unmoving face as she works vigorously. It's as if she's trying to breathe and pump life into a rag doll. It's terrifying to watch. I run to the tap and ring out a cloth in cold water, and dab Linda's face as best I can.

* * *

Dr. Milton calls me to let me know Chuck was pronounced dead on his arrival at the hospital and that the police have lots of questions. I already know that, because Linda and I were questioned as soon as the police arrived, and were told that there'd be follow-up.

Linda's lying on the floor of the family room, exhausted, with her sweaty head resting on a pillow. Both she and I are in shock.

It's as if I'm pushing the replay button again and again. I see Chuck transformed into a threatening, obnoxious stranger and then witness the sudden, unexpected end of his life.

I feel as if my insides have been in a blender and that I've been cut into pieces. I can't pull myself together. It's as if I'm disjointed. I have an urge to join Kelly as she cowers behind the recliner. Instead, I wander aimlessly from the family room into the kitchen and then back again, not knowing what to do.

And I can't imagine how Linda feels, having tried so hard to resuscitate him.

"Linda, I'm dreadfully sorry I put you through this ordeal."

"I'll be fine. I wish I'd helped him though." Her voice still has a breathless sound about it.

"You gave it your best, and I'm truly grateful. You did much more than I could have imagined possible." My voice is shaky and my throat is dry. And I can't stop a couple of tears from running down my face, which seems to have lost some of its feeling. It's as if the shock has numbed several of my nerve-endings. "I don't think anything could have saved him. I honestly think he was gone before he hit the floor."

"It didn't work. I took the course because I thought it worked and I could save someone one day."

"Linda, it doesn't always work. And we don't know what was wrong with him. I bet there's more to this than we realize at the moment. I won't let you accept responsibility for any of this at all. You did so much." I kneel at her side and smile at her, wiping away my tears. She's flushed in the face, but her breathing has steadied. "Let me pour you a bath. I've got some luxurious aromatic stuff which might help you unwind a bit and perhaps help those aching muscles of yours. Would that be okay?" It's good to have something to do.

"Yeah. That'd be nice. Thanks." She stirs and turns her head. Kelly sees this as a signal to emerge from her hiding place, and she licks Linda's face. "On second thoughts, I don't need a bath. Kelly's just seen to it." Linda's bouncing back. What an amazing, resilient woman she is. I'm sure she'll be great for Austin.

"I'll run it, anyway. And I'll put your clothes in the wash. You can borrow a robe while they dry. Won't take long."

"Thanks."

"Don't get up till I have the bath ready."

As I run the bath, mixing in some of my favourite aromatic oil, I think of the question Dr. Milton, or Munro as he prefers me to call him, asked. I don't know what prompted him to query this, but he asked if Chuck was a drug addict. If he was, I didn't know. It makes me think of Dania, his fiancée who left him a couple of weeks before their wedding and sent him into a tailspin. I wonder whether she'd be able to provide any insight.

While Linda's in the bath and her clothes are thrashing around in the washing machine, I do some research. Dania isn't a common name, and I'm pretty sure she still lives in Vannersville. From checking out two of the on-line sites set up to facilitate connectivity, I find email addresses for three people with the first name 'Dania' in this area. I send off an email to each of them asking if they know Charles Alexander Murphy. Dania's reply is almost instant, and it includes her phone number.

"Thanks for your quick response to my email. I'm sorry to have to tell you that I have bad news about Chuck, and I thought you should know."

"What bad news?" Her voice is steady.

"Chuck died today. We don't know the cause of death yet, but it was sudden and unexpected." My voice is wobbling.

"Wow. I'm sorry to hear that. He must have told you about me, then."

"He lived here with me at the farm for a while."

"You must be pretty upset."

"It was a terrible shock." I cough and wipe tears away.

"Sorry. You don't know the cause of death?" She sounds nothing like as shocked as I feel.

"Actually, I thought you might be able to help answer this. Can you think of anything about his health that might have contributed to his death?"

"You must know that we were engaged, and that I called it off." I'm not sure what to make of the sound of disgust that I hear in her voice.

"Yes. I hope you don't mind me asking why you called it off? I only heard one side of the story of course."

"I don't mind. It might be helpful. Things went off the rails when he started talking about some plantation he'd inherited and his plans to make millions by growing sugar cane there, as had been done in the past. All he needed were investors. He'd make them rich, guaranteed. Then he asked me to give him two million dollars! Shit, how crazy can you get! He got angry when I said a flat 'no'. I noticed a change in behaviour, which made me wonder if he was on something. He became erratic and unpredictable and then accused me of scheming against him. I admit I even got a bit scared of him. It got worse. He asked me for money again, and one time he pushed me against the wall when I told him 'no'. I was convinced by then that he must on drugs, and I wanted to find out what. To cut a long story short, I eventually found an empty prescription bottle, and the drug was some kind of amphetamine. I tried to talk to him about it, but he just got mad. You ask why I called it off? Because he didn't love me, he was simply after my money, and he fell apart when I said I wouldn't give him any. And he didn't want me to help him get better. But I'm sorry he's dead, I have to say that. Are you okay?"

"I'm okay. What you've said makes me think he might have died of a drug overdose."

"I don't know what's gone on between you, but if he was thwarted again in his attempts to get the money he seemed to want so desperately, he might have gone back on the drugs. Or that may not have been the trigger. It could have been something else."

"He was wrongly accused of murder."

"That could do it. Chuck is, was, not a resilient person. He seemed nice enough, in fact he could be charming and kind when things in his life were under control, but if things went wrong, and it wouldn't take much, his personality changed. He couldn't cope with stress, or with things not going his way. If he wanted something, he thought he had a right to it. What about his funeral? Do you have his family contacts?"

"I haven't thought about it yet. And no, I don't."

"I don't mind helping to arrange a memorial service in the new year. Whatever he did, he deserves that, at least."

"That would be a tremendous help. Thank you. Do you know anything about a will?"

"There won't be any money and the plantation will have to be sold to pay off debts. As far as I know, he has a nephew in B.C. who will inherit what pittance is left."

"Thank you for being so open and helpful." My intuition tells me that Dania is a kind person. With her help, managing the practical aspects of Chuck's death will be less daunting. I'll have to deal with the few personal effects he has here, and his old Jeep, which is parked in the drive-in shed.

Talking with Dania has nudged a vague memory out of a file in my brain. I recall Frank saying that Chuck had trouble studying at university because he had ADD. Frank convinced him to go to a doctor but then regretted it because Chuck became too reliant, Frank said, on his pills. I remember why it came up. Frank wanted me to let him know if I ever saw Chuck taking anything. He didn't want anyone taking drugs like that on his property. He said that he couldn't condone it, and that it was too much of a liability.

18

Hurley

Despite being shaken to the core, with a myriad of thoughts crashing around in my brain, I remember I should call Neal the trainer to thank him for lending us the nebulizer. It's as if I'm looking for something mundane to do to help quell the powerful emotions running through me like little demons on caffeine.

Linda believes the nebulizer is making a big difference. I've noticed improvement, but I'm still concerned about both Speed and Rose. They've lost shine in their coats just when Linda had them looking sleek again, the sparkle in their eyes isn't back yet, and there's a lot of discharge from their noses. I tell Neal all this, but he doesn't sound concerned. He then says that he's been keeping his ear to the ground regarding Juan's murder.

"Rumour has it that Ferris has disappeared."

"I sort of guessed that," I say. I'm sure that the meeting with Dominic, at which I was present, was part of a plan to get him out of the way and to implicate him in Juan's death.

"That's not all. Dominic has gone. Something must have spooked him good because his gambling business has shut down."

As we end the call, a probable scenario unfurls in my mind. Dominic demanded that Ferris poison Juan. He wanted to get rid of Juan because he could endanger his race-fixing if he talked. And then, because Dominic himself was at risk of being implicated in Juan's murder, he decided Ferris should take the blame and set him up as the fall guy. The two jockeys I met with told me that Ferris is a control freak and that he was mad at Juan for not wanting to play the game anymore. But the jockeys could well be a couple of Dominic's puppets taking part in a play which I've been watching and mostly believing.

The inquiry into his illegal gambling business and the investigation into Juan's murder could have spooked Dominic. I'm certain that the police are after him at last, and that the evidence that Frank sent to Murray will help them. Perhaps he's taken his money and his business to a foreign land.

Kelly moves to the kitchen door, tail swinging. I'm glad to see William standing on the doorstep. He looks well bundled up. A blizzard is just beginning with white curls of snow blowing around in what seems to be permanent suspension, but I see there's a layer of the white stuff on the ground, so some of it's settling.

I tell him about Chuck, including what I learned from Dania, and that Linda is relaxing in the bath.

"I should have been here. I chose the wrong time to be in the wrong place. How are you doing?" He keeps his dark eyes on me as he takes off his tailored woollen coat, dusting the snowflakes off onto the mat.

"I feel numb. I suppose I'm still in shock. And I'm worried about Linda, although I think she's tougher."

"Doubt it." William smiles.

"Can I get you anything?"

We settle for hot chocolate, with a brandy to follow.

"Have the police questioned you?" He asks.

"They asked 'preliminary questions', as they put it, of both me and Linda."

"I wish you'd called me. I would have been here like a shot."

"I have to put Linda's clothes in the dryer. Just give me a minute." As I move the small load from the washer to the dryer, I wonder if I've offended William by not contacting him immediately. I would have loved to have had him here. I should have called. "How was your day?"

"Not as exciting as yours, obviously," William says as he leans against the doorpost, watching me. I select the dryer temperature and time, and we both move to the kitchen table. Kelly is munching on kibble and Cooper is biffing a small piece of ice around the floor, which must have come in with William.

"But I found something out today, during my brief lunch break," he says as he sits down. "Dominic Marcel is missing and the police are looking for him for several reasons, spurred on by the development that one of the jockeys has come forward who's willing to give evidence that links Dominic to Juan's death, and how that's connected to the gambling operations."

"You know who else is missing? Joanna. I think there's a connection. And I'm worried that the plan is to make Ewert the fall-guy for Frank's murder."

* * *

I've had a rotten night, but that won't stop me from making progress today.

Kelly and I trudge through six inches of wet snow in the semi-dark to the back of the large field. I'm enjoying the fresh air and exercise, but I have to encourage Kelly now and then.

I ponder the phone call I received from Dr Milton, Munro, earlier this morning. Preliminary lab tests found a significant amount of an amphetamine in Chuck's blood and Munro explained that the dilated pupils, bloodshot eyes and aggressive behaviour could have been symptoms of the overdose. But he added, off the record, that he wouldn't be surprised if fentanyl shows up in further tests, and conjectured that Chuck might have bought amphetamine which was laced with that lethal drug.

A pang of deep sorrow stings me in the gut. What a sad waste of a life. I should have done more to help him. I should have remembered what Frank said and given Chuck more support. Regret. I have a lot of that.

We turn towards the barn. The lights are on. Linda is already there, presumably recovered from the exertion of the day before. But I know it'll take us both a long time to recuperate from the shock of Chuck's sudden and tragic death in my kitchen.

When I open the barn door, a waft of warm air greets Kelly and me. The barn isn't heated and has mediocre insulation, but it's astounding how warm it can get with four horses inside. I don't like it to get much warmer than outside because sudden changes in temperature can be stressful for the animals. I'm not one to put blankets on, preferring that the horses grow good winter coats. But we might have to dig out the blankets for Rose and Speed this winter if they don't bounce back soon and put some more weight on.

"I haven't had a chance to check the horses yet. Just got here," Linda says as she grabs Speed's water bucket for a refill.

"I'm surprised you came today. Are you okay?"

"It's better than sitting at home. Better to keep busy and be with the horses."

"How's Austin?"

"He's stressed out about Ewert. He's sure the police are wrong, and he says Ewert shouldn't be locked up. I don't like Austin upset."

Linda wipes a couple of tears off her face with the sleeve of her grubby jacket. “He can't believe that Ewert could kill anyone.”

“It doesn't look good for Ewert, does it?”

“Austin got hold of Ewert's doctor. Don't know if he's gone to see Ewert.” Linda sniffs, and more tears roll down her red cheeks. “Sorry, I guess I'm shook up about all of this stuff.”

“Nothing to be sorry about. I should apologize to you, not the other way around.”

“It's not your fault. And I love working here. I met Austin here, didn't I?”

“I'm glad you did. The police have Ewert's raincoat, hat and gun and no doubt they believe them to be linked with Frank's murder. But I'm determined to find out the truth and I'm convinced they'll release Ewert soon.” I smile. “I have to go, but I'll keep you posted for sure. Keep your fingers crossed that I'm right!”

“I will. Yeah.” Linda smiles and sniffs and picks up her travel mug.

“Make yourself some fresh coffee in the house.”

“Yeah. Thanks.”

* * *

Earlier, before I ventured out into the wintery landscape, I called Dominic's mobile, but got nowhere. I then tried to connect with both Benito and Hurley, the two jockeys who told me that Dominic treated them like family, that he's not a murderer. Hurley texted back and said he'd meet me at the farm where he's working. He said he has a break at about 9am.

I find Chestnut Lane Farm about five miles outside of Vannersville. The fencing hasn't been painted in several years and there are some broken rails which have been patched, not replaced. The barn is a large rectangular building with a galvanized steel roof, and wooden siding which is showing signs of rot at the base of the walls. I assume that the people running the operation are leasing from land speculators. There's no evidence that anyone is investing in maintenance and upkeep.

The barn has about sixty stalls according to the number of small, high, barred windows which each mark the home of a horse. It is one of several operations which offer winter lay-up for thoroughbreds and provide preliminary conditioning before the racetrack opens in the spring. This can be helpful in giving horses a head-start on the season. Some of the more expensive horses might winter in Florida or South Carolina, some continuing to race, others just being kept in shape.

Hurley must have been watching out for me because he comes out of the barn door and walks towards me, holding out his hand.

"I expect you had an early start," I say.

"Yep. I'm here at 5am and start riding about 5.15. I like it. It beats sitting around all winter. They have a covered training track here which is nice."

"Thanks for meeting with me. Don't you need to eat?"

"I usually sit in my car and eat my sandwich."

"I don't mind joining you."

"Thanks, excuse the mess."

I notice his keys are hooked onto the antenna. The car is packed with all sorts of riding paraphernalia, including two crops, a saddle, a protective vest, riding boots, two jackets, gloves, as well as old race programs and racing magazines. Hurley chucks the items that are on the passenger seat into the back. I feel as if I'm sitting on the ground. This sports car is so low compared to my pickup truck.

"Thanks, Hurley, for meeting with me."

"You already said that." He smiles, with a mouthful.

"I'll get straight to the point. I want to know more about what Dominic's been up to."

"Since it's just the two of us, I'll tell you how it is. I don't want to get into no court case or anything, though." He talks with his mouth full of chewed sandwich, but I can understand him.

"Thanks. Just tell me what you know."

"Here goes. Not sure how much help it will be. I'll say one thing about him, he's clear what he wants. He demands complete loyalty, no ifs, buts, or maybes about that. That was the start of Juan's troubles with Dominic, when he started saying to the rest of us he wanted out. Dominic sent his boys to see him. I don't know what happened, but Juan wasn't on the race card for about three days."

"So, Dominic doesn't act like an uncle to those of you who are on his payroll."

"I know me and Benito said that, but, no he don't. He's ruthless if any of us don't toe the line. It's bad news. There's no goddam way out once you're in."

"And race-fixing is what it's all about, so that he can make more money in his gambling business."

"Yep. He does pay us, and it's more that we'd earn if we won each of the races, but it's shit awful. I hate it. I hate it so much I'm thinking of escaping by going back to exercise riding in the States. That's one reason I'm here for the winter. I want to see if I can handle it. But it means a hell of a lot less pay."

"Can you think of anything that might help to prove Dominic was fixing races? What about friends, contacts, people who associated with him?"

"I'm sure he did business with a lot of people, but I didn't get to see many and I sure couldn't tell you names. Just now and then I'd notice someone in his private box at the track."

"Can you think of anyone in particular?"

"There was a woman who followed him like some kind of puppy-dog. I was surprised that she wasn't told to buzz off. I don't know why she was hanging around him. Saw her sitting next to him in his box several times, and, yep, I saw her getting out of a limo with him at the track entrance once."

"What did she look like?"

"I didn't get much of a look, but she looked like she was tall, not great looking. She was sure taller than Dominic. That's about it, though."

* * *

Linda and Kelly emerge from the barn as I get out of the truck. Linda waves and smiles. She only has a thin sweater on with her well-worn jeans that are tucked into her black barn boots. I wave and walk towards them. I assume Linda has good news to share, because she's rarely this demonstrative.

"Hi, Meg. I'm so happy. Rose ate all her feed this morning and didn't cough yet!"

"Oh, Linda, that's marvellous."

"I was going to ask you if they could go out for longer today. Although it's slushy, it's sunny. I think it'd do them good."

"You know you don't need my permission, Linda. I consider you to be in charge of the barn."

"Let's lead them out." It's as if Linda's dancing, there's so much bounce in her step.

Both of the horses appear to have turned a corner in the last twenty-four hours. The relief is enormous. I must have been much more worried about them than I realized. Too much going on.

We don't even hear a cough as they each kick up their heels when they're set free in the paddock. Linda puts out fresh hay for them and makes sure the automatic watering system is working. Eagle and Bullet wonder what all the fuss is about and come cantering over to the fence to check things out. Fortunately, they're smart enough not to slide on the slippery ground into the rails. It's such a wonderful feeling to see all four of them outside enjoying the freedom and the sunshine. I thank Linda again for all that she's doing, and make my way to the house. I want to talk to Tammy. Really talk.

William is waiting at the kitchen door.

"Good morning, Meg. I've brought breakfast. Some for Linda too. And a cookie for Kelly, of course." He pats Kelly's head as I open the door. He unloads a huge brown bag onto the table. Two coffees, a tea, three breakfast sandwiches and an oatmeal cookie. Without saying anything, he takes a coffee and breakfast sandwich out to Linda. Kelly finishes her cookie before he's made it out of the door.

I get a plate for each of us and get rid of the wrappers and the bag. He's soon back in the kitchen and has a friend in Kelly for life. She loves cookies, especially oatmeal raisin ones.

"Thanks for breakfast. I hadn't thought about it."

"Glad I got it then."

"Something's on your mind."

"I might say the same about you." He takes another bite and looks at me with his intense dark eyes.

"A lot's on my mind. I think I know who killed Frank."

"Ah. I reckon you think that the police have the wrong man."

"You're right."

"Bad news there, I'm afraid. They found Ewert's fingerprints all over the gun, and they think it was the murder weapon. Mind you, that still has to be proven. That, along with the fact that they've had several reports of sightings of someone tall in a wide-brimmed hat at the time of the murder, means he's the number one suspect. I'm not sure when extradition proceedings will commence, but they will take some time, and there is an opportunity under the Extradition Act to appeal."

"Have you talked to him? Does he have a lawyer? Are you able to help him?"

"No, I don't know, and yes, you know I'm willing to help him."

"My bet is that his gun is not the one that was used to shoot Frank."

"We'll get an answer soon, I expect. Now it's your turn to tell me what's on your mind."

"I think that Dominic and Joanna are an item. I think that they're together in some foreign, sunny clime, enjoying Dominic's wealth which he's accumulated from his gambling business. And he might have plans to set up in business again in his new locale. And it'll be somewhere that doesn't have an extradition agreement with Canada. After all, they're both murderers. I think Dominic had Juan poisoned and I think Joanna murdered Frank because so many people have said they saw someone tall, wearing a wide-brimmed hat and a long raincoat, and she had access to both of them, and the murder weapon, since they all belong to Ewert."

"Motive?" William asks as he takes our plates and puts them in the dishwasher.

"She got rid of her husband and secured her relationship with her lover, by killing Frank and framing Ewert."

"But why did she need to kill Frank? Why not just run off with Dominic?"

"Frank was threatening to expose Dominic. I know he had the evidence because he sent it to Murray. That's why I want to talk to Tammy again. My theory is that there was much more going on between Frank and Dominic than we realize."

"But if you're right about Dominic murdering Juan, he'd have to run in any case. Why bother to have Frank killed?"

"But he thought he'd set up Ferris to be the fall-guy for Juan's murder. He handed Juan the laced coffee."

"He must know that it would unravel. As I told you before, the police now believe Juan's death to be suspicious, and someone came forward with evidence that links his death to Dominic."

"Frank was an intelligent man. If he was determined to bring Dominic to justice, I think he would have found out where he was, and pursued him, preventing him from setting up business again. So, Dominic needed him out of the picture."

"Probably depends on the country. Some places might not have much in the way of gambling laws."

"Then he wouldn't have as much scope to make a lot of money."

"Perhaps. But I have trouble with your conjecture that Joanna killed Frank. I still have trouble with motive." William looks at me with dark, intense eyes as he sips some of his coffee.

"I don't. I have two potential scenarios. She certainly had her own reason. Revenge. Frank wouldn't give her money when she asked for it. As we know, she thought she was entitled to some of Frank's wealth because she's Louisa's sister. And, when she went down to Kentucky and asked him again, and he said no, she shot him."

"But then she would have had to be prepared to shoot him and have already planned to frame Ewert. I'm not sure I buy that scenario."

"It could be some of that scenario, combined with Dominic putting her to the test. He demands absolute loyalty. He killed Juan because the jockey didn't want to be part of the Marcel Team any more. Dominic might have had his doubts about Joanna, or at least wanted to be absolutely certain. He needed to have Frank out of the way and probably thought it wouldn't be a big deal because Frank was considered legally dead in Canada. They could get away with murder, literally. But Joanna wanted to frame Ewert. Her passion for Dominic, and especially his money, made her determined to show her loyalty and love. Getting rid of her husband and murdering Frank, she thought, would guarantee her the relationship with Dominic that she wanted, and, of course, the lifestyle she yearned for."

"But killing two birds with one stone might have backfired on her. I think her attempt to frame Ewert is problematic. For one thing, he'll be able to prove that he didn't leave Canada."

"Anyway, I'm going to call Tammy. I need to know more about the what went on between Frank and Dominic."

"Mind if I hang around for a bit?"

"Of course not. That would be great. I'll put her on speaker phone."

19

Joanna

I'm hoping Tammy still has the same mobile number. I think she's left Louisa's Acres and, if she has, I've no clue where she is.

"Hi, Meg." She sounds more upbeat than I expected. Whenever I've talked to her before, she seemed stressed and somewhat muddled.

"Hi, Tammy. I'm glad I got you. How are you?"

"I'm doing great, thanks."

"Do you mind if I put you on speaker? My friend, William is here, and he's helping me."

"Go right ahead. Sure nice to hear your voice, Meg. Hi, William."

"Hi, Tammy." William moves his chair to be closer to where I've put the phone.

"Where are you and what are you doing?" I ask.

"I'm renting a small place in Hollywood, of all places. I'm doing make-up to help get things going and plan to set up an agency. My aunt has tons of connections here."

"Sounds exciting. I wish you success. The reason I'm calling is that I need to know more about Frank's relationship with Dominic Marcel."

"Mm. I'm not sure what I told you before, and I don't remember much. Frank liked him at first because he was sure great at getting nice horses for his barn."

"But later on, things changed?"

"I can see Frank's thunderous face when he told me he had no respect for cheats like Dominic. I asked him what he meant, and he just said 'race-fixing'."

"Can you remember anything more?"

"Only that, after Frank found out what Dominic was up to, he told me it left a bad taste in his mouth and spoilt his enjoyment of his horses and the barn. And what with so many people finding out he was alive, he grew grouchier every day."

"Thanks, this is helpful," I say, looking at William, who nods in agreement.

Cooper is sitting on William's shoulder, batting at his ear, fortunately with no bared claws.

"I sure want you to find out what happened to poor Frank," Tammy says.

Just as we end the call, we're startled by a frantic knocking on the door. William gets up with a deep frown furrowing his forehead. Joanna bursts in and collapses on the floor. My first thought is please don't die here. I can't cope with another corpse.

"Joanna, what on earth are you doing here?"

"I need help. Lots of help. I'm in trouble." Her body rocks with heaving sobbing as she sits on her heels with her head in her hands.

"We thought you were with Dominic," I say.

"That no-good scoundrel. He's a pig. That's what he is."

William helps her to stand up. I take her wet coat off. It must be raining or coming down with wet snow. I give her one of the barn jackets to wear until she warms up. Her teeth are chattering and her hands are purple. William takes her into the family room and settles her in the recliner while I make a mug of hot chocolate.

It takes just a few minutes and then she talks. She tells us about her gambling addiction, admitting that she lied to me about Ewert.

"He isn't the one owing money to Dominic, it's me." She shudders. I'm not sure if it's because she's still cold, or if it's a sign of how onerous her debts to Dominic are. "I tried to develop a relationship with Dominic, hoping that he'd let me off the hook. I thought I was getting somewhere when he took me to the races. We sat in his private box. But it made no difference. He demanded I pay what I owe him, with crazy interest. It just got worse and worse and I got desperate, real desperate."

"Does Ewert know about all this?" William asks.

"Yes. He couldn't do anything, and the only thing I could think of doing was begging Frank for money. I told Dominic that I was going to see my brother-in-law in Kentucky and that he'd help me, and I'd be back with the money in a couple of days."

"How did you know where to find Frank?" I ask.

"I overheard you and Murray talking. It wasn't hard to track him down. Louisa's Acres, give me a break." She sniffs, as if showing derision, but I'm not sure. "Frank wasn't pleased to see me. He went deathly pale and didn't want to talk with me. I followed him into his office and pleaded with him. I told him everything. When I mentioned Dominic's name, he changed. He said I should do nothing, that there was nothing to worry about. If it was the last thing he did, he would see to it that Dominic faced justice. I wouldn't have to repay my debts."

"When did you meet with Frank?" I ask, remembering that Murray received Frank's letter about Dominic only a couple of days ago.

"Almost two weeks ago, I think. I pleaded with Frank, telling him it was urgent, but he wouldn't listen."

"Did anything happen?" William asks.

"I got frantic, is what happened. When I got back, Dominic asked where the promised money was. He acted funny. He asked if my brother-in-law's name was Fred Simpson. I told him his real name was Frank Sheppard. It gave me the creeps that he seemed to know who he was, although I wouldn't be surprised if he had me followed to Frank's place. He got hold of my shoulders and shook me. He said if I valued my life, I must get rid of that man. He said that Fred, or Frank, was a threat to his business. When he let go of me he sort of calmed down, and said that if I went back there and got rid of Fred, he'd consider my debts paid."

"But you couldn't murder him," I say.

"How do you know?"

"Because he was your brother-in-law and because you love Ewert, despite everything," I say, realizing that the scenarios I described to William didn't fit. "So, why are you here?"

"I didn't know where to turn. I know I don't deserve any help from you, but I don't think there's anyone else who can help. No-one else knows what's going on, other than Ewert and he's locked up for something he didn't do."

"How can you be so sure?" asks William in a quiet, non-threatening voice.

"Because he didn't go to the States. He has an extreme fear of flying, close to a phobia. I reckon it's linked to his capture. He can't bear to be enclosed with no way out." She sniffs. "There wouldn't be any more of this hot chocolate, would there?"

"I can probably figure out how to make it," William says.

"And he wouldn't have had time to drive down," I say.

"No. I'm sure there's a way to prove he didn't go down there."

"You tried to frame him though, by using his raincoat, hat and gun, and that evidence is what's holding him."

"No, I didn't. I just wasn't thinking. I saw them and grabbed them, thinking I'd be less recognizable. I didn't take the gun. It couldn't have been Ewert's gun that killed Frank. The truth is that I knew I couldn't kill Frank. I went there without a plan."

"Dominic somehow knew you were wearing Ewert's raincoat and hat. He told me a shipper had seen someone in that outfit getting into a car outside Louisa's Acres."

"I don't remember seeing a shipper. I was in such a state. It could have been a guy he had follow me who told Dominic. And he could have been following me for a while. It's scary."

"So, you must have told Dominic that you killed Frank?" asks William as he hands her a fresh mug of hot chocolate.

"No. He knew I hadn't. I don't know how he knew, but he did."

"Okay. So, assuming all that you've said is true, the question of who murdered Frank is still out there. Do you have any ideas, since you were there at the time?" I ask.

"When I got there the second time, I was startled and shocked to find Frank lying on the ground in the aisle of the barn in semi-darkness. I thought perhaps he'd fallen and couldn't get up. I remember thinking it was a good thing that the floor was made of that rubberized interlocking brick stuff that they often use in fancy barns. He wouldn't be as badly hurt. But when I looked down at him, my heart pounded as I realized he was dead. And I saw a gun lying in front of him. I shook so badly I could barely make it out to the car, which I'd left in the road. I'm ashamed that I was more afraid for myself than anything. I didn't doubt that he'd been murdered. I thought I'd be a suspect if I was found anywhere in the area, especially because Dominic had told me to kill him." She sobs and puts her hands over her eyes. Her cheeks are flushed. She wipes tears away with her fingers, and then takes the box of tissues from me that I'm offering her. I think I believe her. But I've been taken in by people before, so I'm going to be cautious.

* * *

William and I talk until the early hours of the morning. When he leaves, at about two o'clock, I stand on the kitchen doorstep looking at the sparkling, silvery landscape. The full moon lights up the icy crystals attached to every blade of grass, every fence rail and every twig. I soak in the farm's beauty as it shimmers and glistens, feeling Kelly's tail wafting air around my legs. At this moment, I sense a seed of pure happiness swell inside me. I find it hard to appreciate, because I ask: how can I possibly be feeling this? My husband is dead, my mother is dying, my partner collapsed and died in my kitchen, my horses are recovering from illness, I've lost my job and I can't solve Frank's murder or bring Dominic to justice.

* * *

As I sit with my mug of tea, wondering what to eat for breakfast, Cooper jumps up on the table and rubs against my hand, purring. I put him down and tell him he's not allowed on the table, and that he should know better. Even as I'm telling him off, I feel the little seed of happiness still nestled inside me. It wants to stay. And I want it to, but it's such a strange feeling for me. I know why it's there -William. But I'm scared. I'm no good at relationships. The only ones that seem to work for me are the ones with animals. As if Kelly can read my mind, she puts her head on my lap, which is under the table. I pull my chair back and stroke her. She is always faithful, always loves me whatever happens, and is always honest.

I enjoyed talking to William. But my latest theory takes me in a circle. I don't have all the rationale figured out, but I think I'm getting close. The mobile's ringing disrupts my thoughts.

It's Joanna asking if she can come over. More often than not, she just shows up. I'd rather she didn't come right now because I want to talk with Tammy again. There's something I need to follow up on. But Joanna sounds so stressed that I tell her she can come any time. She says she'll be over in two minutes.

Linda is at the kitchen door beside Joanna, obviously not happy with her visit.

"It's okay, Linda," I say.

"Her husband shot Austin. I know I shouldn't say anything, but I'd like to know what this woman was doing in the barn with the horses. They got real sick after that."

"Come in, both of you, and perhaps Joanna will tell us both what was going on."

Joanna's eyes are red and puffy and she's carrying a wad of tissues in her hand. She hasn't got a coat on, even though it's below freezing, and is shivering.

"Okay, I'm making hot chocolate. Joanna, why didn't you wear a coat?"

"I don't know. I can't think. It's because of me that Ewert's locked up. I can't bear it."

"But he won't be there for long because the evidence won't stand up."

"I know Dominic seems to have disappeared, but I'm scared. He said he knew I hadn't killed Frank. How he knew, I don't know, but he said I still owe him all the money and that the interest is building fast."

"I'd like to know what you were doing in the barn, and why Ewert shot Austin." Linda is shaking. I've never seen her so intense.

"Linda, I'm sorry. It had to do with getting ringers for Dominic so I could pay off an enormous debt I owe to that creep. It didn't work at first because Meg found the horses."

"No, Kelly did," I say. "And it wasn't just because we found the horses, it was because Dominic needs to have matching horses to switch them with, right?"

"I told him I'd got these great horses, but he said they'd need to be a match for two poorly performing horses so they could be substituted for them, and win. I was pretty upset. 'Cause I was desperate, I tried that ransom note. Then you took them back." Joanna stares into her mug. Linda looks at me with disgust written all over her face. "But I couldn't think of any other plan. So, I tried again with Dominic and told him the two great horses I'd stolen were in a barn down the road from me, and that one was a stakes winner. Dominic said if he knew exactly what they looked like, he'd consider it. I was so relieved. I had no other way I could think of to pay off the debt."

"But you'd have to steal them again, and I knew it was you or Ewert who stole them the first time, so it wouldn't be easy for you to do it again."

"Dominic said he could arrange it, if I gave him all the information and if they would be useful as ringers somewhere."

"What were you doing in the barn?" Linda sounds as if she's likely to lose it and do something like punch Joanna on the nose.

"I'd watched the videos of the replays of their races online, but couldn't get enough detail of the horses' markings from them. I needed to take some photos and make some notes. Dominic wanted to know specifics on any white socks, white flashes or stars on their faces, cowlicks, and the colour of their coats, as well as the colour of each hoof." Joanna turns to face Linda. "I didn't make them sick. I didn't touch them."

"Why did Austin have to get shot?"

"Ewert said that he was terrified. He thought Austin was reaching for a gun."

"He wasn't!" Linda blurts out.

"I know, but don't forget that Ewert has PTSD."

"So does Austin, and he got shot for nothing." Linda's voice is squeaky and hoarse at the same time.

"Linda, please let Joanna tell us what happened."

"Ewert thought Austin was reaching for a gun. Ewert was held as a hostage, and at gun-point most of the time. It was traumatic and I don't think any of us can imagine how terrifying that would be. He didn't mean for his gun to go off. He was stressed out. It was my fault. I'm sorry, Linda, that Austin was hurt. I really am. I made Ewert come so I could get into the barn and he could create a diversion if anyone came. I didn't want him to bring his gun, but he was nervous. And he was supposed to keep his gun hidden inside his raincoat, but he got jittery. Oh, it's all so awful. Ewert's locked up and I don't know what'll happen to me when Dominic shows up."

"I have to ask something, Joanna," I say. "Why did Ewert shoot at Kelly?"

"That was my fault too," Joanna says. There are tears running down her face, but she doesn't use the tissues that are crumpled in her hand. "I told you. I was desperate for money. He was supposed to fire a shot, but not hit anyone. It was a ploy to make you feel sorry for me, for us. But it didn't work. I was sure mad at you for not helping us."

"I remember that," I say. "I wish people would stop thinking I have millions of dollars. I don't. Frank left me enough to keep this farm going, but that's it. That was our agreement."

"I'm going back to the barn," Linda says. She puts her mug in the dishwasher and stomps out of the kitchen. I'll have a chat with her later. She leaves the door open and I'm about to shut it when William's face appears and he asks if he can come in.

"Of course, William. Please do. It's nice to see you," I say, as my heart skips a beat and I become aware of my happiness seed swelling a little more. I feel tingly, and need something to settle me down, so I get up to put the kettle on to make some herbal tea. But, as I move past him, I sense some excitement about him, some energy, and know that he must have some news he wants to share. Just as I'm about to ask, he answers my question.

"I'm glad you're here, Joanna," William says, "because you need to hear this. I've just found out that they've released Ewert." Before he can say another word, Joanna faints and falls with a thud onto the floor, looking ashen with sparkling beads of sweat on her forehead. She's crumpled on her side. I move her onto her back and bring her knees up to help her blood circulation to her brain. William calls an ambulance, which is a good thing. We can't be sure that she's simply fainted. I ask William to put the smallest cushion from the family room under her head, and I get a washcloth and wet it with cold water to place on her forehead. This will the third ambulance coming to the farm in less than a week.

* * *

It's a relief for us all to witness Joanna being transferred to the ambulance. She could sit up and drink some water by the time the paramedics arrived, but when they took her blood pressure it was very low, so we thought it best if she was checked out. I think the stress of all that has happened to her and Ewert has taken its toll, and, perhaps of more significance, she probably did what I sometimes do: forgot to eat.

William gets the hint that I want to talk with Linda and returns to the kitchen.

I chat with Linda as the large, square white vehicle rumbles down the driveway. I give her more background on what has been going on with Joanna and Ewert, and I can tell that the antagonism that Linda feels towards Joanna is waning, although not completely gone. She can't forgive Ewert for shooting Austin, nor can she forgive Joanna for stealing the horses.

I don't want to lose her. The horses are doing much better and she works so hard and with such caring and attention to detail. I never have to worry. I decide to tell her as much, and she gives me one of her rare smiles and waddles back into the barn.

William is picking Cooper up out of the sink when I return to the kitchen. The cat's found an empty tea bag envelope, screwed up, just asking to be batted around. Why it isn't in the garbage, I have no clue. He still has it gripped between his two front paws as William puts him down onto the floor.

"So, William, they must have found out that Ewert's gun wasn't the one that was used to shoot Frank."

"I have some updates. Let's go out for an early lunch. I bet you haven't eaten, and I've only had a smoothie. And we won't get any interruptions."

"That would be nice. I'd like that. But I must change." I'm suddenly conscious of my somewhat sloppy appearance. I'm wearing old denim jeans, which look ancient from genuine wear, not from attack by design, topped by a sweater which hangs in ripples. It lost its shape after two washes. Sometimes I wish I enjoyed shopping and bought clothes more often than once a year. At least I'm clean, I say to myself, as I skip upstairs to change, with Kelly in hot pursuit.

"Sorry, Kelly, you're going to have to stay at home."

"We can bring Kelly," William calls up to me. "We can go to this restaurant I know where we can park my car within sight."

"Are you sure you want a dog in your car?" I have to raise my voice because I have my head in the closet, realizing my wardrobe has a lot to be desired. I used to have several smart outfits which I wore when accompanying Frank to functions of various kinds, but I gave most of them to a charity shop this summer. And the clothes I usually wear to work look out-of-date and drab. I want to look presentable. After some rummaging, I'm relieved to find a pair of dark red skinny jeans, and there's a black mohair sweater hanging next to them that I can't remember buying or wearing. I tied up my long, black hair this morning and there are kinks in it. I plug in the flatiron.

I look in the long mirror which is on the back of the bedroom door and think I'll pass. I can't expect much when it only took me seven minutes to get ready.

20

Lunch

William doesn't comment on my appearance as we make our way to his old Jaguar. I must have been hoping that chivalry was still alive, and that he'd say something complimentary.

He tells Kelly to get onto the back seat.

"She might scratch your leather," I say.

"She can't do anything to harm these seats. They've been used and abused for several years."

Kelly looks happy to be with us. Linda's already left to have lunch with her mother, which reminds me I should talk to William again about my job, which I no longer have with the humane society. I need it back. My budget is being stretched too far for my liking by unexpected expenses like hospital bills, legal bills, Linda's work, vet bills, security fees, and more. I have no contingency left.

William parks the car close to the restaurant and puts the windows down a bit for Kelly. Having just opened for lunch, the place is virtually empty and we find a table that has an unobstructed view of his Jag. Kelly is sitting on the front passenger seat, watching us.

In between reading the menu and ordering, William tells me that Ewert's gun was not the one used to kill Frank.

"The police on both sides are admitting there's been some bungling. I think it's because Ewert is here in Canada, and the crime was committed in the US. I have a good friend in the RCMP who's been keeping me informed, while not compromising the investigation of course." William sips some water from a glass that's filled almost entirely with ice.

"That's good. I'm relieved Ewert is no longer a suspect."

"The reason he was detained in the first place is that there's a cop in the States who was convinced that Ewert was their man. But my friend wasn't so sure because it was rather too easy. She knew Ewert's reputation as a smart journalist and found it hard to believe he would smuggle his own gun into the States to commit a murder and bring it back with him."

"I agree it makes no sense."

"And he wouldn't still have the clothes he used hanging up by the front door of his home. I agree with my friend that it was too easy. She followed up on the ballistics report, as well as on the autopsy, reviewed all the reports, asked questions, had them do a couple more tests here and in Kentucky, and one thing that popped up was that Ewert's gun was not the one used."

"That doesn't surprise me."

"What might surprise you is that they've now determined that the gun found in the ditch, with Chuck's fingerprints on, is the murder weapon after all."

"Oh, wow."

"I know. 'Wow', is the word. They messed up with their original analysis. Chuck is the prime suspect again, although I'm not sure how they plan to proceed, since he's not here to defend himself."

"I can't see why Chuck would kill Frank unless there's a new will, which I don't think there is, leaving some of his millions to me. Chuck was after money for his plantation. If he believed there was a new will, he might have asked me to marry him, but the thought of what could have happened next is, well, troubling." That's an understatement. I've not given much thought to what Chuck might have ultimately done in his pursuit of his plantation dream as he faced a probable downhill spiral of addiction. Would I no longer be here?

"There's no evidence, that we're aware of, that Frank drew up a new will. But Chuck could have speculated that you would be the sole beneficiary, if the money exists, and that it would be located and transferred on the event of Frank's death."

"I suppose that he could have done some research."

"Do you miss Chuck?" I can't see William's face. He's looking down at his napkin, which is on his lap. I can only see his shiny bald head.

"Not as much as I should. I feel guilty about it. Looking back, I see we didn't develop our relationship as we should have. We drifted further apart. It's amazing how much clearer things are in hindsight, isn't it?"

"They can be."

I'm a private person and rarely share my inner thoughts and feelings with anyone, but I feel comfortable with William. Perhaps it's because he treats me with respect and is non-judgemental.

"On another topic," William says, as the server places our meals in front of us. He continues to watch his weight, and the butterflies in my stomach won't make room for much food, so we both ordered tomato-basil soup and caesar salad. Why do I have butterflies in my stomach?

"On another topic, as I was saying, there's a manhunt on for Dominic Marcel because Ferris has come forward to the police and given a statement, the gist of which, as you suspected, is that he handed Juan the poison at the behest of Dominic. Ferris swears he was convinced that the purpose was to scare Juan, not to kill him."

"Do you think they'll find Dominic? I'm sure Joanna would feel safer if they did."

"They sound pretty determined. He's such a scoundrel in many regards, and this was a brutal murder to protect his business and to scare other jockeys. Although, I believe it'll be hard to have a murder charge stick. They'll have to lay a lesser charge. But, in addition to the general inquiry, the police are investigating Dominic's gambling business including his use of ringers and his other methods of race-fixing, so I imagine he'll be in jail for a while, once all the trials are over."

"Will Ferris be okay, do you think?"

"He'll be in witness protection. And he might not face charges assuming that he assists them in Dominic's case."

"He shouldn't have done what he did, but I think he got himself into a hole, similar to Juan. Dominic wielded power and control over his jockeys."

"I don't think most of them realized the extreme seriousness of what they were involved in."

We fall silent for a while as we eat our lunch. I glance out to Kelly now and then, and her eyes are fixed on us whenever I check. I realize how comfortable I am with William and how much I relish his company, and a smile comes to my face as I sip my soup. I look up and consider saying something about my feelings towards him, and how much I appreciate the lunch when William breaks the silence. His frown makes me nervous. Intuitively, I know I won't like what he's going to say.

"Meg, I think it would be best if I saw you in a professional capacity only. As a lawyer. I'm willing to help with any legal matters."

"Why?" I know my voice has a tremble and I can feel my face flush.

"I just think it would be more appropriate."

I'm at a loss for words, so say nothing as William pays for our lunch. The wonderful feelings of ease and comfort in his presence evaporate. There is tension in the air. I talk to Kelly like a blabbering idiot all the way home and am relieved to reach my kitchen, where I sit down and sob. I didn't realize how much I care about William. I can't stop the tears. Kelly sits under the table and leans against my legs. I've had partial and peculiar relationships with three different men. Two of whom are dead and the one I really care about doesn't share my feelings. I feel very sorry for myself as I finally sit up and dry my face while patting Kelly whose wide brown eyes show concern and confusion.

The landline phone rings. I reluctantly pick it up. My mother is crying. Her flight is delayed, but I can tell she's scared to leave.

"Meg, I just can't bear the thought of facing all those horrible memories in that grotty house."

"I couldn't go back there, for sure. I don't know how you've stood it."

"Not well. But I don't have the means to move."

"But you need to go back to get the treatment you need. You know, from the NHS."

"I can't right now. I just can't."

"Okay. Get the inn to load up a taxi will all your stuff and you can stay at the farm until you're ready to go."

"Oh, thank you Meg. I don't deserve your kindness."

"Don't be silly, just come. Sorry I can't pick you up." I can't tell her I'm afraid I'll break out in sobs and won't be able to see the road in front of me.

* * *

My mother says she's overjoyed and relieved to be invited to stay at the farm, as I settle her in the family room for a rest. The ordeal of cancelling her flight and coming here has taken a lot out of her. I tell her we'll talk later as I take her suitcases upstairs.

When I come back down, she's sleeping with Cooper curled up on her lap and with Kelly lying across her feet. The bed's made and all her things are put away in the closet and dresser. I've made up my mind that she should stay for Christmas. It's only a couple of weeks away, and I'm sure she'll feel better able to face things in the New Year. Christmas can be an emotional time when one is alone, especially if sick.

After a strong cup of tea, I pluck up the courage to email Annabella. I've a big hunch that Simeon returned to her, despite everything he said, and am banking on him reading the email since he's been the intermediary I've had to communicate through in the past. I simply say that I know who killed Frank, and why, and that I'd love to chat with her.

I check on my mother, who is awake from her nap, but her eyes are heavy as she strokes Cooper. I can hear the cat's purrs from the doorway. Kelly's shiny coat shimmers as she breathes, lying flat on her side over my mother's feet.

"How are you feeling? I expect you'd like some tea."

"That would hit the spot."

I find some cookies which I'd forgotten about, and fortunately the expiry date isn't yet upon us. We sit in virtual silence, although my mother chuckles now and then at Cooper's antics, especially when he chases his own tail, spinning in circles. It's almost as if he feels obliged to entertain us. Kelly is sitting stock-still at my mother's feet, hoping for crumbs to fall.

"I remember your dog, Bertie. He meant a lot to you," she says. Her eyes are watery. "I never dare have any more pets after he was gone."

"Bertie was the best, except for Kelly, of course. But it was because of him that I didn't leave home sooner than I did."

"You were right. Stan would have hurt him."

"Did Stan take it out on you, you know, when I left?" I've not thought of this before, and I glance at her face.

"I suppose he did. But it was nothing to what you suffered. Don't give it another thought. Let's talk about something else. What about that nice William?"

"He's helping with legal matters."

"And?"

"That's it. He made it clear at lunch today that he's helping me in a professional capacity only."

"Piffle." She takes another sip of tea while looking over the cup towards me.

"How can you say that? You don't know him." I feel defensive.

"Your face gives you away. As soon as I mentioned his name, I could tell. I'm your mother, albeit the world's worst. At first, I thought you loved that weird guy Chuck, who should have been called Charles and should have got those brown curls cut, but then I cottoned on to William."

"How do you know about Chuck's hair?"

"I saw him that horrible day when we argued. I saw him before you did. He looked like something the cat dragged in."

"You shouldn't speak ill of the dead. I don't like you talking about Chuck that way."

"You're right. Let's get back to William."

"He's not interested."

"Rot."

"That's not helpful." I'm in danger of getting angry with her. I can feel tension rising and my heart-rate increasing. I would like our relationship to continue to improve, if it's at all possible. I find some deep, warm comfort in the possibility that my mother might become part of my life, even if it will be over a long distance, and for just a short time. I can't explain why I feel this way, especially after what she didn't do when I needed her the most.

She puts her cup and saucer down on the coffee table.

"Call him."

"I can't do that."

"Why ever not? You can say you have a pressing legal matter and that he needs to come here so that you can discuss it with him."

"I can't do that."

"Yes, you can. If I hadn't pursued your father, and not taken 'no' for an answer, you wouldn't be here, and I wouldn't have the best memories of my whole life. Even though I lost him when you were young, I'm very thankful for the time we had together. He didn't want to marry me because he was in the army and knew that his unit would be deployed eventually, and that his life would be in danger. He didn't want to have a wife back home grieving for him. But I told him I wanted to spend whatever time there was, with him. I was resolute. We married and I have no regrets. None. So, phone William."

"Hi! Anyone here?" Linda asks as she stands in the kitchen doorway, letting the cold, crisp December air chase out some of the warm coziness which had been wrapped around our ankles. Kelly shakes and walks towards the kitchen as I follow.

"Come in, Linda, and close that door. It must be cold out there."

"Yeah, it's dropped. The horses are good, though."

"Thanks, Linda."

"I have stuff I need to tell you."

"Okay. Would you like some tea or hot chocolate?"

"No, thanks. I've got to get going. Neal said to let you know he wants your okay to start the horses early next year. He wants them to get some early training before going to the track. I told him they're doing real well now. I was talking to him to make sure he'd take me back. He's going to."

"That's great. But I can't even imagine him not taking you back."

"I like working for him, so it's good. He wants me to help with the early training, too. He didn't go to Florida. He's rented some space at a neat barn that has a large arena. I think it'll be good."

"That sounds like a great idea. I'll talk to him soon."

"The other thing is I wondered if you'd mind if I took a couple of days off over Christmas. Austin's mother has invited me and my mother to go to her place in Sudbury for Christmas. Austin will drive us up there. But I know that it'll be difficult for you."

"I'll miss you a lot, but I don't have any big plans over Christmas. My mother will be here, and we'll be having a quiet, simple holiday. I can manage. Have a wonderful time. You'll need more than a couple of days. Take whatever you need."

"Thanks. I love working here, so I hope I can come back till they go for their training."

"Of course. Have a good evening. See you tomorrow."

"Yeah. Austin is taking me out for supper."

"Have a great time."

Linda smiles as she leaves. I've never seen her look so happy and so full of energy. A sudden pang of envy stabs inside me somewhere. But I shake it off, just like Kelly would shake off anything that was bothering her. Cooper comes bounding out of the family room and collides with me. He's chasing a small moth with no regard for anything in his path. My mother laughs, making me smile.

"I forgot to tell you what the Oncologist said on Monday," my mother says as I sit down.

"I didn't know you had an appointment."

"The Doctor at the hospital got it arranged. I was anxious, not knowing what kind of cancer it was. I had more tests, and the Oncologist wanted to see me. And I suppose I forgot because I thought I'd be leaving. But it's now come back to mind because I'm here for Christmas. The oncologist said that the cancer I've got is not aggressive and that I don't have to be alarmed if I don't get treatment right away. I think she stressed this because she's heard about the appalling state of the NHS and the long waits."

"That's good news."

"The other thing is not good. I have all these bills for the hospital stay, medicines and then this oncologist, so I called the insurance company that I've my travel health insurance with, and they said none of it's covered because it's a pre-existing condition. They asked lots of questions and I stupidly admitted that I've had headaches for some time. Oh dear. I suppose I'll have to sell the house now. But maybe that'll be a good thing."

"Don't worry about it. I'll work something out."

"Perhaps William could look at the insurance policy?"

"I'm not calling him."

"Oh, dear." My mother shuts her eyes and rests her head back on the recliner, as if our conversation has worn her out. Cooper jumps up onto her lap and curls up. Kelly looks up at me.

"Don't you start, Kelly. I'm not calling him."

A loud knock on the kitchen door makes Kelly bark and she rushes towards it. I'm surprised to see Joanna and Ewert holding hands on the doorstep, as if they're teenagers on a first date. Their faces are flushed with the cold. They must have walked here.

"Come in. It's good to see you both on your feet." The last time I saw Joanna, she was being whisked away in an ambulance, and the last time I saw Ewert, he was being taken away by the police. "I'll make some hot chocolate." It's a good job I bought a family-sized box.

"Meg, we want to tell you right off, that we're not here to ask for money," Joanna says. They both smile.

"I like the new clean-shaven look, Ewert," I say.

"Thanks. It's symbolic of a fresh start. We wanted you to know that we're getting things back on track."

"Yes. We've got a meeting with a debt counselor tomorrow," Joanna says. They're still holding hands and looking at each other, rather than looking at me.

"And we've talked to the landlord." Ewert says. "I regret to advise you we're going to be your neighbours for quite a while longer. We've struck a deal with him that, in exchange for painting and repairing the place, we can live there rent-free for three months."

"He's going to pay for the paint and other repair supplies," Joanna says.

"And we can dismantle the barn and sell the beams and boards." Ewert says.

"And I'm registered with the racetrack and casino." Joanna says. "I can't gamble at either of them. Ewert's helping me to work through this gambling addiction thing. I don't think I'm at risk any more, but I'm scared I could go back to it. I'm not going anywhere without him, and I'm not going on-line without his supervision."

"Wow, sounds like you're really serious about getting things turned around, and very quickly," I say, as I place three mugs of hot chocolate on the table and take the fourth one into the family room. I just hope Cooper doesn't help himself to my mother's before she wakes up.

"And Ewert is helping Austin with his new program for PTSD."

"I'm glad," I say, as I sit down opposite them.

"And we're so lucky," Ewert says, as he looks at Joanna. They both smile. "Austin has asked us to spend Christmas at his mother's in Sudbury, and he's even going to drive us there."

"I think Linda and her mother are going too," Joanna says. "I hope we can develop a friendship with both Linda and Austin."

"It'll be so nice to spend Christmas there. Austin knows we can't contribute anything. But next Christmas we hope to make it up to everybody."

"Meg, you might already know, but the lawyer told us that Dominic won't be showing his face because he's a wanted man with several charges against him. We feel reassured." Ewert gazes into Joanna's eyes with an adoring look, reminding me of the way Kelly looks up at William.

21

Murray

I'm glad when Ewert and Joanna finally leave. It's as if I've been watching a couple of love-birds cooing, courting each other. I'm pleased for them and relieved, but they make me feel awkward and alone, sort of isolated. I sit down in the family room, stroking Kelly's head, contemplating Christmas. The last thing I would have wanted a year ago was for my mother to be with me, but this year is different. I don't want to be alone, although I was on my own that Christmas and was fine. I enjoyed walks in the fields, time in the barn grooming the horses, and sitting with Kelly in the family room reading. Murray dropped in. And that thought reminds me I should ask him to come for Christmas Day. I'm sure he was feeling lonely last year, even though he was in the Lighthouse Rehabilitation Centre.

Before I have time to rethink, I send him a text message and invite him. I will remember to check with him more often. He has no other family, is a recovering alcoholic and must still be reeling from having had a stroke.

As I'm about to put my mobile down, he texts back that he'd love to come and that he'll bring the turkey. I'll have to plan a menu and get some groceries, not my forte. And there are many other things I need to accomplish before then.

The most important ones are to work out my finances so that I can pay all the unanticipated expenses, and to do my best to ensure that Frank's murderer is caught and charged.

As far as my finances, I'll have to get a loan. And to help me repay it, I'm going to have to eat my pride, such as it is, and call the Interim President of the Humane Society to see if there is any interest in the Board rehiring me. I loved my animal welfare work and, although it could be frustrating and challenging, I felt we were making a difference. I search the Humane Society's website, confirm that they still have an Acting Executive Director, and send a brief message to the Interim President, Marcia Callwich, to ask if she'll talk with me.

My mother wakes up and I can't think of what to get for supper. I have virtually nothing edible in the house except for dog food and cat food. Since she's not up to going out, I must go out and pick something up. I tell her I'll lock the doors and Kelly will stay with her, and that I won't be long.

The cold air makes my nose tingle and my eyes water. The seat in my truck saps any residual warmth I had right out of my body. I should have worn my heaviest coat. The engine protests a little when I turn on the ignition. I sense reluctance, but it roars into life as if it knows it has to make an extra effort. Kelly is usually with me, and a sense of aloneness surrounds me, just like the darkness enveloping the truck.

William is never far out of my thoughts. I've grown far more attached to him than I've allowed myself to contemplate. My mind wanders to Joanna and Ewert, and Linda and Austin. I startle myself as warm tears run down my cold cheeks. I try to step back and think about what's really upsetting me. Is it that I've lost both Frank and Chuck, or is it that I've lost William, or some or all of the above?

The answer comes in choking sobs as I think of William and how much he means to me. And I'm letting him walk away. My mother is right: I need to call him. I need to find out why he said what he did. I'm owed an explanation for his sudden coolness and his pulling away.

I can't take the time to phone, so I text him as soon as I'm parked by the restaurant, and ask him if he can come to the farm since I have a couple of legal matters of some import that I need his help with.

I play it safe with the food. I get several servings each of broccoli soup and cauliflower soup, and two large containers of salads. I also buy some of their fresh rolls and they give me some butter pats, which is just as well since I can't remember if I have any butter or margarine. They put it all in a cardboard box which I place carefully on the floor in front of the passenger seat. Just as I step into the truck, my phone dings, making my fingers tremble as I take them out of my gloves so I can check the message.

"Can come this evening. Is 7 OK?"

"Great. Tx," is my response. I'm buoyed up because he's coming so promptly. Instead of crying on the way home, I catch myself singing along with the radio. I shut it off. He's coming to meet me on legal matters, nothing more. I force myself to be more sensible and to get things into perspective.

My mother is up and about and has laid the table, found napkins, made some tea and is wiping the countertop when I come through the door oozing cold air.

"I hope this is alright with you," she says. "I thought you might bring something hot, and it'd get cold."

"That's great. I won't have to reheat the soup."

"By the way, William's coming."

"How do you know?"

"I called him."

"You did what? How did you know his number?"

"By chance I noticed his business card on the fridge with his mobile number."

"You shouldn't have interfered, even if you are my mother."

"I know, but life is too short."

"What did you say?"

"I said you're potty about him and that you can't live without him and that he should get himself here presto." She smiles at me.

"What did you really say?"

"I asked him if he would go over my insurance policy, that I was very worried because you might be landed with most of the bills, and I didn't think it was fair. He said he could come this evening, but I said that we needed time to eat supper first. He asked if 7 would be okay and I said it would be great."

My elated reaction to his coming this evening is dampened by the revelation that he believes he's coming to help my mother review her insurance policy. He must have thought my text was odd, since he'd already agreed to come. We eat in near silence until the landline phone rings, making my mother jump and Cooper leap off her lap.

"Hello. Annabella here."

"Thanks for calling."

"That is fine. I want to talk to you as well."

"It must be very late wherever you are."

"I am in Florence and yes, it is late, but I am a night person. You say that you know who killed Frank. I know too. I hope we agree on who it is."

"I think we will."

"Simeon returned to me, but I told him to leave. I didn't want him to tell me what he did. I did not want to believe that my assistant, Simeon, could be a murderer. It is too terrible. I tried to drown my suspicions in drink. And then you said someone else was there. Someone in a big hat. That was a relief, but the awful thing is that the hat made me think of Tammy."

"That shook Tammy up."

"I know. I wanted so much for Simeon to be innocent. I feel bad about accusing Tammy. When I talked to her again, I believed her. I was puzzled by the big hat person you told me about, but I kept coming back to Simeon."

"I think you're right."

"I know he was in love with me. But it was not a selfless love. It was a controlling love, a jealous love. And he was very, very angry with Frank for letting me down, even though Frank was my lover. He saw how upset I was and knew that I needed the money to continue in my career."

"Whose idea was it to blackmail Frank?"

"I was so angry with Frank that I came up with the idea, and told Simeon to confront Frank. But it did not work and worse, Frank died because of it."

"You told me Simeon delivered some personal items which Frank had left behind."

"I had to think up a reason for his visit. I did not want to tell you of the blackmail plan."

"I see."

"And I sent him back! What a stupid fool I have been. And when he returned to me the second time, I could tell that something awful had happened. It was on his face and it hung in the air. I did not want him near me. I told him to go. He went to see you?"

"To think I harboured Frank's killer under his own roof. I can't forgive myself for being taken in by Simeon for so long. He was an obvious suspect from the beginning."

"Perhaps. But there were red herrings, as I think you call them. Things like the big hat, and Frank's anger with some man called

Dominic, which Tammy told me about, and other visitors like Chuck, and his fingerprints on the gun, and Frank's brother. Tammy told me they all had arguments with Frank."

"Yes, they did. Thanks for helping me feel better about being so slow to figure it out."

"And I have good news."

"Wonderful. What?"

"I have a beautiful man in my life. He is kind and has a generous spirit. He is a tenor. We are both here in Florence and will spend Christmas here together. And, he has helped me to get an audition. I am falling in love. It feels magnificent."

"Oh, Annabella, that's such splendid news. I wish you happiness and success."

"Thank you. I hope you have a happy Christmas. I hope you can enjoy some time with family and friends."

"Thank you."

"I'll make a fresh pot of tea," my mother says. "I can tell you're tired."

"I do feel shattered." I'm annoyed that I was so easily duped by Simeon into believing that he couldn't possibly be the killer. It was smart of him to come running here, asking for help. But he must truly love Annabella because he didn't try to frame her. In fact, he dug up her rock-solid alibi. But Annabella pointed out that his love was a controlling love, it wasn't a selfless, caring, giving love.

I'm glad that Annabella has a new man, but thinking about love sends me into a funk again.

"Here's a fresh cup." My mother prefers cups and saucers, and has found some at the back of one of the many cupboards. She must have a nose for them.

"Thank you."

"And there's time to change before William comes." She doesn't look at me, but watches Cooper, who's rolling around on the floor just for the hell of it. I glance down at what I'm wearing. She's right. I should change.

The unexpected and loud knock at the door causes me to nudge the cup, and so it now sits in a pool of tea caught by the saucer. My mother opens the door. It's not William arriving early. It's Murray, and my mother introduces herself and hands him a cup of tea as he sits down, his sheepskin coat still on.

"I had to come and see how you're doing," he says as he wrestles out of his coat and lets it fold over the back of the chair. "I'm looking forward to coming for Christmas, by the way. Thanks for the invite."

"You're welcome. You'll be good company for us." I sit up. I almost feel as if there should be a drum-roll. "I have good news. We know who murdered Frank and think we know why."

"Wow, that is good news. Someone I know?"

"Annabella's assistant, Simeon."

"Okay. Why?"

"He was doing it for Annabella. He was angry with Frank for hurting Annabella so badly. She was devastated that she lost Frank both as a lover and a sponsor."

"Seems a drastic reaction."

"Simeon, in his own way, loved Annabella. She told me that his love was a jealous, controlling love, not a selfless love. Annabella made a big mistake when she launched a plan to blackmail Frank, using Simeon as the messenger. I think Simeon's emotions got the better of him when he confronted Frank. He said that Frank laughed in his face and told him he was scum and that he should get the hell out, amongst other things."

"Annabella would have needed some better threat than revealing that he was still alive, because so many people knew that he'd faked his death."

"You're right. And they had nothing better. Simeon said that Frank made some crack about putting up a billboard with the words

'Frank is alive', so Simeon must have felt humiliated and probably grew even more angry. I think he killed Frank because he lost his temper, and because he saw no other way of avenging what Frank had done to Annabella. And don't forget, Frank's sudden desertion of Annabella affected Simeon. His life was wrapped up in Annabella's success as an opera singer and she needed Frank's sponsorship."

"I still think it's a pretty drastic response."

"It was. But my guess is that Simeon believed his action would convey to Annabella how much he loved her. In his mind, he killed Frank for Annabella. He hoped Annabella would feel eternally indebted to him and that this would develop into love for him. He must have been devastated when she kicked him out. Why else would he have killed Frank but to gain Annabella's love?"

"Have you talked to Annabella?"

"Yes. She believes Simeon is the killer. We agree."

"What weapon did he use?"

"The gun found in the ditch, with Chuck's fingerprints on, is now believed to be the murder weapon. But what killer, with any sense at all, would leave fingerprints? I'm convinced that Simeon used gloves and left the gun beside Frank's body, believing it couldn't be traced back to him. He'd feel safe back in Europe."

"Where's Simeon now? Have you talked to the police?"

"I don't know and I will."

"I have good news too." Murray finishes his tea and puts the cup on the table, rather than on the saucer. I can sense my mother's mild annoyance as she picks them both up and puts them in the dishwasher.

"Thank you," Murray says. "That was nice tea. Yes, I have good news. Well, I hope it will be, but it's a touchy subject. It's about Frank's money."

"Oh."

"As you know, there was no mention in Frank's will of any additional money, but we know he has money off-shore somewhere, and we believe it's a lot of money, likely millions."

"You're determined to track his money down."

"Yes, I am. You would be the beneficiary, Meg, and I think you deserve his money. You were his wife when he died."

"But he kept his side of our bargain."

"Anyway, I've done some digging and thinking, and I thought of the lawyer our parents used. In a nutshell, turns out he has a key to a security deposit box in Frank's name which he thought we knew about. I don't know who's to blame, but no point going there. I have an appointment at the bank tomorrow to open the box. Do you want to come?"

"No thanks."

"I hope I find what I'm looking for, because I don't know where else to look. I would really like to get this sorted in the early new year. As Executor of Frank's will, I should be able to figure it out. I might ask William to help if I need to. How is he, by the way?"

"He's due any minute now. In fact, he's late." The clock shows that it's 7.15pm and I feel a pang of unease. He's usually on time. I put my hands on my thighs and realize that I haven't changed my outfit yet.

"My goodness me, you're going to be rich," my mother says, as if what Murray said has only just sunk in. She sits down at the kitchen table, looking as if she's going to faint. The colour, such as it was, has left her cheeks. I think of brandy, but check myself. It's not fair to have alcohol around Murray. I would hate to contribute towards Murray's return to alcoholism after all that he's been through. I check the pot of tea, find there's enough for a cup, and add lots of sugar and some milk, and encourage my mother to drink it.

"I don't know how this will work out," Murray says, "but I hope Meg will get enough to make up for her unemployment status." He looks at me and smiles.

The funny thing is, all I can think about is William, and wonder if he's alright.

I look at my mother.

"I'm fine. It's too much excitement, that's all," my mother says as she picks Cooper up. They've become the best of pals.

"Okay. Do you want to sit in the family room, in the recliner?"

"No, I want to be in the centre of the action." A rare smile lights up her eyes. Even though I can see her uneven, stained teeth, her smile warms my heart.

Kelly moves towards the door and whines. Usually, she just stands by the door and doesn't make a noise when she asks to go out. But I can't remember the last time we went outside. Perhaps it's been a while, and she's desperate. I open the door to let her out, but she looks up at me. I know what that means. She wants me to go out with her.

"Sorry, have to go out with Kelly. Be back in a few minutes," I say, as I grab my warm jacket, boots and gloves. Rather than ambling towards the barn, she dashes around the house. As I reach the side of the house, I can see her jumping up and down at the side of a car, which appears to have two people in it. When I get closer, I see it's William's car, and he's on his mobile phone, with a woman sitting next to him. William sees me and gives me a half-wave and mouths something which I don't understand. I tell Kelly to come with me and decide we should check on the horses. I need to overcome my disappointment that he's not alone, and the best way is for me to refocus with a visit to the horses' world.

All four horses are grinding their teeth as they munch on their hay with loud crunches. They raise their heads for only a second when I put the lights on. The warmer, stiller air feels good. Kelly sniffs around the floor of the aisle, looking for grain that the horses drop as they hang their heads over the half-doors while eating, to see what's happening. They can be agitated at feed time, but they look the picture of calmness now. And the results of Linda's work are clear to see. Their coats gleam and their eyes sparkle with their regained health. Their hooves are clean, their manes and tails combed, and their halters are oiled. While I've always taken good care of them, I have to admit that they've never been this well attended to during the winter. There's no sign of the trauma they suffered at Joanna and Ewert's place, or of the nasty virus they both suffered with. Even the barn cats look fatter.

I feel better and tell myself at least William is here. I need to get into the house, brew some fresh tea and make him and his woman-friend feel welcome. Although, I can't imagine what would possess him to bring a woman here.

I switch off the lights, say goodnight to the horses, and Kelly and I make our way back to the house.

22

Departures

"William and a friend are out in his car at the front of the house. I think they'll be in soon," I say, as I hang up my jacket by the door. And sure enough, I hear them approaching outside and let them in.

"Hi, William. Thank you for coming." I hope I sound relaxed and welcoming. "You know Murray and my mother."

"Yes, of course."

"You can call me Miriam," my mother says, surprising me. "I know people here use first names and I don't like my surname. I never have."

"Okay, Miriam, I'd like you to meet Leya, Detective Leya Channing," William says. "And this is Meg Sheppard and Murray Sheppard, Leya."

The Detective is in civilian clothes, but her pant suit fits her tall frame perfectly. She has her blond hair tied back into a knot, and her black shoes shine. She stands almost at attention and gives us only a faint smile as she shakes each of our hands with a firm grip. Cooper takes an instant liking to her, rubbing against her navy pants, no doubt depositing a generous gift of tabby hair in the process. Before I can do anything about it, my mother picks the cat up.

"Isn't Cooper wonderful?" She says, looking at William.

"He sure is," William says.

"Please sit down," I say. "I'll get another chair from the office."

Murray leaps into action and beats me to it. My mother puts the kettle on and says she'll make tea. William says he's brought some chilled bottles of water which he takes out of a tote bag and distributes on the table, and also some oatmeal raisin cookies, which Kelly is keenly interested in.

William apologizes for not letting me know he was bringing Leya. He says that the opportunity arose just an hour beforehand, so he took a chance that I would be okay with it. He explains that Detective Leya Channing is a dedicated policewoman with the RCMP and became a friend because of a case they were each involved with several years ago.

Of course, I say I'm fine with her being here, but inside I'm reserving judgment.

"Thanks, Meg. I'm grateful for Leya being willing to come here this evening. She's off-duty as of 6pm but, when I told her I'd be meeting with you, Meg, the widow of the murder victim, Francis Sheppard, she agreed it would be within protocol to come and give you an update in person."

"I think that you and Detective Channing should start," I say. "And then we'll share our information and see where we're at." I thank my mother for the tea which she's served in mugs, perhaps for the first time in her life. I suppose she couldn't find enough clean cups and saucers. And she's even put the milk in a jug and put it on the table, along with the sugar, rather than automatically assuming that everyone takes it. I'm noticing all these details when I should be focussed on William and Leya. I'm apprehensive about what they're going to say.

"I'm sorry for your loss, Meg." Leya looks into my face with such sincerity that I feel a wince inside. She must know that this is the second time that Frank has "died", and must guess that my grief is not raw and heart-wrenching. But perhaps it should be.

"Thank you," is all I can say, and all I should say, I think.

"While I can't share anything with you that could jeopardize the case, I am at liberty to update you on some findings of fact." She explains that her unit has been given authorization by Foreign Affairs to act as a liaison with Kentucky State Police, and to ensure that the applicable Canadian authorities co-operate in the investigation. She tells us that Foreign Affairs is in a process of renewal, and is working to improve its communication and support to foreign investigative authorities in murder cases on behalf of bereaved Canadian families, such as the Sheppards. Hence her role as liaison. She looks at Murray.

"I'm pleased to hear that," Murray says. He looks at me. "I didn't tell you, because I thought it wouldn't do any good, but I contacted Foreign Affairs and asked them if there was anything they could do to help with the investigation into Frank's murder. I was concerned about the apparent lack of action."

"That was a good move, Murray," I say. It also makes it absolutely clear to me he had nothing to do with Frank's murder, so why didn't he tell me before? And I recall, with shame, that I planned to contact Foreign Affairs some time ago, and forgot.

"Here are the facts I can share," Leya says. "Mr Sheppard was found, fatally shot, in the stables located on a property called Louisa's Acres in the State of Kentucky. A gun was recovered from a ditch not far from this location. It has been determined that this gun was the murder weapon. Fingerprints were found on the gun which matched those of Mr. Charles Murphy. Notwithstanding this, the Kentucky State Police investigated the ownership of the gun and, after extensive work, they found evidence that it was purchased at a local sports-store the day of the murder. The State Police interviewed the owner of the sports-store and he was able to provide a description sufficient for a facial composite to be issued."

"Can we see a copy?" My interest is piqued.

"Of course. The Kentucky State Police is asking for our co-operation in locating this individual. But I'll finish what I have to say first, if that's okay."

"That's fine." I take a cookie.

"Kentucky State Police have advised that Forensics determined, based on the autopsy findings and other evidence collected at the murder scene, the trajectory of the bullet which killed Mr. Sheppard. This trajectory leads investigators to believe that the killer is small in stature. And it is useful to note that this is consistent with the description given by the sports-store owner."

"We can tell you who we believe the person is," I say. "Let's look at the picture after we've shared our conclusions."

"Go ahead." Leya picks up her mug of tea. I have a feeling that she prefers coffee, and probably likes it strong.

"I assume everyone is familiar with all the names I'll be mentioning," I say. "We have been told that Frank, my husband, was murdered between 3 and 5pm. Chuck, or Charles, had an argument in the aisle with Frank at about 3pm, which was witnessed by Murray. At approximately 4pm, one of the barn workers saw someone matching Simeon's description arrive, carrying a small backpack. The next visitor is Joanna, Ewert's wife, who arrives at about 5pm. She discovers Frank's body on the floor of the barn, before Chuck arrives at about 6pm. Chuck wouldn't have returned if he'd already killed Frank. He picks up the gun and tosses it into the ditch. Murray isn't a suspect, so that leaves Simeon. No-one saw him leave. No-one knows what he was carrying in his backpack. Simeon Boulet is therefore the prime suspect."

"What would the motive have been?" Leya asks as she enters Simeon's name.

I explain, as succinctly as I can, Simeon's passionate, controlling and obsessive love for, and reliance on, Annabella; his determination to avenge Annabella's devastation on Frank leaving her as a lover and especially as a sponsor; his attempt to blackmail Frank (on behalf of Annabella) and Frank's reaction; and his attempt to confuse me in my efforts to find out the truth. And then I describe him in as much detail as I can, including his stature, his complexion and his accent. Leya shows me the facial composite on the tablet she pulls from her bag. It's a pretty good likeness.

"Okay. The Kentucky State Police Service is looking for him and we're looking for him, but from what you say, he's likely to be in Europe."

"He returned to Annabella, but she kicked him out. She was in London then, but she's now in Florence. I've no clue what he would do, or where he would go."

"I expect my bosses will connect with Interpol. This has been useful, thank you."

Leya stands and shakes each of our hands again, and leaves a few of her business cards on the table. William asks if he can return, after he's taken Leya back to her vehicle, to review my mother's insurance policy, since he'd promised to do that. As the two of them walk outside, some snowflakes flutter into the kitchen, melting as they float down, disappointing Cooper, who was preparing to catch them.

"Thanks, Murray, for contacting Foreign Affairs," I say.

"When I contacted them, I was concerned that the police in the States might not assign a priority to solving Frank's murder. All their attention seemed to be on the school shooting. I thought it might help if the Canadian Government picked up the phone. I didn't know that Detective Channing's involved. I think that's good."

"We've done all that we can. Interpol will have to do the rest. Annabella probably has some photographs of Simeon, and she might know where his family lives. Sometimes people go back to their families when they're in trouble. You never know."

"On another subject," Murray says, "I got to open the security box today, and I found documents relating to an account held in the Cayman Islands in Frank's name. I need to follow up. I'll let you know what I find out."

Frank's money is the last thing I want to think about right now.

After he's left, the house seems quiet and cold. My mother looks pale and tired.

I get a text from William saying something has come up and could he come tomorrow evening instead, at about the same time. I imagine him and Leya having a drink in a pub somewhere, or a meal together.

"What's the matter, Meg? You look like you've seen a ghost."

"I'm fine. I'm just tired. William is going to come tomorrow evening. He says something has come up."

"Ah. Oh dear." My mother gets up from her chair. "Cooper and I are going to rest in the recliner, if that's okay?"

"Of course. I'll clear up."

* * *

Sleep eluded me for most of the night. All I could think about was William and Leya and what a fool I've been. And in my most fitful moments, Frank's face and then Chuck's face would loom in my mind's eye. They each seemed to accuse me of not loving them. And perhaps I didn't. But I cared. From Frank's perspective, our marriage had been one of convenience for both of us. And I'm grateful. I know that I'm lucky to live on this farm and to have animals around me, and it's all thanks to Frank. It's the lifestyle I'd always dreamed of having. I thought I loved Chuck at first, but I discovered I didn't know him as well as I thought I did. He became more withdrawn, and was often away. We seemed to drift apart, rather than grow closer together. And I didn't do anything about it, and I should have.

But the night could have been worse. With my mother sleeping in my house for the first time, I thought I'd have flashbacks of my life in England. I have those terrible nightmares infrequently now, but it doesn't take much to trigger their reappearance. And her presence brings back some unbearably painful memories. But I was spared the horrific dreams.

It's time to get up at last. So, I draw the drapes and look out on fairyland. There must be about six inches of fresh, powdery snow, softening the landscape. The sun is peeping over the horizon, and is casting a pinkish, shimmering glow. The horses will love being outside with the cushiony footing, the still air and the clear sky.

Linda is already working in the barn, so Kelly and I take her a mug of coffee and an oatmeal raisin cookie. Then I venture into the large field. I feel as if I've been cooped up indoors too much recently. I miss being outside. But Kelly isn't enthusiastic. The snow is clinging to the hairs in between the pads of her paws, and forming into balls of ice, which must pull her skin. She stops and chews away at the ice and then looks up at me as if she's searching for sympathy.

"You're supposed to be a tough farm dog, Kelly." But I relent, and we turn for home. At least we got a little fresh air.

My mother is in the kitchen when we return, even though it's not yet eight o'clock.

"Good morning. You look better," I say, as I hang up my jacket.

"I slept well. That's a comfortable bed, and the room is nice and warm. I've made a bit of breakfast. I don't know what you have usually." She places some scrambled eggs on some toast and hands the plate to me. William must have bought eggs.

"Are you having some?" I ask.

"I'll have a little. What about William? What are you going to do?"

"He's coming this evening, remember?"

I'm saved by the phone. It's Neal, the trainer. He asks how the horses are doing and we chat about plans for the next racing season and confirm that they will start their training early.

"I thought you'd be really excited today. I couldn't wait to call," Neal says.

"What do you mean?"

"Haven't you heard?"

"Heard what? Neal, just tell me!"

"They've arrested Dominic Marcel."

"That's fantastic. Where was he?"

"They caught him trying to fly out of the US."

"I thought he'd left for faraway places a long time ago, but perhaps he laid low for a while, thinking he'd stand a better chance of getting out."

"No telling. I just wanted to thank you and your friend William for what you did. And a bonus is that they're doing a full review of the illegal gambling scene including race-fixing, the whole shooting match. It'll be good for racing."

"Does Juan's wife know?"

"I'll make sure that she does, but I think the news is going to spread like lightening."

"I'll make sure Linda knows, and William. I just hope they keep Ferris safe in the witness protection program."

"Yeah, I hope so."

"It's because of him that Dominic was on their radar."

"Yeah. But he's going to be in trouble because he gave the poisoned coffee to Juan and knew it was poisoned. Tell Linda I say hi, and I'm looking forward to working with her soon at the barn and arena, where I've rented stalls."

"Will do."

My mother has her head lying on her crossed arms on the table.

"Aren't you feeling well?" I ask.

"Not too good. Bit under the weather." Her voice is muffled. She lifts her head up. Her eyes are red and her nose is running. She grabs a tissue and blows her nose. "Actually, I'm scared."

"What do you want to do? Do you want to go home?"

"No."

I've been admiring her strength and courage and was surprised that she so readily accepted my invitation to stay for Christmas. I would want to have a brain tumour treated immediately, despite the specialist advising that it's not an aggressive cancer. I wouldn't want to delay. If it was me, I'd have been on a plane home by now.

"You still want to wait until after Christmas?"

"I don't want to go home."

"Oh." I don't know what cancer treatment would cost here, without insurance. We're in ignorant bliss, most of the time, regarding the true costs of our health care. I now wish I'd paid attention to what Murray said about Frank's money, but I doubt that I'm going to see any of it for quite a while longer, if at all. "Okay. Perhaps we can arrange for treatment here, but I'm not sure how long you'll be permitted to stay. I'll have to find out. I've no idea what the laws are about foreign visitors. Perhaps I could sponsor you."

"No. No." She stands up and straightens her brown woollen cardigan. "I've started packing my bags. I have a flight tomorrow. I've made up my mind. I'm going to move into the retirement place down the road and sell the house, which I hate. You can get meals and cleaning and laundry and other services in that place. And then I can get my treatment through the NHS. That's what I'm doing, and don't argue."

"If you're certain that's what you want: you're sure you don't want to stay for Christmas?"

"I'd love to. I really would love to, but I'm too scared. I've been trying to block it all out, but the headaches and funny feelings I get remind me, and they frighten me. I know they said it isn't aggressive but I want to get going on treatment. I'm hoping to have a few happy years without Stan, living my life, doing things I want to do, making friends. And I want to visit you, Kelly and Cooper when I'm better." She looks at me, holding the tissue to her nose, tears running down her flushed cheeks.

"You'll always be welcome."

"You go after that William before it's too late."

"What would you like to do today?"

"I'd like to sit in the family room, with Cooper on my lap, drinking tea." She looks down at Cooper, who's rubbing against her legs. "He's such a gentle, friendly cat. I didn't know cats are such super company. I think I can have a cat in the retirement place."

"That would be a great idea. I'll make the tea while you and Cooper get comfortable."

My hands shake as I fill the kettle. I feel stupid and insensitive that I didn't realize what must have been going on inside her: the torment and anguish. Although I'm a bit shaken that she's decided to go home and has already booked a flight, I'm relieved that she'll be starting treatment. I'll spend the rest of the day focussing on our time together.

* * *

My mother ate a small lunch. She wanted only a little soup, managing about a quarter of a cup. I think she's stressed about the flight. She's now resting in the recliner in the family room, with Cooper curled up on her lap. The cat's going to miss her, and Kelly and I will too. I never dreamt that I would ever feel that way about my mother.

I sit at the kitchen table, gazing out of the window, watching the snow melting and the icicles forming. Kelly looks at me with her big brown eyes. I know she wants me to take her out, but I don't want to leave the house. I text Linda and ask her if she could take the dog round the paddock. When Linda comes into the kitchen, I give her the good news about Dominic's arrest. Her face lights up with a bright smile, making her rosy, shiny cheeks look even chubbier. I remember how upset she was when she and Neal told me about Juan.

"Linda, you must take some credit for this, because you told me you and Neal wanted to find out the truth. And you convinced me to help. Nothing would have been done otherwise. They were treating it as an accident, remember?"

"Yeah. I remember. I hope that guy Dominic goes to jail for a long time."

"Let's hope so. And let's hope that they do a better job of preventing illegal gambling and race-fixing and so on."

"Yeah."

As Linda and Kelly leave for their short walk, Murray phones me on my mobile.

"What's up?" I ask.

"I hope you won't mind, but I won't be coming for Christmas after all."

"Oh. Are you off to some exotic place?" I try to sound nonchalant.

"Exotic might not be the right word. A couple of friends I met at the Lighthouse have booked a flat in London, through Airbnb, and asked me if I'd like to go. Frank and I were born in London, as you know, and we have cousins in England. I'm pretty excited. But I'm sorry to let you down."

"Don't be silly. It sounds like a great idea. When do you leave?"

"In four days' time. We'll be away for three weeks."

"Have a wonderful time. See you in the new year."

23

The Fall

Kelly is back from her short walk and lying under the kitchen table. My mother and Cooper are both fast asleep. The house is so quiet that the ticking of the clock, which I usually don't notice, seems intrusively loud.

It'll be just me, Kelly and Cooper for Christmas, and Eagle, Bullet, Rose and Speed, of course, and the barn cats. The animals will be good company, and looking after them all will keep me occupied. But.

I set up the laptop and start work on some of the bookkeeping, hoping that it'll keep my mind off the fact that there will be no-one around soon.

My mother wakes up after two hours' sleep. Whenever I checked, Cooper was in the same position. They both stretch as they wander into the kitchen. It's going to be hard to see them part company tomorrow. I hear the kettle buzzing and realize my head's throbbing, probably from working on my finances while being frequently distracted by thoughts of William, as well as of my mother and the future of the farm.

Murray called an hour ago to let me know that what he thought was going to be pretty straightforward won't be the case after all. I might not see any of Frank's money for a long time since there are strict bank secrecy laws in the Cayman Islands: they demand documentation, including death and marriage certificates and so on. This was just as I was trying to work out a new budget which reflects the loss of my work income. I've used up all of my contingency on paying security guards, Linda's salary, my mother's bills, legal bills, and other unanticipated expenses.

And, almost at the same time as Murray's phone call, I received an email response from the Interim President of the Humane Society saying that she'd love me to consider a position on the Board (which I'm not interested in). So, they won't consider re-hiring me in the paid position of Executive Director. Perhaps that's just as well. I think it would be hard to return.

Despite all these challenges, I think my revised draft budget is workable, as long as no more unusual costs occur. I plan to cash in my savings account and arrange a line of credit to help with cash flow. I'll have large bills to pay as soon as the horses go back in training and I'm not counting on any revenue from them until early summer. I get a sudden lump in my throat as I remember how thankful I am to Frank for giving me the incredible opportunity to continue in this lifestyle, even though he's gone. I don't think he'd bargained on my keeping his racehorses, but I don't have the heart to let them go. Without their expenses, my budget would be a very different kettle of fish.

I might offer to help Neal at the track for a small reduction in costs. That would help financially and would probably do me a lot of good.

I accept the mug of tea from my mother.

"No cup and saucer, then?" I smile at her as she sits down opposite me.

"I think I've been converted to mugs. I'll soon fit right in. But I need to get a new wardrobe, a new hairstyle and a new handbag."

"I hope you'll be able to do all those things when you get back."

"I might give it a whirl. If I sell the house and rent at the retirement place, then I'll have some spending money, which would be nice. When's William coming?"

"I haven't heard. What about supper? Is there something you'd like? I can pick it up."

"I do seem to have a bit of an appetite."

"In other words, you're starving."

"I'm hungry, but I'd just like cheese on toast. That's what I fancy."

"Okay. I might be able to rustle that up."

"I'll do it. I'd like to."

"That's nice. Thanks. I've finished what I wanted to do. I'd like to see Linda in the barn before she goes."

I nearly fall over as I step onto a layer of shiny ice which has encrusted my doorstep and everything else all around. It's a sudden change in landscape from the fresh powdery snow of the morning, and not welcome. There are no lights on in the barn. I check my phone and sure enough there's a text from Linda saying she's leaving because the freezing rain is worsening and she doesn't want to sleep with the horses, much as she loves them. I smile. I can imagine her bedded down in one of the stalls. But, as I slip and slide over to the paddock, encouraging Kelly to stretch her legs a bit, I feel the cold, damp air sink inside me. I won't see William tonight. He won't venture out in this. I'm surprised that he hasn't let us know he's not coming by now since he's always professional and courteous. And my mother is leaving tomorrow, so he won't get a chance to go over the insurance policy for her, as he said he would.

Kelly looks miserable. The icy rain is relentless and her beautiful, silky coat is already looking bedraggled. Water is running down her nose and she has her ears pinned to her head and her tail between her legs.

"Okay, Kelly. We're going back to the house." She picks her way to the kitchen door and waits for me as I skate my way over to her.

"Oh, my goodness me," my mother says as we bring in cold, damp air and lots of drips into the kitchen. My jacket is not as waterproof as it claims. Kelly and I need to dry off. I rub her down with an old towel, making her look even more unkempt, and go upstairs to find a dry sweater for myself.

I hear the landline phone ringing, and my mother answers it.

"Meg! Can you pick up the phone?" She sounds agitated and I only just catch what she says.

"Yep. I'll get it."

"Is that Meg Sheppard?" asks a woman whose voice I can't quite place.

"Yes."

"I'm Ramona, William Porter's Assistant, and he asked me to connect with you because he's not able to come this evening."

"Because of the weather." Why couldn't he have called himself?

"No, well, yes, in a way. He's had a nasty fall and is in the hospital. I think he's broken some ribs. He fell as he was walking towards his car and hit his ribs on one of those low concrete barriers."

"Oh, how awful. Thank you for telling me."

My hands are shaking as I put the phone back. The fact that William is hurt has upset me more than I could have ever imagined. I'm an expert at bottling up my feelings, denying my emotions and quashing my reactions. But I'm having a hard time right now.

"Meg, what are you going to do?" my mother shouts from below.

I walk down the stairs, wishing I was alone. Cooper is licking Kelly as if trying to dry her off as they lie under the kitchen table. My mother has cheese on toast, cut in strips, on a plate on the table, and has cut up some apple I forgot I have.

"What do you mean, what am I going to do? There's nothing I can do."

She munches, while keeping her eyes fixed on me.

"I know lovesickness when I see it, even in you." She pushes the plate towards me, but I don't take a piece. My stomach is churning and my hands are still trembling. I wish I could do a better job of concealing how disturbed I am by the news. My reaction is worse than when they told me that Frank had been murdered, and even when Chuck collapsed and died on my kitchen floor. William's only broken some ribs. He'll get better. But it's not just that. I'm hurt, beyond comprehension, that his assistant called, rather than him, just as if I really am only a client to him. I've lost him, that's for certain, but the real question is: did I ever have him?

"What do you mean, 'even in me'?"

"You know what I mean. I'll tell you what you should do. You should go to the hospital."

"You listened in."

"Of course. I've been worried about William too, and the woman told me she's his assistant."

"How can I go to the hospital in an ice storm?"

"You've got those spiky things over there, and I expect you put them over your boots."

"Very observant. But the roads will be bad."

"I thought you Canadians put salt and sand down all the time. I'm sure I heard the plow just now. Be careful, though. And eat something first."

"The driveway will be lethal."

"Meg! Enough! Do you want this man or not?"

I start to cry.

* * *

I turn on to the road leading towards the hospital parking lot.

It's all very well for my mother to tell me to go to see William, but I'm convinced he won't want me here. I fooled myself into believing that we had a relationship which was growing. I feel comfortable with him, partly because he knows about my baggage and doesn't seem to judge me for what happened to me. But perhaps he's given it more consideration and realizes that I'm damaged goods, that I carry scars from my past, and he can't handle it. He has his own scars from his wife's death and I know he mentioned he had a struggle with drugs for a while, although it wasn't anything like as serious and life-threatening as Chuck's struggle apparently was. I didn't know enough about Frank or Chuck. And I don't know much about William, really. And it's probably going to stay that way.

I hesitate before I press the button to get the parking ticket in front of the hospital. I contemplate turning around and leaving, but just as I put the truck into reverse, someone behind me slams on the horn. I'm trapped. I get my ticket and park. I'm lucky that there's a spot close to the entrance. I check the footing. There's salt everywhere, and the asphalt looks wet with puddles. I don't need my ice grips, so I take them off my boots. But I hesitate.

My mobile rings, giving me a reason not to leave the truck.

"Meg, oh, gee, I'm sure glad I've reached you." Tammy sounds frantic.

"What's the matter?"

"Annabella told me everything, and Simeon is here. I'm scared."

"He's with you now?"

"He's having a shower. I don't have long to talk."

"You must call the police."

"I'm frightened. He'll know I've called them. What if he takes me hostage when they come, or they let him out on bail or something?"

"Let me talk with him."

"I don't know if he'll want to talk with you."

"Let's try."

"Okay. When he's out of the shower, I'll call you and try to get him to talk to you."

So, I'm trapped in the truck whether I like it or not. I can't go inside the hospital. And I'm worried about Tammy. Is she safe? Annabella and I believe Simeon has killed a person. My anxiety grows as I sit watching the rain run down my windshield, the rivulets lit up by the fluorescent lighting beaming out of the hospital's expansive front lobby. The temperature must have risen.

Despite my serious concern for Tammy, I'm hit by an intense urge to see William now that I'm this close. I'll go into the hospital straight after my phone call with Simeon.

Each minute that passes feels more like ten. I'm getting cold and damp. I do, and I don't want to tell William I'm here. I decide not to, using the excuse that I don't want to risk messing up answering my phone when Tammy does eventually call. If she doesn't call in the next five minutes, I'm calling the police. Which police? I don't know who to call. Detective Leya Channing, I suppose, and then I don't have Tammy's address. That was dumb. My phone rings and it's Tammy.

"Meg, Simeon is here. He'll talk with you."

"Hello, Meg."

"Hi, Simeon. What are your plans?"

"I'm on my way to Canada. It's a big country and easy to get lost in."

"So, you're a fugitive. And you'll always be on the run. Do you want that?"

"I'm used to moving around."

"Not when you have to watch your back all the time, not knowing if you're being followed, not knowing if someone has discovered who you are, and not being able to live a life. No job, no friends, nobody you can trust."

"I'm good at disguise."

"Maybe you are, but the police are pretty good at finding people, and social media is a tremendous asset. I just think it would be better for you if you gave yourself up. I think you'll be treated a lot better than if they pick you up somewhere."

"They might kill me in a shoot-out. That might be best."

"I don't think you mean that, Simeon."

"I do. I did it all for Annabella. Nothing else matters to me."

"There's no point making your life any more difficult, hurting yourself even more. Do the sensible thing and give yourself up now."

"I don't think so."

"Even though you killed my husband, Frank, I know that you're not a terrible person. You deserve fair treatment. You don't deserve to be running in fear. There's nowhere to hide. And you can't escape what you've done. I know what it's like to be haunted by the past. I remember it disturbed you to hear about what had happened to me: the abuse I suffered. I'm sure that you're haunted by what you did and I can tell you that those flashbacks and nightmares never totally disappear, even after years and years. I know."

Silence.

"The only way to make yourself feel better about the whole thing, and to give yourself some peace, is to confess to the police."

"He's handed me the phone back, Meg." Tammy's voice is quivering. "Thanks for talking with him, anyway."

After we've ended the call, I remember to text her to get her address and the phone number for her local police service, and to tell her I'll call the police if he's still there in an hour's time. From the tone of Simeon's voice, and the fact that he talked with me and didn't smash Tammy's phone, I don't think she's in any imminent danger. But I suppose I can't be certain.

Now the battery's low on my phone and I have to plug it in. Another reason not to leave the truck, but this time I know I want to go to William. No ifs, buts or maybes.

Tammy sends me a text saying that she's taking him to the police station in town and going to watch him go in, and that she'll return home straight afterwards. It should take about twenty minutes. I text back that I'd like her to let me know when she's home.

I decide to give my phone longer to charge, and then I'll go into the hospital.

Someone knocks on my window and I just about jump out of my skin. I get out of the truck, despite the rain.

"I thought it was your truck," William says, as he moves his large black umbrella so that it covers both of us.

"How are you? You must be in a lot of pain."

"It's not that bad."

"But you have broken ribs. Shouldn't you still be in hospital?"

"Ramona saw me fall in the parking lot behind my office, and was convinced I'd done a lot more damage than I have. I have bruised ribs. The only reason they kept me in for a couple of hours was because I banged my head. But they confirmed it isn't serious. Just a bump. So, I'm a free man, thank goodness. Hospitals are not my scene."

"I don't think anyone enjoys having to be in hospital." What is wrong with me? Why can't I say something meaningful?

"Anyway, sorry about this evening. How about tomorrow evening? Or have you already set that up with Ramona?"

"My mother leaves tomorrow afternoon. I'll be taking her to the airport about lunch-time."

"I see. I'll have Ramona check my schedule for tomorrow morning. No, I remember, I'm in court tomorrow, at least for the morning."

"Never mind. I've paid the bills, so there's nothing for my mother to worry about. We can probably deal with it later."

"That's good. I'm going now. I'm feeling tired from all the excitement." He smiles, turns, and ambles away from me. My heart quickly sinks into my boots. I blew it. He made the effort to come over, but he didn't give me much opportunity, did he? He didn't even ask me why I'm here. But I didn't wish him a speedy recovery, or tell him I hope he gets better soon, or something preferably not so trite. I could have at least done that.

I get back into the truck, pick up my phone, and no text from Tammy. It's almost twenty minutes since our last exchange. I'm going to stay put until I hear. I'll give it three more minutes.

Just as I'm hovering over my phone, about to enter the number for the police station, Tammy calls.

"Are you okay, Tammy?"

"I'm fine, Meg. Something you said must have hit a chord. He sat for about five minutes, then said he was ready to go to the police station. He just has a small backpack, so it took him no time to get ready to leave. So, we left. I made sure he went inside the building, and waited about three minutes before I had to drive off. I was in a tow-away zone so couldn't wait longer. He didn't say a word. I just wished him good luck when he left the car."

"I'm glad he's done that, for everyone's sake."

"I think he feels terribly alone and miserable. Annabella is the only person he cares about, and since she turfed him out, he's lost."

"Why are you feeling sorry for him? He shot Frank."

"I feel partly responsible because I knew about the blackmail plan."

"You didn't ask him to shoot Frank."

"Yeah, I know. Anyhow, I don't think he would have gone if you hadn't talked with him. Thanks. I owe you a lot."

"No, you don't, Tammy. Thanks for believing that Frank didn't commit suicide. It was you who got the ball rolling."

"I'm going to soak in the bath. I'm exhausted. Thanks, Meg. I sure hope we keep in touch."

"I hope so too."

24

New Beginnings

My mother is asleep in the recliner with Cooper curled up on her lap, but he opens one eye to see what I'm up to. Kelly is dry and doesn't look eager to move from her spot by the chair, but I know she should go out for a short walk. I leave a note on the table beside my mother, just in case she wakes up and realizes Kelly isn't here.

The rain has stopped, but much of the treacherous ice remains, with a layer of water on top, making it even more perilous than a flawlessly groomed ice-rink. My ice grips are back on my boots as Kelly and I venture out into the black night. The lights from the house seem dimmer in this dismal darkness. With my bright flashlight I scan the fence-line, and Kelly follows the beam looking for any eyes reflecting the light back at us. We can't see any, so I think all the creatures must be hunkered down in their warm beds, as I'd like to be.

I didn't tell William about Dominic Marcel's arrest. And I must update him on Simeon Boulet. I expect he'll find out sooner rather than later, but after all he's done to help, he should hear it from me. I'll call Ramona in the morning and set up an appointment to see him, if that's the way he wants it. I'll go there as soon as I've made sure that my mother is through airport security.

* * *

I drive back from the airport, surrounded by grey mist and soggy fields, feeling more alone than I've ever felt. It's as if everyone has peeled away, leaving me vulnerable, unneeded and forgotten. I used to cherish being alone, and that's how I lived my life for many years. My animal friends, with their unquestioning, unconditional love, kept me company. Without their loyalty and faithfulness, I'd be sinking into a funk right now. Nevertheless, I am feeling sorry for myself.

It was more traumatic saying goodbye to my mother than I could ever have expected. When she arrived at the farm unannounced, I was flabbergasted and outraged that she would have the audacity to show up, and her unwanted appearance caused painful and hurtful memories to fight their way through the chinks in my armour. But, when I think of her now, I see a vulnerable woman who was abused by her second husband, my stepfather, who felt trapped in that relationship and who knows that she seriously and severely let me down. I know she has lots of regrets. I'm now glad that she came and hope that she recovers enough to visit us again next year.

Cooper will miss her the most, but we all will.

The only bright light today is that I have an appointment with William. Ramona had to squeeze me in between two clients. I'm not optimistic that the time allotted will allow for anything other than the briefest update from me, with no opportunity to find out what has caused William to back away. I've been thinking about him a lot, and I can't believe that we weren't, at the very least, developing a warm and close friendship. What made things suddenly go cold?

I'm not sure what's made me so determined to see him, even if it's only for a brief appointment in his office, but the last words from my mother were to "go get William". She blew me a kiss and disappeared into the security area.

I left Kelly in the house with Cooper, so I'm keen to get home and see that they're okay, although I know Linda checked on them before she left for lunch with her mother, as well as when she returned.

When I get home, Kelly is nowhere to be found. It's as if my stomach does a somersault, but then I see a note on the kitchen table from Linda. Kelly is in the barn with her.

"Hi, Linda. Thanks for looking after Kelly."

"No problem. She's been following me around."

"How are things going?"

"Good. The horses are great. I'm collecting the water buckets. I want to give them a scrub. Can I get some hot water from the house?"

"Any time. Thanks. You're on top of everything, as usual. I'm leaving again in a bit and I'll take Kelly with me."

"I'll be going home soon, if that's okay? I'm about to bring the horses in. I know they haven't been out long, but there's still a lot of ice around. And this mist is bad."

"That's fine. Thanks. See you tomorrow." Linda is more alive than I've ever seen her before. It must be love, I think to myself, as I wander slowly towards the house, with Kelly at my heels.

* * *

I park the truck outside William's office, which is an improvement on his previous decrepit location. He bought a large, old house just inside the Vannersville city limits, and renovated it. He told me he lives upstairs in a spacious, airy apartment. There's a small parking lot behind the house, but Ramona told me it's still icy. The person who salts and sands in the area has a major problem with his truck and hasn't been able to get to them in two days. I leave Kelly in the truck and make my way up the wet, salted steps to the front door.

Ramona is warm and welcoming, but says I'll be waiting a few minutes. My hands are trembling and even my knees are wobbling, so I sit down and pick up a magazine, but I have an urge to get out of here. I put the magazine back on the coffee table. I look at Ramona and she smiles.

"Shouldn't be much longer."

"Thank you." My voice sounds raspy and my lips feel dry.

"Would you like some water?"

"Yes, please."

I try to distract myself by looking around the reception area. There are three beautiful watercolour paintings hanging on the walls in elegant frames.

"Mr Porter painted those," Ramona says, as she hands me a glass of water. "Mr Porter is a talented man."

"They're beautiful. I especially like the colours in this one that shows a lake at sunset."

"That's my favourite too." Ramona focuses back onto her computer.

My eyes are drawn to a large photograph of a black dog, perhaps a labradoodle, sitting beautifully for the camera. It almost looks as if he's smiling. I'd forgotten that William has a dog. I'm drawn to the picture, and get up to walk towards it.

"That's Mini."

"She looks beautiful."

"He. His name is spelt like the car. You know, the Mini."

"Oh."

"But don't mention him. Mr. Porter had to have him put down last week. He was thirteen years old and had cancer of the liver. He's pretty cut up about it. He can't talk about it yet."

"I had no idea."

"He wouldn't expect you to know."

"Oh." Oh dear. I know so little about William. I can't even tell when he's grieving the loss of his beloved dog. And the dog must have been sick for a while. I turn away from the picture. I should go home. But someone is leaving through the front door, the previous client, presumably. My exit isn't clear and William's walking towards me.

"Hello, Meg. Glad to see you." William extends his hand. It feels odd to be greeting him with a handshake. His grip is firm and his hand is warm, but his eyes are not sparkling as I've seen them in the past. William guides me to his office.

"Thank you for meeting with me," I say. The furniture is elegant and modern, such a contrast to his previous office, which looked worn out and tired, as if its occupant had given up. The three windows let in natural light, which brings unexpected brightness to the room, even though there's no sunshine today.

"You had something you wanted to discuss with me?" William sits behind his desk, rather than at one of the easy chairs which surround the coffee table. I feel as if I'm being put in my place, wherever that is.

"Yes. I'm not clear what you already know, but I'm here to make sure you're aware. First, Dominic Marcel was arrested while attempting to cross the border into Canada."

"I know about that, yes. I thought it curious that he would choose to go to the US, and then attempt to return to Canada. But he must have had his reasons."

"He's pretty resourceful. I wouldn't be surprised if he had forged documents, but something blew open his fake identity."

"Perhaps."

"And Simeon Boulet has turned himself in to the police in Hollywood. He admits he murdered Frank." I have a lump in my throat.

"Yes. Leya called me this morning with the news. And, from what I hear, you counselled him and whatever you said to him had some influence on the outcome. So, I think congratulations are in order." His mouth smiles, but his eyes don't. It's as if a current of cold air is keeping us apart, and it's growing stronger at the same time as my resolve is grower weaker. I get up out of my chair, and, on my cue, William stands. But I sit down again with a thump.

"William." I hesitate.

"You have something else you want to talk with me about?" He's sitting back in his chair, as if he might catch something if he gets closer to me. I force myself to believe that this is a good sign. I need a little hope to inspire me to continue.

"William. I've enjoyed your friendship and company very much. I don't understand why you've decided that our relationship should revert to being simply a professional one. I miss you." He looks at me and says nothing. Then he moves forward to lean his arms on his desk.

"Meg, I miss you too. But you've lost your husband and your partner within a two-year period. I realized I was growing too close to you when you're grieving and you're vulnerable. I didn't think it was right for me to be around so much. I think you need time to process all that has happened. I thought you might think I was taking advantage of the situation."

"You didn't ask me."

"True. I didn't."

"You should have talked about it with me. You're as bad as Murray. As you know, he tried to get money from Frank on my behalf without discussing it with me. You should not assume that you know what other people are thinking and feeling." I shouldn't lecture someone when I do just the same thing myself.

"You're right."

"Frank's murder and Chuck's sudden death have not left me distraught, unable to function and incapable of thinking straight. You know that Frank and I had a marriage of convenience, and while I admit I wanted us to be in love, it wasn't to be. I didn't realize how deeply, and apparently permanently, Frank was damaged by Louisa's death. I grieved when he vanished nearly two years ago, and I was very sorry to hear that he was murdered. He didn't deserve that. And I admit losing Chuck was a shock. A terrible shock, actually. I didn't know Chuck had a drug problem, and I knew nothing about this plantation business. One thing I do know, is that I don't want a repeat of any of this. I hope you'll give me a chance to get to know you. Everything about you. I want to know what makes you sad, what makes you happy, what you're thinking when the sun comes up, what you dream about, what makes you angry, what makes you laugh, what colours you like, where you like to be: everything one can possibly know about someone else. Will you give me the chance to find out?" I look into his eyes through a blur of tears, which are about to trickle down my red-hot cheeks. I grab a tissue from the box on his desk and dab my eyes, blow my nose, and try to stand, but my legs are shaking and seem to have lost most of their strength. I stay seated. At least I've told him.

Hot air blows on my neck. William has drawn a chair round to sit next to me, and he's wrapping his arms round me.

"Meg. I'm sorry. You mean so much to me. Please accept my apology."

"You sound like a lawyer." I turn and smile at him, but I'm still not sure where things lie between us. I need more.

"I am a lawyer."

"Will you give me the chance to get to know you, as a person?"

"Yes, on the condition that you'll give me the chance to get to know you. And that will be hard for you." He holds me closer. It feels wonderful but awkward at the same time, because we're each sitting on a chair. And I don't think I've allowed anyone to hold me for this long before.

"I don't think it will be hard to be open and honest with you."

* * *

I hope that the new year will bring a new beginning for me, with William.

And I wish a new beginning for my mother as well. And I never thought I would ever make that wish. It's a good feeling.

That seed of happiness has re-emerged and is beginning to germinate.

www.ingramcontent.com/pod-product-compliance
Lightning Source LLC
La Vergne TN
LVHW010604100826
845148LV00014B/2839